Ghost at the Wedding

"Michael," Toria cried frantically. "You can't go like this, you can't."

"And how do you want me to go?" Michael asked. "Would you prefer it this way?"

He swept her into his arms, crushing her wedding dress and pulling her lace veil from her head with the roughness of his embrace. She felt his mouth, hard and brutal against her lips. His violence was frightening, and the passion behind his kiss seemed almost to devour her. Then just as she felt she could not breathe, but must suffocate by his very strength, he flung her away from him.

And then Michael was gone—and Toria's husband was waiting for her to come to him!

LOVE
IS
MINE

Barbara Cartland

PYRAMID BOOKS ▲ NEW YORK

LOVE IS MINE

A PYRAMID BOOK

Pyramid edition published December 1972
Sixth printing, November 1976

Printed in the United States of America

Pyramid Books are published by Pyramid Publications (Harcourt
Brace Jovanovich, Inc.). Its trademarks, consisting of the word
"Pyramid" and the portrayal of a pyramid, are registered in the
United States Patent Office.

PYRAMID PUBLICATIONS
(Harcourt Brace Jovanovich, Inc.)
757 Third Avenue, New York, N.Y. 10017

1

Charles Drayton was bored.

He yawned as the Air Ministry car carried him swiftly through Barnet and Potters Bar, and he yawned again as they turned off the main thoroughfare through twisting lanes leading to a patch of country which was still surprisingly rural although within easy reach of London.

It was Saturday and Charles had planned to spend the weekend at his own home in Worcestershire.

There he would have been riding round his estate or walking over the fields with his bailiff.

Instead he had been forced to make arrangements to have luncheon at Lynbrooke Castle and inspect an invention which he was already certain in his mind would not be of the slightest use.

He had protested at this change in his plans, and with no avail. His Chief was adamant.

"The Minister has asked personally that you go yourself, Drayton. I know it's inconvenient; but what do the 'powers that be' care about our inconvenience? It need not take you long."

However short the time he must spend at Lynbrooke Castle, Charles knew it had ruined his weekend.

It would be too late by the time he left for him to get down to Worcestershire till the evening, and it would not be worth while going at all under the circumstances, for he had to be back in London on Sunday night.

Charles told himself that he loathed Ministers who were asked special favours by their friends.

If the Earl of Lynbrooke wanted his nephew's invention vetted, why couldn't he let it go through the ordinary and proper channels for such matters?

Why should he, Charles Drayton, be brought into it?

Actually he knew the answer to that, although he was

5

too modest to admit it himself. His own career in the Royal Air Force had been meteoric.

The youngest Air Vice-Marshal in the Service, he owed his success not only to his brilliant leadership and daring exploits in the War, but also to the fact that peace had found him to be equally successful in another branch of the R.A.F.

It was his desire for efficiency which had made him design his first improvement to a fighter plane, and it was the realisation that he could see a fault and know how to correct it which made him eventually Number Two in the Department of Aeronautical Research.

Three of Charles' inventions were already in production as standardised parts of the new Fighters.

Unfortunately from his point of view, the newspapers had got to know of this. The public were accordingly informed that "One of the Heroes of the Air"—as he was called to his disgust—"has now turned inventor."

And there was nothing he could do to stop his picture from appearing in every national newspaper with paragraph after paragraph of inaccurate information beneath it.

It was for this reason that one of his few days of relaxation had been taken from him and he had been sent off on what he was already convinced was a fool's errand.

The car turned and then unexpectedly drove in through some high lodge gates. Charles looked around him.

The Park on a bleak February afternoon was not particularly prepossessing. The ground looked sodden from the recent rains and the trees, bleak and leafless, made it hard to believe that spring would soon be back again in all its verdant beauty.

The car bumped uncomfortably and Charles was forced to crouch down to prevent his head being bashed against the roof.

The driver took his foot off the accelerator, but not before another bump caused Charles to swear softly beneath his breath as he put out his hand to steady himself.

6

The drive was undoubtedly in a disgraceful state of repair. With a sense of relief Charles saw the house in front of them, noting at the same time that it was quite one of the ugliest buildings he had ever seen.

Lynbrooke Castle was mentioned in the Domesday book; but the eighth Earl had fancied himself as an architect and in 1890 had destroyed the last remnants of the Queen Anne house which had been built on the site of the original Castle and had erected instead a red brick building in excruciating taste.

It stood squarely facing an avenue of oak trees which, having been planted four hundred years earlier, were resolute enough not to faint away at sight of the new edifice.

There was no sacrilege against Art and Architecture that the Earl had not committed. He had liked ornamentation, and in consequence the house was adorned with columns, porticoes and pediments.

Battlements, spires and turrets peppered the roofs and there were even a dozen Victorian statues perched in niches between the first floor windows.

It was with a sense of stupefaction that Charles surveyed the Castle. It was farcical that such an outrage against good taste should have survived the war.

The house was in almost as bad repair as the drive. The paint on the windows had long since peeled and blistered into a dirty grey uniformity, several panes were missing from a horrifying mosaic of coloured glass over the front door.

Charles pulled the front door bell with the conviction, which was obviously not unfounded, that it would not work.

After some minutes' wait a dog began to bark and after a further delay there was the sound of slow, shuffling footsteps approaching the door. Charles turned to his chauffeur.

"You had better try to get some food in the village if there is one," he said, "and be back here at 2.30 sharp."

"Very good, Sir."

The man saluted and got back into the car as the front door opened slowly and wheezily. An old man

7

with grey hair and a brown, weather-beaten face stood there wearing a shabby uniform coat trimmed with silver buttons.

"I'm sorry if I've kept you waiting, Sir," he said, "but the bell's been broke these last three months."

"Wouldn't it be a good idea to have it mended?" Charles asked as he stepped into the hall.

"We'll get round to it in time," the old man said cheerily as he took Charles' cap. "We ain't had time recently for falderals."

Charles nearly retorted that that was obvious. The hall, dark and cheerless, was as untidy and uncared-for as the outside of the Castle.

Tables and oak chests were littered with a miscellaneous collection of caps, hats, whips, gloves, pieces of string, old magazines, tennis racquets and rubber balls.

In one corner wellingtons and galoshes rested beside two dog-baskets and a bowl of water.

The old servant led the way across the hall and into a large room on the other side of it.

The room was unexpectedly pleasing. It was shabby and the chintz covers were almost white with innumerable cleanings, but the walls were half hidden by books, and where there were no books there were windows opening on to a view which stretched across the parkland.

Charles had not imagined there could be such a magnificent view so near to London and instinctively his feet carried him towards the window. Then, as he stood looking out, he heard a gay young voice beside him say:

"I suppose you are admiring our view. Everyone does!"

He turned quickly, not having realised that anyone had come into the room. To his astonishment he found himself looking at one of the loveliest children he had ever seen in his life.

She could not, he thought, be much more than twelve or thirteen. Her hair, naturally wavy, was the pale gold of jasmin blossom, and her eyes were the deep, vivid blue of the Mediterranean Sea. She was small and deli-

8

cately made with a tiny pointed chin, and the fingers of the hand she held out to him were long and sensitive.

"You are Air Vice-Marshal Drayton, aren't you?" she said. "I am Xandra Gale. I am sorry my father is not here to meet you. He has gone down to the stables as we are rather worried about one of the cows."

Her self-possession and grown-up air of assurance made Charles feel almost at a loss.

"How do you do?" he said a little stiffly. "Perhaps I am early! I was not sure how long it would take me to get here."

"I think it is only a quarter to one," Xandra told him, "but all the clocks in the house are broken and we have to rely on Mrs. Fergusson's wireless for the right time. As she is cooking the luncheon, I can't ask her now."

"No, of course not!" Charles said. "And it doesn't matter much as I am here, does it? It would have been much worse if I had been late."

"Much worse," Xandra informed him solemnly. "We are having a very special luncheon today because of you. We have even killed one of the hens and as we have only got ten left, it makes it quite an occasion."

"I am indeed honoured," Charles said with a faint smile.

"It is so very important that you should like Michael's invention," Xandra said.

"Is it?" Charles asked.

Xandra nodded her fair head.

"You see, if you don't, Michael will have to marry 'Phone and Photo', and that would be too awful!"

" 'Phone and Photo'?" Charles repeated bewilderingly.

"That is what we call her, of course," Xandra explained. "Her real name is Susan Butler and her parents live on the next Estate to this. They bought it last year. They are frightfully rich and what Michael calls 'frightfully suburban'."

She smiled.

"Susan talks about the ' 'phone' and a 'photo', and 'going up to town'. She uses 'perfume' instead of 'scent' and calls their sitting-room 'the lounge'. It sets Mi-

9

chael's teeth on edge but she is crazy about him, and is always ringing him up. We can't bear her. That is why it would be so awful if he had to marry her."

"Is such a course really inevitable?" Charles asked in all seriousness.

Xandra nodded.

"Unless you take Michael's invention, there will be nothing else for him to do," she said. "He can't keep a job of any sort. He has tried two or three since the war, but nobody will keep him for long. He just loathes being ordered about. We Gales are all like that."

"Michael is your brother, I suppose?" Charles asked.

Xandra shook her head.

"Oh, no, he is our cousin. His father and mother were killed in an aeroplane accident in America, and Michael seems like a brother for he has always been here. That is why we couldn't bear him to marry 'Phone and Photo'. You do understand, don't you?"

"Yes, yes, of course," Charles said unconvincingly.

With a sense of relief he saw the door opening. But it was another child who entered. As she crossed the room, Charles stared at her in surprise, for he could hardly believe his eyes.

She was indeed a complete replica of the little girl to whom he was already talking. They were also dressed alike in old, well-washed sweaters of dark green with skirts of a matching tweed which even to Charles' experienced eye appeared unnecessarily short.

"This is Olga," Xandra explained as the other child drew nearer. "Olga, this is Air Vice-Marshal Drayton. I have just told him how important it is for him to like Michael's invention."

"It is very nice of you to come down and see it," Olga said, holding out her hand to Charles.

He looked down at the children as they stood together. It was, he decided, impossible for anyone to tell them apart.

"You must be twins," he said.

"Of course," Xandra said briefly, as if the remark were unnecessary, which indeed it was.

"Where is Toria?" she asked, turning to Olga.

10

"She hasn't come back yet," Olga replied. "You know she said she might be late."

Xandra smiled.

"Toria's our sister," she explained to Charles. "She had to go to London. She poses for photographers and gets awfully well paid for it; but she was angry that she had to go up today, being a Saturday, and especially as you were coming."

"Look here, before anyone else arrives," Charles said, "just tell me briefly of what your family consists. It is all rather muddling for a stranger, you know."

"It is not very difficult really," Xandra said. "There are only six of us in the house. Daddy, Toria, Olga and myself and Lettice and Michael."

"Who is Lettice?" Charles asked. "Is she another sister?"

"No, she is Michael's sister," Xandra explained. "There are only three of us. Three unwanted girls, because, of course, we ought to have been boys. It will be the first time for generations that the title hasn't descended from father to son."

"And Toria is how old?" Charles asked.

"Oh, what is she?" Xandra enquired of Olga. "Twenty-one or twenty-two, I never can remember."

"Twenty-one," Olga said quietly. "Don't you remember, she said she ought to have had fireworks on her last birthday, but no one made any fuss of her because she was only a girl?"

"Of course I remember now," Xandra exclaimed. "Yes, Toria is twenty-one."

"It is a very unusual name," Charles said.

Both twins smiled simultaneously.

"Everyone says that," Xandra said. "Her real name is Victoria, of course. Our Mother loved Royalty and we are all called after Queens. Toria after Queen Victoria, I'm after Queen Alexandra. . . ." She stopped and looked at Olga.

"Shall we take him on?" she asked, and without waiting for an answer she turned to Charles.

"I bet you a shilling you can't tell us what Queen Olga is called after."

11

Charles thought hard. As far as he could remember, there had never been a Queen Olga.

"Was she Russian?" he hazarded at length.

The twins went into shrieks of laughter.

"Pay up," they said.

Solemnly Charles took a shilling from his pocket and handed it to Xandra.

"Now we'll tell you," she said. "Olga is named after Queen Mary."

"Queen Mary?" Charles exclaimed in astonishment.

"Yes, it's her fifth name. Nobody ever knows, and we make an awful lot on bets, don't we, Olga?"

Olga looked worried.

"One day someone will know, and then we won't be able to pay them. What shall we do then?"

"We will have to give it to them in bits," Xandra replied. "What do you call it? The instalment system."

Olga looked doubtful.

"Would that be all right?" she asked.

"Of course it would," Xandra said scornfully. "Wouldn't it?" she enquired of Charles.

"Perfectly all right," Charles re-assured her.

"I knew it would," Xandra said. "Olga needn't fuss; nobody ever guesses correctly. But she is very particular. She is religious, you see. She has found out that we were a Catholic family before Cromwell started fighting them and the second Earl joined his Army. Olga wants Father to turn back again, and of course he won't."

Charles fortunately had not to reply to this because the door was opened and two dogs hurled themselves into the room, followed by Lord Lynbrooke.

The dogs rushed at Charles, barking ferociously and at the same time wagging their tails, while their owner and the twins screamed at them at the tops of their voices so that the noise was almost deafening.

When the dogs had been dragged away from Charles and petted into silence, he found himself facing a middle-aged man with a bald head, a long fair moustache and vague, apologetic blue eyes which seemed to have difficulty in focusing on anything in the immediate foreground.

12

Charles was to learn, as he knew him better, that Lord Lynbrooke invariably spoke with an air of deliberate courtesy as if it was an effort for him to make conversation and he was choosing every word with care.

It was a disconcerting habit, especially as the Earl never took part in any general conversation and had a way of starting a subject of his own regardless of what had been going on around him.

People who were deeply engrossed in a friendly argument or a conversation in which everyone had joined would find it confusing to say the least of it when Lord Lynbrooke would suddenly enquire if they suffered from rheumatism or if they did not think the weather had been very wet recently.

At times it seemed remarkably like a snub or a reminder that they were becoming too obstreperous; but after a time they grew to know that nothing was further from his lordship's thoughts.

It was just that he lived in a world of his own. The hurly-burly of everyday life went on around him, but he did not notice it.

Only on the subject of the First World War could he come voluble and expansive. It had been the happiest time of his life, a time when he had known comradeship and enjoyed the company of his fellow-men.

His stories were out-dated and incredibly boring to the younger generation who had never known the mud of Flanders, the blood and tears of the trenches.

But to Lord Lynbrooke the horrors and privations, the battles and bombardments were as fresh in his mind as if they had happened yesterday.

He moved around the Castle like a kindly ghost always accompanied by his two spaniels, named with what he erroneously imagined was a streak of original humour—Brandy and Soda.

Brandy was a golden Cocker Spaniel, and Soda, exactly the same size, was white with brown patches. They accompanied the Earl wherever he went and slept at the foot of his bed.

If by any chance one of them was shut outside a door or parted from him by some mistake, its howls and vio-

13

lent onslaught of scratchings and bangings would reverberate throughout the Castle.

"I am sorry I was not here to meet you," Lord Lynbrooke said to Charles. "Did you have a good journey down?"

He spoke as if London was far distant and the journey long and tedious.

"It took me a shorter time than I expected," Charles said, feeling his early arrival required explanation.

"Luncheon should be ready," Lord Lynbrooke said. "Let us go in."

He walked across the room and the dogs, who were being fondled by the twins, broke away from them and followed closely at his heels.

The twins stood back for Charles to precede them. He did so, feeling that the procession was somehow an odd one.

The dining-room, an enormous room, hideous and unprepossessing, which opened off the other side of the Hall, was covered from floor to ceiling with pale brown oak.

There were two very badly executed family portraits on the wall and the carpet, Charles noted, was so threadbare that one was lucky if one reached a seat without catching one's foot in a hole.

The Earl sat down at the head of the table in a high-backed chair. Charles hesitated, and as no one said anything to him he seated himself on his right. He had no sooner sat down than he had to rise again. In the doorway, which they had left open behind them, appeared two people.

One of them was a girl of about twenty with dark hair parted in the middle and a strange, rather arresting face which would, Charles thought, have struck one as being exceptionally pretty if one had not already looked at the twins.

"Come along, come along," the Earl said testily. "Luncheon is ready."

The third girl crossed the room to Charles' side.

"I am Lettice Gale," she said. "I am so glad you have come."

14

"It seems a pity no one could tell me that the Air Vice-Marshal was here," a deep voice said bitterly, and Michael Gale, entering the room behind her, glared at the twins before he shook hands with Charles.

"I meant to be on the doorstep to meet you, Sir," he said, "but I did not know the time. The clocks never seem to go in this house."

"It is quite all right," Charles answered. "I was early, and was well entertained as it happened."

He looked at Xandra as he spoke, and she smiled back at him.

"The Air-Marshal is terribly nice, Michael," she said. "I am sure he is going to like your invention."

Michael merely scowled, and as he sat down next to her at the table Charles saw that he tried to kick her under the table.

Michael Gale was exactly as Charles had expected him to be, having looked up his confidential report at the Air Ministry before he left London.

It had told him that Squadron-Leader Gale was brilliant in action but erratic and not dependable at other times.

He had won the D.F.C. and Bar for conspicuous gallantry, but had fallen out with the authorities on the ground and had received one bad report after another from his Commanding Officers.

Charles had a mental picture of Michael before he arrived, but like everything else at Lynbrooke Castle he, too, was unexpected. He was, Charles thought, almost as good-looking in his way as the twins in theirs.

He was as handsome as any film star, tall, broad-shouldered and with the clear-cut features which one expected to find in the illustrations of a woman's magazine.

But what spoilt him was his expression. He looked sulky and even disagreeable, and he had not smiled since he entered the room, not even when he had greeted Charles.

Yet there was doubtless an explanation for this, the latter thought. He had been kicking his heels since the War. He had found himself to be yet another post-war failure, and it would not have come easily to him to accept defeat.

He was the type who wanted to be top dog, to enjoy life, to spend money. Charles had seen so many of them —young men who were only at their best when they were riding the skies and who in consequence found an office or disciplined life completely intolerable on their return to earth.

By this time they were all seated at the table. Lettice had taken her place on Charles' right and the twins were on the other side of the table, one on each side of Michael.

There was, however, an empty place at the end, and just as the old man-servant had reached Charles' side with the chicken, Toria came in.

Once again there was pandemonium. The dogs rushed at her, yelping with delight, and the twins shouted above the noise, while their father thundered at them to be quiet.

As Charles rose to his feet, he found Toria beside him. He had expected her to be pretty, having seen the rest of the family, but he was not prepared for her to be utterly and breath-takingly lovely.

At the same time he realised that her face was somehow familiar and remembered after a moment how often he had seen it looking at him from the glossy pages of *The Tatler* or the other illustrated newspapers. "Lady Victoria Gale, beautiful eldest daughter of the Earl of Lynbrooke."

He could remember at least a dozen photographs, and yet not one of them had ever begun to do her justice.

Her hair was fair, like the twins', and fell in one heavy golden wave over her forehead, the ends curling faintly an inch above her shoulders. Her eyes were as blue as Xandra's but appeared twice as large, while her face was a perfect oval though almost too thin.

In repose, her mouth drooped a little wistfully, and she was like, Charles thought unexpectedly, a nymph who had got lost in an enchanted forest.

For the very first time in his life he wanted to protect

16

a woman. There was something infinitely pathetic about Toria, something exquisite about her pale, golden loveliness.

She was like an Easter lily, so delicate, so fragile, that one felt that the slightest breath of wind might destroy her.

"I am sorry to be late," she said.

Her voice was the most unexpected thing about her, Charles thought. It was deep, low and a trifle husky. Charles felt her hand touch his and then she had taken her place at the bottom of the table.

She took off her coat as she did so. She was dressed in a very smart, tight-fitting gown of black satin.

"I've had an exhausting morning," she said, speaking to no one in particular, but to the table in general. "I had to model six different dresses, each one more nauseating than the last. It took them hours and hours posing me against cellophane and bits of newspapers, but I didn't dare complain for fear it would take longer. And when at last I got away I simply flew to the Tube."

"You had left your car at Barnet, hadn't you?" Lettice asked.

Toria nodded.

"Yes, and the beastly thing wouldn't start, but a taxi driver helped. He had to give me a tow, and that all took time. I thought I should never get here."

"The Air Vice-Marshal arrived," Michael said, "but nobody bothered to tell me."

"Oh dear, I am sorry," Toria said.

"We entertained him," Xandra said. "Didn't we?"

"You did indeed," Charles replied. "I am afraid I was early."

As he said it, he decided he was sick of apologising to this erratic household; but as Toria smiled at him, his irritation vanished.

"Nobody is ever on time here," she said. "The next time you come to see us, arrange to be half an hour late and then we shall all be waiting for you."

The chicken had at last gone the round of the table. There was very little left except the carcass when it finally reached Lettice. Charles, looking at his portion, wondered if he dared eat it before it got completely cold or if he must wait for the vegetables.

He had just decided that he would not wait while the old man fiddled on the side-table with dishes, when a woman put her head round the door which led into the pantry.

"Jim's here to say her be a-startin'," she announced.

Charles looked up in surprise. The woman's tone sounded urgent. The old man put down the dishes with a crash.

"It's Daisy, m'lord," he said to the Earl, and went hurrying through the door, taking his uniform coat off as he went.

Charles was not in the least prepared for what happened next. There was a cry of "Daisy!" from the twins and then they, Toria and Lettice sprang to their feet.

"You'll have to help, Michael," Toria said as she went, and reluctantly Michael too followed the others.

A moment later Charles found himself alone in the Dining-room except for Lord Lynbrooke.

"We'll have to help ourselves," the Earl said unconcernedly.

"What has happened?" Charles enquired.

"It is Daisy, one of our cows. I think she is having twins. We have been expecting her to calve all this week and the Vet said when he looked at her yesterday that she might have a difficult time.

"I am sorry it should have happened just at this moment, but that was our Cowman who was waiting on us. He was in the house before the war, but now he is on the Farm and he only comes back when we have important people to meals. Servants are difficult to get nowadays."

"Yes, indeed they are," Charles said, helping himself somewhat gingerly to some cabbage which looked as if it had been incompletely washed rather than boiled.

"I find these sort of things always happen at meal-times," Lord Lynbrooke remarked. "I remember in the First World War, 14-18, that the Germans always started a barrage whenever we sat down to a decent meal. Once we had killed a calf, and just. . . ."

18

Charles' thoughts wandered away from his host's somewhat boring story. He was thinking of Toria.

Why hadn't he realised that the beautiful Toria Gale was Lord Lynbrooke's daughter? He supposed it was because he never moved amongst the smart, social set, whose movements were reported in the Gossip Columns and whose doings were as well-known as any film star's.

His Mother entertained a great deal in the country for him, and when she came to London, which was seldom, she would insist on giving dinner and theatre parties to which young women were invited automatically as partners for him.

Toria had never been among them, and Charles had the feeling now that his mother would not approve of her.

He remembered some of the things she advertised. There was Pond's Cold Cream, of course, a well-known woollen manufacturer's jumpers and cardigans, dresses by famous designers—hats—shoes and gloves.

He had seen her wearing them all, and even without his knowing it her face had haunted him a little so that the young women his mother presented to him seemed somehow gauche and rather heavy after the delicacy of Toria's gentle beauty.

". . . and I said then," the Earl was saying, " 'Damn it, can't these fellows ever let us have a meal in peace?' "

Charles laughed as Xandra came rushing into the room.

"Daddy, they're heifers, both of them."

"Good! That is splendid," the Earl said. "And Daisy's all right?"

"Yes, she's all right. She bellowed like the bull of Basan and everyone helped except Olga. She just prayed."

"That helped too," Olga retorted, coming into the room.

She was followed by the rest of the family.

"Isn't it splendid, Daddy? Two heifers," Toria said, "and Daisy is as pleased as Punch."

She sat down in her seat at the end of the table.

"My chicken is quite cold," she said, "but I suppose it does not matter."

"Shall we pass round the vegetables?" Xandra asked. "It is no use waiting for old Fergie. He won't be able to leave Daisy yet a-while."

"Oh, let us wait on ourselves," Lettice said. "I don't see why we have to have Fergie anyway. I don't think he impresses anyone and he smells of the cowshed."

"He doesn't," Xandra said angrily, "and I think he waits very well. He polished his buttons for hours last night. You were impressed by him, weren't you, Air-Marshal?"

She turned appealingly to Charles.

"I thought he looked extremely efficient," Charles lied.

"There, I shall tell Fergie that," Xandra said. "He will be frightfully disappointed at not being able to finish the luncheon."

She slapped some cabbage down on her plate and looked across at Lettice who, however, was not taking the slightest notice of her.

"You have got an estate of your own, haven't you?" Lettice said to Charles.

"Yes, a small place down in Worcestershire," Charles replied. "How did you know?"

"I had heard of it," Lettice replied, and her eyes were raised to Charles' face in what he thought was somehow meant to be a flattering manner.

"She didn't hear of it at all," Xandra whispered to Michael. "She looked it up in *Who's Who* last night. I saw her. Ouch!"

There was a shriek of pain and Charles knew that Michael had kicked her under the table. He wanted to laugh, but something in Lettice's face prevented him. He forced himself to go on talking as if he had heard nothing.

"I farm a little," he said, "but my land is only arable. I do not go in for stock."

"My uncle used to farm here in quite a big way," Lettice said, "but now the farms are all let or sold, and all we have got left are the stables where the cows are kept and some pig-sties adjoining them."

"Yet that must be an interest," Charles said.

Lettice raised her eyebrows.

"Not really," she replied.

A fruit salad made with apples long past their best, pears that were as hard as bullets and a few sour oranges followed the chicken. After that there was a plate of tired biscuits and mousetrap cheese, accompanied by some superlative port which made Charles look at his host with a new respect.

"I have only got a few bottles of this left," Lord Lynbrooke said, "and Michael persuaded me to bring one up for you today. I hope you like port?"

"Very much, Sir, when it is as good as this."

"That reminds me of a story I heard in India . . ." the Earl began.

Charles looked down the table at Toria. She was sitting with her elbows on the table, her chin resting on one hand. She was looking at Michael, and it struck Charles suddenly that, although they were not speaking, they were in some way communicating with each other.

He looked across the table at the young inventor and decided that he definitely disliked him.

There was something about Michael Gale—he could not put his finger on it exactly—but there was something in his general air, the way he lay back in his chair, the expression on his face, which made Charles feel uneasy.

Toria suddenly got to her feet.

"I must go and change," she said. "This is my only decent dress and I can't afford to sit about in it. Don't let Daddy keep you too long over your port, Air-Marshal. You want to see Michael's invention and we shall want to know what you think about it."

Charles felt his heart sink. He knew already what he was going to think about Michael's invention. If he had a good idea, which Charles doubted, it was very unlikely he would be able to carry it out.

The port was being passed to him again. He filled his

21

glass for he felt he was going to need sustenance during the next half hour.

Lord Lynbrooke finished his story. Michael was waiting. There was an air of tension about him even though he appeared to sprawl relaxed in his chair. Charles suddenly felt sorry for him.

He really cared about what he had done, and it was difficult to possess his soul in patience while his Uncle meandered on with his long stories and his judge and jury drank the family's best port. Charles finished his glass and looked across the table.

"Shall we go now and see what you have to show me?" he asked.

Michael nodded and rose to his feet. He was scowling, but Charles with a sudden perception realised that his air of sulky disagreeableness was merely a trick of nerves.

It was then he felt a hand on his arm and looked down to see Lettice's dark eyes raised to his.

"I do hope you like it," she said very softly.

2

Toria walked into the room which was commonly known as "Michael's Workshop".

It had originally been the Billiard Room. Looking north, it was cold and bleak, although the view over the gardens and the fields beyond sloping down to the woods was very lovely in the spring-time.

Today, in honour of Charles Drayton's visit, a log fire had been built in the big open fireplace; but usually when Toria watched Michael work she sat curled up in one of the old dilapidated armchairs, and when her teeth really began to chatter she would wrap herself in a rug.

She looked, as Michael had told her more than once, like an Eskimo maiden peeping out of an igloo.

Michael never seemed to feel the cold. Sometimes he

would work in his shirt sleeves on the coldest day with the windows wide open and the wind whistling round the room.

Today, with the fire blazing and the room for once quite pleasantly habitable, Michael looked pinched and cold.

He was standing with his back to a dais covered with models and blue prints which stood in the middle of the room, and his hands were deep in the pockets of his corduroy trousers.

His lower jaw was thrust forward, giving him an expression of surly aggression which Toria knew only too well was a sign of one of Michael's moods.

She came quietly into the room and closed the door behind her. She had changed from her black satin dress into a jumper and skirt.

Toria crossed the room and slipped her arm through Michael's.

"Well, it wasn't as bad as we feared," she said, "and —not as good as we had hoped."

"It is hopeless," he said harshly, shaking himself free of her arm and walking across to the dais.

He stood looking down at the model of his last invention and Toria sat down in the window-seat.

"The Air-Marshal said he was coming again," she said reflectively.

"He looked at you as he said it," Michael retorted. "It is hopeless! I knew from the moment he entered this room and saw the expression on his face and heard the way he carefully chose his words so as not to hurt me more than he could.

" 'Very interesting indeed, Gale,' he said in that superior tone of his. 'Of course our fellows have been working on this idea for some time. Actually I am a little out of touch with them at the moment; but I will find out exactly how far they have got, and if there is any chance of your suggestions fitting in, I will let you know'."

Michael spoke in a mocking travesty of Charles' slow, serious tones and then in his own voice he continued:

"I may be a fool, but I'm not a damned fool. I may just as well smash the thing right away. It is just another failure."

"Don't take it so hard, Michael," Toria said. "It may be better than you think. Charles Drayton didn't strike me as the type who would gush."

"I didn't ask him to gush, did I?" Michael enquired savagely. "But I've had it, I'm too late. This has all been thought of already. Perhaps this is the worst thing of all, to know one hasn't an original thought in one's brain."

"Oh Michael, Michael!" Toria cried. "We have all got to face disappointments sooner or later."

"How many have I faced?" Michael asked. "Do you think I liked losing one job after another? Do you know what the last man who sacked me said?

" 'You are unemployable, Gale,' he remarked. 'What you want is a factory of your own—in Paradise'."

"Poor Michael!" Toria's voice was soft. "But I believe in you—and you will find the right place one day. It is just a question of waiting and not getting too despondent."

Michael strode across the room and back again.

"I think those kids have got the only right idea," he said. "I had better marry a rich wife and let her keep me for the rest of my life."

Toria laughed.

"But not 'Phone and Photo'," she exclaimed. "She rang up again after luncheon. I forgot to tell you. I said you were engaged, but that you would ring her back when you were free."

"I shall do nothing of the sort," Michael growled.

"She wanted you to go to a Hunt Ball or something equally nauseating," Toria said. "I told her I would give you the message. There was nothing else I could do, was there?"

"Damn the girl! Why can't she leave me alone?"

"They don't, you know, when they are smitten," Toria said lightly.

"You should know!" Michael retorted. "Has Pennington been after you again?"

Toria nodded.

"He was in the party last night, and of course he contrived to get me alone during the evening."

"What did he say?" Michael enquired.

"Everything that he said before," Toria replied in a bored voice, "but actually he added one new bit! I said for the nine hundredth time that I had no wish to marry him; then he suggested that I should live with him. He said he would make it worth my while and he would even buy me emeralds from Cartier's."

"What damned impertinence!" Michael spluttered, then added in a different tone, "All the same, I wonder you don't, seeing how hard up we are."

"I couldn't stand Pennington for one thing," Toria said, "and for another sin is so untidy. I couldn't be a Mrs. Hagar-Bassett."

They both laughed with the easy familiarity of those who encounter a family joke and laugh through sheer habit.

Mrs. Hagar-Bassett lived exactly opposite the Lodge gates. She had a small house with what the twins called an "IN" and "OUT"—a tiny circular drive in which there was only just room for one car to pass IN between a clump of larches up to the front door and then drive OUT through the front gate.

A retired stockbroker's widow, Mrs. Hagar-Bassett was a woman in her late thirties or early forties. She kept a maid and a small ten-horse-power car in which she drove about the roads very slowly, but with an utter disregard for the Highway Code.

How the Earl had come to know her and why he had taken a fancy to her no one knew.

She was certainly not pretty or even good-looking, but she had a manner of concentrating intently on the person to whom she was speaking, raising her face to his, and keeping her eyes fixed on her audience almost hypnotically.

And she could listen as well as talk. Perhaps that was her attraction. She gave the impression to anyone to whom she was speaking that he was the one and only person with whom she desired to be.

25

No one was quite certain what the relationship was between Mrs. Hagar-Bassett and Lord Lynbrooke, or if indeed there was any relationship at all save his desire to talk and hers to listen.

But practically every afternoon, as soon as he had finished his after-luncheon nap, Lord Lynbrooke, with Brandy and Soda at his heels, would set off across the park, pass through the lodge gates, walk through Mrs. Hagar-Bassett's IN gate and raise her highly-polished brass knocker which was shaped like a dolphin.

The children talked about her amongst themselves; but although they occasionally mentioned her name to their father, he would not be drawn into discussing the lady.

Nor indeed did he ever ask her to the Castle. Daily they would see him go to call on her and two or three hours later they would see him come back, always at the same time, always accompanied by his two spaniels.

"If only Brandy and Soda would talk, what a lot they would tell us," Toria said, when she and Michael and Lettice were discussing the mystery of Mrs. Hagar-Bassett.

"Perhaps they would merely repeat Uncle Arthur's stories to us," Lettice suggested, "and that would be more than I could bear."

The three of them laughed, but somehow Toria hated to see her father walking off across the park.

"It is all so untidy," she had said once, and Lettice looked at her in surprise not understanding what she had meant.

But Michael had understood.

"You can't expect all human relationships to all end like a book with marriage or death," he said. "There are other endings, you know."

"But this is not an ending," Toria expostulated; "it is just one of those nasty rambling episodes which go on and on without a beginning or an ending."

"You are intolerant of other people's frailties," Michael had accused her; and now, looking at her sitting in the window seat with her fair head silhouetted against the grey afternoon, he said it again.

"You are intolerant of other people's frailties, Toria."

"I like that from you, Michael," she said. "No one is more intolerant than you. Besides, why am I intolerant? Because I don't like Pennington?"

"He is not the only one you have refused," Michael said.

"You sound like an ambitious Mama trying to thrust your débutante daughter on to the first eligible bachelor who comes along," Toria laughed. "I am waiting to fall in love."

Michael was suddenly very still.

"That is rather old-fashioned, isn't it?" he asked.

"Perhaps," Toria replied, "but then inside I am rather an old-fashioned sort of girl. People think I am fast because I go to any party at which I can get a free meal, because I try to pick up an honest penny now and again with the only assets I have got—my looks and my figure.

"I can't see why it is more reprehensible to be photographed in a Hartnell evening dress than to bang a typewriter all day long. The only real difference is that I can't type and haven't got brains or the ability to learn."

Michael walked across to the fire and stood looking down at it for some time as if he had never seen flames before.

He did not speak, so Toria uncurled herself from the window seat and walked across to her usual chair by the hearth. There was no need for the rug today, and she kicked it on to the floor before she sank back against the battered velvet cushions.

Michael, she thought to herself, was being more incomprehensible than usual this afternoon. She was afraid he would be upset when Charles Drayton had not said right off that his invention was workable.

But she had been encouraged when the Air Vice-Marshal had asked if he might come down another day and inspect the model again. Now, thinking it over, she realised that he had looked at her as he had said it.

She tried to remember if there had been any particular expression of admiration or interest in his eyes. She was used to seeing men's eyes light up as they looked at

27

her, and she was used to feeling them reaching out towards her either figuratively or physically, and she had grown adept at avoiding them.

But Charles Drayton was different somehow. There was a reserve, an aloof kind of dignity about him which had made her consider him only in the light of being useful to Michael and never for one instant as of interest to herself.

She had been nice to him because so much depended on it, but she would have been nice to anyone if she thought he could be of use to Michael.

How vulnerable the latter was, she sighed, how absurdly ultra-sensitive about himself.

She knew so well what Michael was feeling, that mixture of failure and impotence, of isolation and loneliness which was inevitable when he was unable to achieve what he had set out to do.

She racked her brains for words of consolation and knew that the last thing Michael would want from her would be pity.

She remembered how difficult he and Lettice had been when they first came to Lynbrooke Castle, after their father and mother had been killed in an accident when flying across the American continent.

It had been the obvious solution that the two orphans should come to Lynbrooke and live with their cousins, and Toria had not exactly disliked the idea.

But she had been afraid of those strange, unknown relations and Michael, too, had made everything as difficult as he could. A boy of sixteen can be very overwhelming to a child of ten.

But Toria knew later that Michael's air of superciliousness, his apparent dislike of anyone and anything, and the scorn with which he seemed to regard his new home and everybody in it was due to an acute sense of pride.

A feeling that he and Lettice were being taken in on charity, a feeling that they did not belong, that they were not wanted.

But a ten-year-old child is not a philosopher and Toria wept many bitter tears into her pillow at night before she learned that Michael did not hate her half as much as he pretended.

She slaved for him, of course, and both she and Lettice ran at his heels in the holidays rather like two well-trained dogs.

Then suddenly they had grown up and their relationship changed.

When Michael went to the war Toria was only a child. When the war ended, he did not come home immediately but finished his service abroad.

It was therefore a considerable shock for him to find when he did return that Toria was an acknowledged beauty, a lovely, fêted and acclaimed young woman about whom all social London was talking.

It took them some time to get acclimatised to their new relationship. Sometimes, when Michael was in one of his moods, difficult, sulky and vindictive all at once, Toria found herself forgetting that the years had passed and discovered that the tears were rising to her eyes as easily as when he had first come to Lynbrooke. But when he was enjoying himself and things were going right, no one could have more charm.

Toria always said there was nowhere where she could laugh as she did at home, and now that the twins were growing up they added to her conviction that they were all one family against the world.

In fact it was Xandra who put what they all felt into words.

"Whatever happens," she said once, "there is always 'us'—us against the rest."

It was this feeling of unity which had guided Toria through her first years of being grown-up. However many parties she enjoyed, however many invitations were given to her, she always wanted to come home.

There was such a cosy, comforting feeling about it all. She would tell everything that had happened to Lettice, flatteringly attentive, to Xandra, wide-eyed and smiling with excitement, and to Olga—dear little saintly Olga whom one always had to be careful not to shock.

Sometimes Toria would think whimsically to herself

that, if she really considered doing anything wrong, it would be Olga who would stop her.

She would not be able to face that serious, earnest little face with the feeling that guilt might be written on her own.

Last but by no means least there was Michael. Michael, who could not keep a job of any sort since the war, who always seemed to be at the Castle, waiting for her, ready to sneer and jeer at her friends, at her amusements, her work and her interests.

Poor Michael, he felt things so deeply and was so hard to help!

Watching him now staring down at the fire, Toria wondered how it was that he invariably managed to be a round peg in a square hole.

She knew so many men, far less good-looking, far less intelligent, who managed to make a brilliant success of their lives just by being commonplace, ordinary and unimaginative.

That was perhaps the crux of the matter. Michael was too imaginative.

"Daddy will be disappointed," she said suddenly.

"I can't help that," Michael snapped.

"I know," Toria said, "but be nice to him. He took a lot of trouble to contact the Minister for Air. You know how he hates asking favours."

"Who doesn't?" Michael asked; then savagely kicking the fireguard with his foot as he spoke, he added: "Do you suppose I like staying on here, contributing nothing for my keep, sponging on Uncle Arthur when you know as well as I do that I ought to be making money, supporting a wife and perhaps some beastly children."

Toria began to laugh.

"Oh, Michael, they need not be beastly; but somehow I can't see you as a family man, catching the 8.15 with a bowler hat, a rolled-up umbrella and the *Daily Telegraph* under your arm."

"You can't imagine me doing it," Michael said, "for you know damned well I am incapable of earning a salary of any sort. I'm a rotten failure, that is what I am."

"Does it matter very much," Toria asked, "except to your own self-esteem?"

He stopped kicking the guard and turned round to look at her.

"What do you mean by that?" he asked.

"What I said," Toria replied. "We are all failures if it comes to that. We are all rather badly educated, incapable of settling down to anything, drifting through life aimlessly and as pleasantly as possible, living on other people and an overdraft, and hoping that somehow everything will clear up one day."

"That is all right for a woman," Michael said.

"Not now it isn't," Toria replied. "I ought to be a nurse or a charwoman or something equally useful. Instead of which I pick up a fiver here and a fiver there, and I spend it on clothes to wear among my friends, the majority of whom are as feckless as I am myself. And then I come home. What do any of us do here?"

She paused before she went on.

"We leave the cooking and the housekeeping to old Mrs. Fergusson and those half-witted girls from the village. We just wander about the place being happy. But the main thing is, Michael, that we are happy—far happier than people who think they always ought to be in the right place at the right moment. We are 'us' and nothing and nobody can stop us being that."

Toria's low, rather husky voice was still, and now Michael suddenly and unexpectedly knelt down beside her chair.

Toria was sitting with her legs caught under her, her head against the threadbare, faded velvet cushions. Michael put his elbows on both arms of the chair and his face was level with hers as he said:

"Tell me something honestly, Toria," "What do you want of life?"

"It is an awful thing to admit," Toria replied, "but not much more than I have got now. I would like a lot of money to spend—the twins want new dresses, Lettice longs for some furs, Daddy needs a new suit, and you want a hair-cut."

"Is that really all?" Michael asked.

"I daresay I can add to the list," Toria said, "but those are the essential things. Oh yes, and I would like a blue Persian kitten. I have always wanted one, but the good ones are at least ten guineas."

"You have never really grown up, have you?" Michael asked.

"If being grown-up means walking about looking gloomy and taking a serious view of the economic, national and atomic situation, then thank the Lord I have not," Toria replied.

"I don't mean that," Michael said. "You said just now that you were waiting to fall in love. Haven't you ever been in love with anyone?"

"I don't think so," Toria answered frankly. "Sometimes a man has made my heart beat faster when I first saw him; but it was usually because he was very good-looking or had a crooked smile or something equally irresistible. But then, when I got to know him, I have usually found he was incredibly dull. My heart would then go quickly back to normal."

Michael got to his feet and stood staring down at the fire again.

"I shall have to go away," he said at length.

"But, Michael, why?" Toria enquired.

"Because I love you!"

He spoke in such an ordinary, unemotional tone of voice that for a moment Toria thought she could not have heard him aright; then she sat up very straight in the chair and said:

"Michael! What do you mean?"

"I told you you hadn't grown up," Michael said. "Any woman who had any intelligence would have known what I have been feeling all this past year, that I have loved you with every part of me that can feel at all —utterly and hopelessly! I can't bear life without you and it's just perfect Hell to see or think of you with any other man for two minutes!"

"Oh, Michael, it isn't true! You can't love me, not like that!"

"I do!" Michael replied: "I have loved you for years, I think, ever since you were the child whom I used to

32

order about and tease until you cried. Your poor wet little face used to haunt me when I was out in Burma. I used to tell myself how kind I would be to you when I got home. But when I got back, you had grown up and it was you who were being kind to me."

"Poor Michael!"

"That's right—we must all be kind to Michael! Just throw him a bone which somebody else doesn't want!"

There was too much bitterness in Michael's tone to be borne.

"You are not to talk like that," Toria said. "It isn't true! I never guessed . . . I never thought . . . yet now somehow it seems natural and inevitable, as if it had to happen. You and I. . . . Oh, Michael, I couldn't think of life without your being in it."

"You had better get used to the idea, because I shan't be," Michael said. "If this venture had been successful, I might have begun to hope. But no, it was impossible from the very start. Everything is against us! We are cousins for one thing, and there is no money for another. I'll clear out! I don't know where I'll go, but I'll go somewhere."

"No, Michael, no, you mustn't do that," Toria said. "Don't do anything hasty, nothing that we haven't considered, thought about and talked about, and. . . ." She stopped.

"And what?" Michael asked.

"I don't know what I was going to say," Toria replied. "I am trying to believe that this is true, to realise that you did say it. Oh, Michael, say it again so that I can be certain."

"I love you! Is that what you want to hear?" Michael asked, and the words were a question.

He looked down at her, her face in the firelight seeming strangely white.

"I love you, love you, love you! Oh, Toria, damn you, why did you do this to me?"

He dropped down on his knees as he spoke and laid his face on her lap, his eyes hidden against the roughness of her tweed skirt.

Swiftly her hands went out to him, touching his hair,

33

caressing his neck. They were silent for a long while; then at last in a whisper, Toria said:

"Michael, I'm happier than I've ever been in my life. I can feel it tingling all over me, a wonderful golden happiness just as if I was sitting in the sunshine. It is as if I've been waiting for something for a very long time and now it has happened. Michael, do you think that it could be?"

He raised his head and putting out his hands took her by the shoulders.

"What are you trying to say to me?" he asked.

"I think . . . I think that I love you too," Toria said. "I'm not sure, but, Michael, make me sure."

He pulled her roughly into his arms; his mouth was on hers, fierce, possessive, demanding.

He held her for a long, long moment; then suddenly he flung her from him. He got to his feet.

"Why did you let me do that?" he said. "Don't you understand it is going to make it worse—much worse for me now?"

He strode across the room and flung open the window. It was raining now, and the chill wind swept in, stirring the papers on the table and swirling them across towards the fireplace.

"Michael, your football pool! It will be burnt!" Toria cried suddenly.

Michael turned at that and slammed the window.

"My football pool!" he sneered. "It is about the only work I am capable of doing."

"Perhaps one day you will win a prize," Toria said.

"What should I do then?" Michael enquired. "Marry you?"

Toria suddenly put her hands up to her face.

"Don't, Michael, don't laugh about it."

"Do you think I am joking?"

His voice was tender for the first time.

"Oh, my darling, my sweet, don't you understand how much I adore you? If you did, you would realise a little of the agony which I am suffering. I want you, Toria, I want you for my own; and to see other men talking to you, to know that they make love to you

34

when my back is turned is simply killing me. It is worse than being wounded a thousand times."

The tears brimmed into Toria's eyes and overflowed down her cheeks.

"Oh, Michael, Michael, how I hate that you should be hurt because of me! Yet how can I help it?"

"You are too lovely," he said. "Even when you were a child I was afraid something would take you from me, something would hurt you, and then I would not be able to save you; but now I know it is myself I cannot save."

"Michael, don't talk like that," Toria begged. "It all seems hopeless—a miserable, unhappy tangle; but somehow we will find a way out of it. We simply can't be parted. We must be together, all of us."

"I don't want anyone but you," Michael said.

"I know, but that is selfish," Toria replied.

She was smiling at him, but he would not smile back. His eyes were devouring her face hungrily, taking in every detail of her small, tip-tilted nose, of her eyes bright with tears, of her lips parted in a smile that had something pleading about it.

Toria put up her hand and touched his cheek.

"It doesn't seem somehow as if it is real. I just can't get used to the idea that my Michael, the boy with whom I grew up, has become someone who loves me."

"It was mad of me to have told you," he said. "You realise how much I've got, don't you? Three hundred a year is all that is left of my father and mother's money, and out of that I have to support Lettice."

"We never had any money," Toria said, "and we have all been very happy."

"As children," Michael said.

"And now?"

"Do you think we can go on being happy like this?" Michael asked. "Darling, it is impossible; we have got to do something, but what I don't know. I thought of going to Australia, but what shall I do when I get there? Besides, I am quite certain I am not the type of emigrant they are looking for."

"Michael, you are talking wildly," Toria said.

"And what if I am? Is it not enough to make anyone

35

wild, to see you sitting there, so content, so happy in your own way, while I stand outside in the cold, a beggar at your gates? That is what I have always been, ever since I came here."

"That is nonsense, Michael, and you know it."

"It is not nonsense. Lettice and I have never really had a home of our own. Your father took us in. What do you think he would say now if I told him I wanted to marry his daughter? I—the penniless ne'er-do-well nephew, the boy who has never managed to make good."

"Michael, will you stop being sorry for yourself?" Toria asked. "You did brilliantly in the war and we were all terribly proud of you. It is only now, when you want to find a job, that things seem to go wrong—but I'll find you one."

"And how long shall I keep it?"

"Couldn't you keep it for my sake?" Toria asked.

"No! That is the damnable part about it. I know I couldn't, not for anyone's sake unless it was what I wanted to do."

"But, darling, what do you want to do?"

"I don't know. Don't you understand—that is the torture of the whole thing? I don't know what I want to do. I am only certain of one thing in the whole world, and that is that I love you, Toria. I love you, I love you."

He caught hold of her fiercely and would have kissed her again; then suddenly, as she raised her flower-like face to his, he changed his mind.

"Go away," he said. "Go away and leave me alone. I am no use to you and I never shall be."

He walked away from her and Toria got to her feet. She stood there indecisively, her eyes wide and a little frightened, the firelight picking out the gold of her hair.

It was growing dark and shadowy in the room and Michael's broad shoulders seemed to fill the whole window.

Quite suddenly Toria felt as if the frustration and bitterness within him was enveloping her like a cloud. She felt an unutterable sadness, a sense of desolation well up within her.

She wanted to cry out, and yet her voice seemed imprisoned in her throat and there was nothing she could say; she could only stand there watching Michael, unable to help, unable to reach him.

At last, as if her anguish and indecision percolated into his consciousness, Michael turned.

"Go away, Toria," he said. "I have got to be alone."

There was a finality as well as a command in his voice, and obedient to him, as she had been when she was a child, she went towards the door.

She felt battered and bruised, as if she had encountered a wind of great violence and it had almost torn her limb from limb.

As she reached the door she paused for a moment, looking back, hoping that Michael would ask her to stay, yet almost fearful that he might.

It was all too overwhelming, this thing that had happened to her, this confession that she had never expected or anticipated.

Michael did not speak, and Toria opened the door and passed through it, closing it quietly behind her.

For a long time after she had gone Michael stood at the window, and then at last he turned round. His invention stood in the centre of the room and it seemed to him to be waiting there for him.

Suddenly with an almost indescribable sound he went towards it. There was a hammer lying on the table. He picked it up and brought it sharply down on the work which had taken him nearly a year to complete.

There was the sound of the hammer striking metal, but the blow fell on solid steel and did no harm. Then, as if he could not bring himself to destroy what had for such a long time held all his hopes, ambitions and interest, Michael hurled the hammer from him with all his force. It sped across the room, knocked against a lamp standing on a side table and brought it crashing to the ground.

Michael did not even look to see what damage he had done.

He walked across to the fireplace and throwing himself down on the chair in which Toria had recently sat, he buried his face in the cushion against which she had lain her head.

3

Charles stopped the car at the drive gates.

It was a lovely day, the ground was crisp with frost and the sun, warm and golden, seemed to promise that spring was not far away.

Charles wanted to stretch his legs and also he had learned from bitter experience that the drive to Lynbrooke Castle was no pleasure ride.

"Take everything that is in the back of the car into the kitchen to Mrs. Fergusson," he told his driver.

The man saluted.

"Very good, Sir."

There was the suspicion of a grin on his face as Charles walked away. "Everything in the back of the car" included a ham, a stilton cheese, a succulent pork pie and a jar of *pâté-de-foie-gras* from Fortnum & Mason.

Charles had discovered that it was quite easy to become a visitor to Lynbrooke Castle so long as one invited oneself and just turned up without making any fuss. In fact, after a visit or two, he had been taken for granted and had almost become one of the family.

The preparations for his first visit were never repeated, and he had no reason to fear now that the Gales might put themselves out for him.

Shortly after his first luncheon at the Castle Charles had telephoned to Michael—a difficult monosyllabic conversation—that he had decided to look at his invention again and had told him on what day he proposed to come.

Michael had certainly not been effusive in his manner. But Charles had informed him that he would arrive at tea-time; and on that occasion he was late for a meal.

There was nothing left to eat and only a cup of very weak and cold tea could be offered to him in the way of hospitality.

But he had seen Toria, and that, he admitted to himself with an unusual degree of self-honesty, was enough. Since then he had gone down to Lynbrooke again and yet again, making Michael the excuse, yet gradually ceasing to pretend even to the family that Michael's invention was of paramount importance where he was concerned.

He felt as if he were drawn by an invisible magnet, and while he admitted frankly to himself that the magnet in question was Toria, he was too shy and far too reserved to be able to convey the fact to her.

Charles was a strange mixture—of dashing bravery when it came to action, of an embarrassed reserve when it concerned anything emotional or to do with his own feelings.

Yet, being generous both in thought and deed, he soon found that the one thing he wanted to do more than anything else in the world was to help the Gales.

It was not very difficult to see that their cry of poverty was a very real one indeed. The Earl was practically bankrupt, his daughters spent as little as possible, yet even that was too much.

Michael and his sister were in the same position. It was in fact a miracle that the family had survived as long as they had. And while the practical course was, of course, for them to abandon the Castle and what remained of the Estate, Charles realised that to them it was home and that to part them from it would be to tear up the very roots from which they sprang.

It was, however, a case of acting quickly, but how he could contrive to help or rather save them was a problem which Charles was finding himself pondering over to the exclusion of everything else.

Michael was, of course, the first nut to crack, but Charles knew that unless he took his invention as it stood—and it was in fact utterly useless—Michael was resolved to accept no other favour from him.

He was for some reason unknown to Charles actively aggressive to him. There was no mistaking the antagonism in his manner or the hostility in his voice.

The only time when Michael could forget his grievance and be carried away was when studying or discussing the technicalities of aeronautics. Then the frown would vanish from between his eyes and he would become eagerly interested and vitally alert.

It was impossible for Charles not to realise then that he had a charm and an almost compelling attraction; and yet he had to admit to himself that he personally disliked the younger man and found his attitude on the whole unsatisfactory.

But, he told himself, Michael had to be found a job. It would help the household, it would help Toria, and that was all that mattered.

He had been thinking of the Gales' financial position all the way down from London, and now as his car drove away down the drive, bumping drunkenly in the pot holes, Charles looked around him and noted once again, as he had done so often before, that the lodge gates were liable to collapse at any moment.

Architecturally beautiful, they were rusty and crumbling with age and neglect, while the heraldic animals which stood on the stone pillars on either side of them had long ago lost their heads and legs.

Charles was just about to walk through the gates when he saw that a notice had been fixed on one of the stone gate-posts. He stopped to read it and saw that it was written in untidy block capitals which had been outlined with red and blue crayon.

"COME TO THE HOLY GROTO," it invited, "AND YOU WILL BE CURED OF REMATISIM, ARTHERITIS AND ALL YOUR ACHES AND PAINS. ADMITTENCE 6d."

The spelling made Charles smile. He walked down the drive and soon saw a large cardboard arrow, also ornamented with coloured crayons, which pointed the

40

way to the right where a small path wound through a clump of laurel bushes.

Charles followed the arrow and found himself in an untidy, unkept shrubbery. A few Scotch firs which should have long since been felled rose above a thick undergrowth of laurels, rhododendrons and briars.

Charles was wondering how far this path would take him when he overheard voices behind him. Looking back he saw that two women were walking after him down the drive.

Quickly he abandoned the path and pushing his way through the rhododendron bushes was soon hidden from sight. It was an impulse which made him hide himself, but he did not regret it when he heard one of the women say with an American accent:

"Be a sport, Betty, let's have a look while we're here. You know I'm anxious to complete my paper on the holy spots of old England."

"I've never heard of a Holy Grotto in these parts," the other woman remarked curtly in an uncompromising and unmistakably English voice.

Charles could see them now and he noted that they were both middle-aged, both plump and well upholstered in Scottish tweeds, with felt hats, set at a jaunty angle and ornamented with dyed pheasant feathers, on their greying hair.

"Now which way do we go?" the American woman asked. "Ah, here is another arrow."

They disappeared from Charles' sight and he followed them cautiously. A moment later he heard their voices joined by another and recognised immediately Xandra's gay, lilting tones.

He avoided the path and cut directly through the bushes to where the sounds came from. It was only a second or two before he was able to see and yet not be seen.

There was a small clearing surrounded by fir trees, and in the middle of it was a stone-encircled pool. At one end there was a statue, or what remained of one, and Charles thought he recognised the remnants of a cornucopia held by a green and crumbling goddess.

It was, he was sure, the Victorian idea of a pleasure garden; and while the cornucopia had once gushed water, now the stream trickled far below it, oozing untidily over the stagnant banks of what had originally been a tidy, compact water-lily pond.

Xandra and Olga were standing beside the pool. They wore their green jumpers and out-grown tweed skirts, but their hair was magically gold and their lovely little faces had almost an ethereal look against the background of dark green bushes and beneath the shadows of the firs.

Olga had a wooden box in her hand and Xandra was explaining to the two visitors the magic properties of the pool.

"This water is a cure for all your aches and pains," she informed the American woman.

"But how do you know that?" the woman asked.

"We live here," Xandra explained, "and we often talk of the wonderful properties of this Grotto."

"Wal, isn't that interesting!" the American exclaimed.

Her companion, however, looked sceptical.

"It doesn't look very old to me," she said; "not more than a hundred years at any rate."

Xandra looked indignant.

"It is much more than that. I am quite certain that the Holy Grotto was here when the Castle was first built, and that was when the Normans first came to England."

"1066," the American exclaimed, a tone of awe in her voice.

"That is right," Xandra said. "That was the date of the old Castle. Of course it has been altered since, but I am sure this Grotto must have been there then. Why, it might have been one of the places where the pilgrims stopped on their way to Canterbury."

"But this is not on the way to Canterbury," the English woman remarked.

"Canterbury can't be the only place where they had pilgrimages to," Xandra retorted. "Can't you see the people come riding up on their horses to drink from this wonderful spring? Perhaps they brought their relations with them to be cured of their ills. I am not certain, but I think there is a picture of people being cured at a Grotto just like this."

"Wal, I think this is verry, verry exciting!" the American said. "I will certainly put it all down in my book. Do you know to what Saint the Grotto is dedicated?"

Xandra looked at her twin.

"St. Thérèse," Olga said.

"But St. Thérèse is quite a modern Saint," the American woman exclaimed. "Unless you mean St. Teresa, but she was Spanish."

Xandra could see that Olga was out of her depth. She cast a quick look round and then exclaimed in the tones of a pantomime chorus girl heralding on the principal boy:

"Oh, look, here comes a crippled boy! I am sure he has come to be cured of his ills."

As if he had been waiting for his cue, a boy of about eight or nine, whom Charles was sure he had seen hanging about the back door of the Castle, came limping into the clearing. He was supporting himself on what was apparently a crutch, but which Charles recognised as a croquet mallet.

Ignoring both the twins and the visitors, he hobbled up to the head of the pool, and kneeling down, cupped his hands for a drink of water. He only took a sip, then rising to his feet he threw away the croquet mallet and announced in flat, unemotional and rather surly tones:

"I'm cured."

"Cured?" the American woman exclaimed.

"I were a cripple an' now I can walk," the boy announced.

Her English friend took her by the arm.

"Come along, Sadie," she said, "these children are, I think, rehearsing some private theatricals."

Xandra looked from one to the other in perplexity.

"I think it is wonderful," she said. "Aren't you impressed?"

"I think we have seen quite enough," the English

woman remarked crisply. "Come on, Sadie, we must be getting along."

Sadie, however, was more tender-hearted and hung back.

"We haven't paid our sixpence yet, and I am sure you children are giving all you collect to a very good cause."

"Yes, indeed," Xandra said. "We are giving it to the poor."

"You surely couldn't have a better cause than that."

She fumbled in her bag, pressed all the silver coins she had in Xandra's hand, and then hurried after her companion. As they passed down the path within a few feet of where Charles was hiding, he heard the English woman say:

"I am not certain they weren't trying to trick us into believing we had seen a miracle. I think we ought to report them to the Police."

"Wal, I thought it was real interesting," Sadie remarked. "Those two little girls were quite lovely. They looked like angels themselves."

Charles heard the English woman snort, but her reply was inaudible. He was just about to step forward himself and suggest that he should pay sixpence for the pleasure of seeing the drama enacted once again, when he realised that an altercation of some violence had broken out. The boy was saying:

"Three shillings be what I ought ter 'ave."

"But we said we would give you a third of what we collected," Xandra expostulated. "A third of seven shillings isn't three."

"Two and six then," the boy conceded.

"And it isn't two and six either," Xandra answered. "Wait a minute while I work it out."

"Two an' six is what I'm a-going ter 'ave, or I don't do it no more. That water fair freezes me inside, it does. T'aint healthy."

"What is three into seven?" Xandra asked of Olga, ignoring his protests.

"Suppose I tell you?" said Charles, stepping into the clearing.

Xandra looked up and gave a cry of welcome.

"Hullo, Charles. How nice that it's you!" she smiled. "What is a third of seven shillings?"

"Two and fourpence," Charles replied.

"There," Xandra exclaimed. "I knew it wasn't two and six. Two and four is all you can have, Jimmy."

"Two an' six or I don't do it again," Jimmy retorted stubbornly.

"You can't say that," Xandra replied. "That's black . . . black something, isn't it, Charles?"

"Blackmail," Charles replied. "Yes, I am afraid it is, Jimmy. But you won't be wanted any more today. Here is five shillings, and go and take that notice off the gate."

Jimmy immediately stopped being aggressive.

"Thank you, Sir. Yes, Sir, I'll do it at once."

He took the money and ran off on feet which looked as if there was never the slightest chance of their being crippled.

"Now, Xandra, what is all this?" Charles asked.

Xandra looked up at him.

"Well, this is a Holy Grotto, and. . . ."

"I've heard all that. The English visitor said she thought she ought to inform the Police."

"Oh, she didn't, did she?" Xandra said.

"I told you we ought not to do it," Olga cried. "I knew it was wrong, and now something terrible will happen to us."

"I don't think you need worry too much," Charles said, seeing that Olga was really upset. "The American had a kind heart. You wouldn't have got seven shillings out of her if she hadn't; and now what is the idea of all this . . . pageantry?"

Xandra linked her arm in his.

"We are trying to make money."

"That is obvious! But why?"

"It is really to help Daddy and Toria. They were talking last night and Toria said, 'If only we had a decent old house, we could open it to the public at two-and-sixpence a time.'

"And Daddy quoted all the enormous sums his

45

friends had made by having their houses on view. Then they both started complaining bitterly that the Castle was Victorian and no one would pay anything to come and see it, so Olga and I thought of having a Holy Grotto in the garden.

"Olga has been reading *The Song of Bernadette*. You know the story of the girl who had visions at Lourdes. Now millions of people have been cured of their ills. They throw away their crutches and hang them up on the wall.

"We thought this looked awfully like a Holy Grotto. After all, it might be Holy for all we know. Olga cut her finger and when she put it in the water she said she couldn't feel the pain any more."

"That was because I couldn't feel the finger either," Olga said. "The water was so cold, it froze it."

"Well, anyway, we thought it was a brilliant idea," Xandra said, "and we got Jimmy to come and act the part of a cripple boy. But he wasn't very good, was he?"

"I am afraid he wouldn't have convinced anyone," Charles smiled.

"I don't think that part was right," Olga said seriously. "It was like making fun of miracles. That is sacrilege."

"I don't think you need worry unduly," Charles consoled her. "Jimmy wasn't convincing enough to deceive a blind man."

"He would have been if he had done it properly," Xandra said. "He was so terribly bad. I could have done it, but as I am so like Olga, the visitors might have suspected something when they saw Olga was collecting the money."

"I think you will both end up in prison eventually," Charles said. "In the meantime we must think of some better way of making money than trying to extort it from an unsuspecting public."

Xandra sighed.

"It is terribly disappointing," she said. "I did think we might retrieve all our fortunes. I lay awake for hours working out what six thousand sixpences came to. That is how many half-a-crowns some of Daddy's friends received for opening their houses."

"It is certainly very unfortunate that the Castle is not as William the Conqueror built it," Charles said. "I liked the American lady for remembering the date, didn't you?"

"If she hadn't had her silly English friend with her, I believe she would have swallowed the whole story," Xandra complained.

"I shouldn't be surprised," Charles said, "but perhaps it was all for the best. You would have got very tired of crowds of American tourists coming here and having to stand all day taking their sixpences. Any job of routine work gets rather monotonous after the first day or two."

"We thought of that," Xandra said. "Olga and I were going to take turns, and have a little hut erected for when it rained, like a sentry-box. We planned to ask Mrs. Fergusson to give us sandwiches so that we wouldn't need to go home for meals. But I daresay we would have got tired of them, too."

"You might find these more appetising," Charles remarked, taking a box of chocolates from his pocket.

Xandra gave a little cry of excitement.

"Oh, Charles, you are an angel, and they are scrumptious ones too. Look, Olga, they are just the kind of chocolates you like."

She held out the box to Olga, but the latter turned away.

"Oh, do make her take one, Charles," Xandra pleaded. "She is punishing herself because she thinks that we have been making a mockery of holy things. She will starve for days and deprive herself of everything that is nice."

"Now listen to me, both of you," Charles said, unable to resist the appeal in Xandra's voice. "What you have done wasn't wrong at all. Anyway, not from a moral point of view. It was quite obvious from the beginning that Jimmy was acting, and Olga never said anything except to suggest a Saint, so she can't be accused of trying to deceive innocent and unsuspecting tourists. After

47

all, there is nothing wrong in acting a religious scene. They have a whole Passion Play at Oberammergau."

Olga smiled.

"Perhaps it would be all right for me to have a chocolate," she said. "And I would like one."

"Then you had better hurry up and eat your share," Charles cautioned her, "or Xandra will wolf the lot."

Eating chocolates and talking nineteen to the dozen, the twins escorted Charles back to the house. They were met by Mrs. Fergusson in the hall.

"Thank you very much indeed, Sir, for the food," she said to Charles. "That ham's a real beauty. And it's taken a big load off my mind, for the fish which we were having to luncheon today had definitely gone off, and there's no sign of that butcher's boy. I was at my wit's end to know what to do."

"Well, let us have the ham by all means," Charles said hastily.

He had suspected Mrs. Fergusson's fish on more than one occasion.

The twins stuffed a chocolate into Mrs. Fergusson's mouth to prevent her from saying any more and ran upstairs to get ready for luncheon.

Charles opened the door of the sitting-room and went in.

Toria was sitting at the far end of the room on the window seat. He went towards her. He was wearing crepe-soled shoes and they made no sound on the carpeted floor.

He was close beside her before he realised that she had a handkerchief to her eyes and that she was crying. It was too late for him to retreat and he stood for a moment embarrassed and self-conscious before he said her name.

"Toria!"

She turned round, startled at the sound of his voice. Her face was very white and her eyes seemed larger than ever as they brimmed over with tears which ran unchecked down her cheeks.

There was something so intensely pathetic in the expression on her face, that Charles forgot everything, even his own shyness.

"Toria, my darling, what has upset you?" he asked.

"Oh, it's you, Charles."

She was not aware that her voice had flattened slightly as if she had expected someone else and had been disappointed.

"What has happened?"

"Nothing."

She turned her face away from him, mopping her eyes fiercely with a childish violence which was somehow infinitely appealing.

"But something must have gone wrong," Charles said. "Is it money?"

"Yes, money," Toria replied, her voice somehow relieved, as if the suggestion made an explanation easier than it might have been.

Charles sat down beside her on the window seat.

"Listen, Toria," he said. "I am rich—disgustingly rich when I think about it. Won't you let me help you? Can't you. . . . ?"

He stopped suddenly.

"Toria," he said, and his voice was very low and deep. "I've wanted to marry you ever since the first time I saw you. I suppose you couldn't think of me in that way?"

Toria said nothing for a moment; then without looking at Charles, she put out her hand blindly. He took it in both of his.

"I suppose that would solve everything," she said at length in a deep, rather breathless little voice.

"Oh, Toria, if only you would," Charles said.

His fingers tightened on her hand until they hurt, but she made no attempt to move it away from him. Instead she turned suddenly and looked up into his eyes.

Hers were vividly blue, and there was something in the glance she gave him which made Charles think that she was asking a question, though what it was he had no idea. As if seeing his face re-assured her, she said after a moment:

"It would solve everything. You are quite sure you want me?"

"Then you will . . . you will marry me?"

Charles hardly recognised his own voice bursting from between his lips. He felt for a moment as if he had got into a dive in his aeroplane and couldn't get out of it.

He felt as if he could never draw his breath again, and then suddenly Toria's hand was against his lips and he heard himself saying:

"I can't quite believe it. I somehow never dreamt that you would."

"Must you be so modest?" Toria asked with a faint smile.

Before Charles could answer, the door was flung open and the twins came bursting in.

"Luncheon is ready, and oh, Toria, we have got ham! Charles has brought us an absolute whopper. It must have been the biggest pig in the world. Won't Daddy be pleased? He adores ham."

Toria got slowly to her feet. Charles had relinquished her hand as the twins burst into the room, and now for one moment he wondered if he had dreamt the whole thing or if it had really happened.

"Don't say anything yet, please," Toria said in a low voice.

He shook his head as Lettice crossed the room to welcome him.

She was looking unusually pretty, he thought. A red ribbon tied round her dark hair matched the red cardigan she wore over a stone-coloured jumper and skirt.

"Nobody told me you were coming," she said, glancing at Toria accusingly.

"I don't think anybody knew I was," Charles replied quickly. "I ought to be working at the Ministry, but I played truant. It was too lovely a day to stay in a stuffy office."

There never had been a more golden day he thought to himself as they went into luncheon, being joined in the hall by Lord Lynbrooke and his two spaniels.

There was only one place that was empty and that

was Michael's. As Lord Lynbrooke glanced towards the empty chair, Charles heard Lettice say to Toria:

"Where is Michael?"

"Gone out," Toria replied.

"But where?"

Toria gave a little shrug of her shoulders and Lettice said no more.

When luncheon was over Lettice suggested that Charles might like to come for a walk. He was longing to be alone with Toria, but she said nothing and in the end no one made a move.

They drifted back into the sitting-room, where the twins put on the new records which Charles had brought on his last visit, and conversation for the moment was impossible.

It seemed to him that Toria was restless. She sat down on a chair by the fireplace, then she rose and walked to the window seat.

She had only been there for a few moments when she rose and went to the writing-desk. After that she walked back again to the hearth. He was content in some ways to watch her.

Her movements were exquisitely graceful and every time she passed in front of the window the sunshine touched the pale gold of her hair and Charles felt himself thrill with an almost physical pain at her beauty.

Yet it was impossible for him not to be aware that she was worried. Something was perturbing her, and then he told himself that she was troubled by the decision she had made just before luncheon.

Perhaps, he thought, she wanted to be alone with him, even as he wanted to be alone with her, and had no idea how to contrive it with all the others grouped around them.

Had he but known it, Toria's thoughts were chaotic to a point when she could not disentangle her feelings and emotions one from the other or put them into any sequence or form.

Over and over in her mind one name was repeating itself, hammering at her brain incessantly:

"Michael! Michael! Michael!"

The whole week had been dreadful—too dreadful for her to know what she felt or thought. Ever since Michael had told her that he loved her, she had known that his love was tearing him to pieces and making him more miserable than he had ever been in the whole of his life before.

She had not realised, until Michael told her of his love, how close they were to each other in many ways. It was true that she had always thought of Michael as a brother; and yet surely brothers and sisters were not so perceptive to each other as they were?

There was some bond between them which Toria could not begin to analyse, but which she knew drew her irresistibly to Michael's side and made her share his feelings, whether she would or whether she wouldn't.

Never after that first kiss did he attempt to touch her again. It seemed that in declaring his love for her he had released nine thousand devils so that he must take a delight in torturing them both.

Toria wished more than once that she had never been born, and the days seemed to be long drawn-out miseries of pain with only very occasional moments of happiness to relieve the darkness of them.

She had never known that Michael could be quite as difficult as this, and yet she told herself that perhaps it was her fault too.

She should have understood about him, she should not have waited until he was almost driven insane by his sense of failure.

She tried to talk with him reasonably, but somehow such conversations always ended with Michael being either in a fury of anger or in the depths of despair, a despair so miserable and so depressed that somehow she could not reach him and help him back to a more sane outlook.

What was so astonishing, it seemed to Toria, was that no one in the house seemed to realise that anything untoward had happened.

Not even Lettice who loved Michael and who at moments was aggressively possessive towards him, seemed aware of it.

Sometimes Toria thought that she and Michael were alone in some kind of terrible No Man's Land, hovering between the past and the present and unable ever to find a future for themselves.

It was there in this No Man's Land of emotion that they really lived during those days, while their bodies moved like automatons through the days, coming down for meals, walking in the gardens, going to bed; apparently they were ordinary, unemotional people, but really they were torn, possessed and devoured by their own feelings in this strange, unknown, mystical existence of which no one else was aware.

"We can't go on like this, Michael," Toria said more than once. "It is killing me. Besides, where will it end? What will happen to us? You say that you love me, yet in the same breath you say that neither of us can ever mean anything to each other. If we can't live like this, if we can't get married, what is going to happen?"

"I don't know," Michael snarled; "if I did, do you think I wouldn't tell you?"

"But, Michael, why can't we do something about it?"

"What do you suggest?" Michael asked savagely.

Toria knew there was no answer. She was as well aware as he was that they could not get married without any money.

Sometimes when she was alone at night, lying wide awake in the darkness, Toria would tell herself that other people managed. A man could get a job as a farm labourer at five pounds a week.

There were people who lived in workmen's cottages, who cooked and cleaned for their husbands, had babies and looked after them with no help.

She knew quite a number of girls who had married since the war into that sort of existence. When she saw them occasionally, perhaps on their one night out in London in a year, when they managed to get a baby-sitter to stay with the children, they seemed gay and happy enough.

They managed. They didn't tear themselves into pieces and torture their minds and souls about it.

But even as she thought about it she knew it was impossible for Michael. Granted that she would not make him a very good wife under these circumstances, however hard she tried, she knew that his pride would never let him attempt it.

He would fail, he would drag her down, even supposing they had got over the obstacle of being first cousins, and all the other things which Michael seemed to put in their way as if he enjoyed conjuring them up.

And then today of all days she had known that a climax had been reached.

It all started with a bill arriving for Michael for some material he had ordered for his invention.

It had been sent for the third time and accompanied by a letter which said that unless the account was paid promptly, the matter would be put in the hands of Solicitors.

Michael could not pay it and he had to ask his Uncle if he could help him.

Lord Lynbrooke had enough bills of his own, and he told Michael so in no uncertain terms.

"You shouldn't order what you can't afford to pay for, my boy," he said sharply.

"I will pay you back, Sir, as soon as my next dividend comes in," Michael said stiffly.

"Well, I suppose I shall have to see to it," Lord Lynbrooke remarked, taking up the bill and scrutinising it. "It appears to me that all this was very unnecessary. What is Drayton doing about it, I would like to know? Is he taking your invention or isn't he? He has been down here often enough."

"It is no use, Sir," Michael said stiffly.

"No use?" the Earl enquired. "Then what is the point of wasting time and money on it? Good lord, boy, there must be something you can do to make an honest living."

Lord Lynbrooke was not particularly unkind, but his words touched Michael on the raw.

He came out of the Library scowling and sullen, and finding Toria alone in the sitting-room, he gave vent to his feelings.

"There is only one thing I can do, and that is to sell

myself as dearly as I can. If one is going to be a gigolo, one may as well be an expensive one. I am going over now to ask Susan Butler to marry me."

If Toria could have laughed at him, perhaps he could have taken himself less dramatically; but his words hurt her, as they were intended to do.

"But, Michael, you can't marry poor 'Phone and Photo'," Toria said. "You will be terribly unhappy, and you will make her utterly miserable. Besides, you don't love her."

"What has love got to do with it?" Michael asked savagely. "Where has it got us? Loving you has perhaps been the most damnable thing that ever happened to me. I can stand the rest, but not that."

"Oh, Michael, must you say things which hurt so frightfully?" Toria gasped.

"Why should they hurt you?" Michael asked. "You, the beautiful Lady Toria Gale, who can marry anyone. Why don't you marry Pennington? He is rich, isn't he? But you're useless, as we all are. You can't do anything in life except look for someone to marry you. Like me, you might as well sell yourself as dearly as you can."

"Michael, Michael, don't talk like that," Toria begged. "Can't you see you are hurting us both? You are spoiling everything that was beautiful and lovely, you are making it all horrible, besmirched and dirty, and I can't bear it."

"I am not going to stay here any longer," Michael said. "I won't go on living on charity, being made to feel useless, having your father kick me around. I can't even earn the wage of a garden boy, but Susan will be pleased to keep me."

"There is no doubt about that," Toria said, "but will that solve anything? Will that help what we feel about each other?"

"I have told you before and I tell you again," Michael retorted, "I can't bear to see you any longer. This is your home, so it's quite obvious that I'm the one who has got to go, isn't it?"

He had laughed then rather horribly and gone from the room, leaving Toria in tears.

She did not cry often, in fact it took a great deal to make her cry, especially about herself; but it suddenly seemed to her that everything had gone horrible and she was lonelier than she had ever been in her whole life before.

Everything had been such fun, despite having no mother, despite their poverty; and then Michael had told her that he loved her and everything had changed.

It had taken away the laughter and gaiety from the house, and she had felt herself drifting into that strange and horrible place in which there was only Michael's anger and no happiness whatsoever.

And then as the darkness of her misery closed over her like a cloud and all she could think of was that Michael had gone and that he would never come back so long as she was there, she had looked up to find Charles beside her.

He seemed so strong and dependable, so sane and unemotional. What Toria wanted after those nerve-racking emotions was a harbour in which she could rest her weary mind and soul.

She felt tired out and utterly fatigued, in fact her brain at times felt as if it did not belong to her. The strength of Charles' fingers, warm and strong and somehow dependable, were unexpectedly comforting.

He always did the right thing, she thought—coming to the Castle without fuss, always bringing food with him, being nice to the twins and keeping her father in a good temper.

He did not revolt her by trying to maul her as Lord Pennington did; and when he asked her to marry him it was not his money that mattered and the fact that, as he said himself, he was "disgustingly rich", but that he was there like a life-buoy to cling to in a very bad storm.

Marrying Charles would settle everything, Toria told her poor tired mind. She would go away from the Castle and Michael could go on living there.

Perhaps he would invent something else and Charles would help him, and then he would have some money, enough at any rate so that he would not be obliged to run up debts and upset her father.

It was impossible for Michael to go out into the world and make his living. He had failed so often and so dismally before.

There was nowhere else for him to live save at the Castle. He did not seem to have any friends and he hadn't any family except Lettice.

Poor Michael—he really was poor.

Toria suddenly felt very maternal towards him, like a mother with a tiresome, ill, querulous child whom she loved much more than all the strong healthy ones put together, for his very weakness made him so dependable on her.

It was Michael's weakness, Toria thought, which made her feel responsible for him. He was so ridiculously good-looking, he had so much charm when he chose to exert it, and yet he was as helpless as any newborn kitten.

He simply could not look after himself—while she could. She had friends, she had a resilience and a sense of adaptability which would always see her through, whatever happened.

Yes, she must be the one to look after Michael—for Michael could never look after himself.

The luncheon was over and Toria wandered around because she wanted Charles to go. She wanted to be alone for when Michael came back.

She did not believe for one moment that he had gone over to propose to Susan Butler. He was always threatening to do so, but it was too much a family joke for him to do such a thing.

No, he had gone off in a rage, walking through the woods possibly with a stick with which he would slash at the undergrowth. He would walk and walk until he was tired and hungry, and then he would come home truculent and difficult, ready to say some more hurting, bitter things which would make her feel that knives were being thrust into her heart.

But he would come home; and when she told him about marrying Charles, he would understand, although he might not like it, how it would solve a great many problems.

57

Charles had money for one thing, and he had influence for another. Something could be done, and at any rate Michael could stay at the Castle while she could go away.

For a moment Toria's thoughts shied at the thought of going away anywhere; but as she looked at Charles at the other side of the room, apparently listening to the noise of the gramophone, she felt re-assured.

His lips were smiling, yet his eyes were serious as they rested on her. He looked so safe. She had never heard his voice raised in anger, she had never heard him querulous or irritable. She had never seen him frown.

Perhaps he does all these things, she thought, and then realised that they would not hurt her if he did. She knew he had no power over her, because she did not love him.

It was Michael she loved—Michael, who had rushed away in a rage, leaving her to cry for him.

"Where can Michael be?" Lettice said suddenly, as if she could read Toria's thoughts. "I have never known him to be as late for luncheon as this."

"Perhaps he is thinking up a new invention," Xandra said. "Charles, are you going to buy Michael's invention? You are taking an awfully long time and we want the money frightfully badly."

"I am afraid it is not in my power to buy it even if I wanted to. It is the Air Ministry that has to decide. I have talked to them about it, but I am afraid it is not exactly what they want at the moment."

"Oh, Charles, do you mean there is no hope?" Lettice asked.

"I am afraid not as the thing stands," Charles said honestly. "Michael might be able to work on it from another angle. I must talk to him about it."

"He will be so dreadfully upset, he pinned all his hopes on it," Lettice cried.

"I think Michael has known for some time that Charles does not want it," Toria said unexpectedly.

Lettice looked towards her with a thoughtful expression on her face.

58

"Has he said so?" she asked. "Is that what has upset him today? Did you tell him you did not want it?"

She asked the question of Charles but he shook his head.

"I have not seen Michael today. I only arrived a little while before luncheon."

"Oh, the poor boy," Lettice said. "Why can't he even have a break! It doesn't seem fair somehow."

Toria got to her feet and walked towards the window.

"I don't know quite why we should expect things to be fair," she remarked. "Everything in the world is unevenly arranged, if one thinks about it."

There was a bitter note in her voice. Charles got to his feet and crossed to her side.

"Don't worry," he said to her quietly so that she alone could hear. "I will find something for Michael to do."

"He won't take it from you," Toria replied.

"I will get him a job," Charles promised. "It need not come from me. I will find something, somehow. I don't like you to be worried about him."

Toria looked up at him. He was so very much taller than she was and her head barely reached to his shoulder.

"You are a very kind person, aren't you, Charles?" she asked. He smiled down into her troubled eyes.

"I want to be kind to you," he said softly, "and to anyone connected with you."

Toria gave a little shiver and looked away from him.

"It is not easy to be kind to Michael."

"I will find a way," Charles said with a confidence he did not feel was entirely justified.

Toria did not answer and after a moment Charles said, still in a voice that no one could overhear:

"Can't we go somewhere alone, I want to talk to you?"

Toria looked vaguely around her.

"There is nowhere," she said. "Besides. . . ."

She hesitated, and Charles prompted.

"Besides what?"

"I have got something to do this afternoon."

"Would you rather I went away?"

"That seems horrid after you. . . ."

"If you want me to go, I will go at once," Charles interrupted. "May I come down to dinner or shall I send a car to fetch you so that we can dine together in London?"

"Send a car—we will dine together in London," Toria said. "I would prefer that. We have got a lot to arrange, haven't we? And oh, Charles, will you marry me quickly?"

He drew in his breath at the sheer delight of hearing her say it.

"How quickly?" he asked. "Tomorrow or the next day?"

Toria smiled then, but her eyes were still troubled.

"Next week, I think. Have we got to have a grand wedding? You could get a special licence or something, couldn't you?"

"I will get one this afternoon," Charles said; "then you can choose any day you fancy."

"It must be soon," Toria said.

Charles could feel her sense of urgency, but it was difficult to question her about it. The gramophone was blaring in his ear and he was conscious that Lettice was watching them from the other side of the room.

"We will talk about it tonight," he said. "Do you mind if I telephone my mother and tell her that we are engaged?"

"Your mother? Of course, let her know."

Toria spoke as if she had not been aware that he had any relations or any connections of any sort.

"She will want to meet you," Charles said. "If there is no time for you to come down to our house in Worcester, I will ask her to come up to London."

"Thank you."

Toria's expression of gratitude had a finality about it.

"Good-bye then until this evening. I will send the car for you about seven o'clock."

"That will be very nice. Good-bye, Charles."

Toria could hardly look at him, then she moved forward on the window seat and swung her legs over the

60

window-sill and slipped down into the garden. She moved away through the untidy flower beds towards the park.

Charles watched her go and then turned back into the room.

"I am going now," he said to Lettice.

She got up and linked her arm in his.

"I will see you off. You do pay us such short visits, we don't really see enough of you."

"I have been here more times than I like to count this week," Charles said, merely for something to say.

Lettice would have answered him, but at that moment the twins realised what was happening and came running from the end of the room.

"Oh, Charles, don't go," they said. "It can't be time for you to leave yet."

They forgot the gramophone as they went with him into the hall, but Toria heard it playing as she moved away from the house down through the garden and into the park.

The twins had put on "Some day my heart will awake", and she wondered bitterly, as the clear sweet voice of the singer followed her through the open window, why anyone wanted their heart to awake.

If this was love, it was curiously like hell, this burning misery of being tortured almost unbearably.

Why, she asked herself, as she had asked herself so many times before, had Michael told her of his love?

She had been worried about him before that, but there had not been this agony of longing to help him and knowing there was nothing she could do.

She remembered how she thought that one day she would fall in love and how she had refused young man after young man because she had known the feelings that she had for them, even when they were those of affection, were not love.

Now she wondered if all the time she had been in love with Michael and not known it, or whether this feeling that she had for him was not love at all but something quite different for which nobody had ever found a word.

But of course it was love!

The pain of being burnt up inside, of being consumed by one's own feelings. It was love to feel that whatever the sacrifice one made, whatever the subjection of oneself, one was at least doing something for the other person, so that one's own feelings in the matter were of no account.

Now she asked herself whether it would be such a sacrifice to marry Charles. Wouldn't any other existence be better than what she had experienced these past weeks?

And then with a sudden pang of unhappiness she realised that by marrying Charles she must leave Michael for ever, go away from him, forget him save as a brother with whom she had been brought up.

It seemed to her then as if something within herself were lost, shut out in the cold, abandoned for ever. She did not know what it was, she only knew it was a part of herself and she could not retrieve it.

Now, when she was almost out of sight of the house, she saw Michael coming towards her.

He was walking, just as she had expected, through the park, bareheaded, a stick in his hand slashing at the shrubs as he passed. He cut a briar and it clung to him, then another and yet another.

It was as if he wielded a sword savagely. Somehow she could not help smiling because it was so characteristic of Michael, this violent outlet of his feelings, this need for action.

Michael had seen her. She saw him miss an easy stroke with his stick. She thought that he squared his shoulders, put his head back almost with an assumption of bravado.

She hurried on quicker and quicker towards him and she was almost running when finally she reached him. She forced herself to speak quietly, to make her words as casual as possible.

"You are terribly late for luncheon, but I expect Mrs. Fergusson has kept you something."

"I have had luncheon."

The words, mild enough in themselves, were spoken

aggressively. Toria felt a cold hand clutch at her heart.

"Where?" she asked, even while she knew the answer.

"At the Butlers'."

"So you did go there?"

"I told you I was going to."

There was a long silence, and almost instinctively Toria turned and walked beside him. They moved evenly together.

They could see the Castle ahead of them, its ugly Victorian battlements silhouetted against the pale sky.

"Well," Michael said at length. "I am engaged to be married."

"And so am I," Toria retorted. "I am going to marry Charles."

4

Toria sat in her bedroom and looked at her reflection in the glass.

Behind her, thrown over the chair and ready for her to put on, was her wedding dress. Her veil was draped over the end of the bed waiting to be arranged under a sparkling diamond tiara which lay in its blue velvet case on the dressing-table.

Toria stared at her face as if she had never seen herself before; yet in reality she was not seeing herself but a thousand other faces, seeing them, hearing their voices, trying as she had tried these past weeks to disentangle what they were saying and to make some coherent sense before it was drowned by the tumult within her own heart.

She was tired, desperately and exhaustibly tired, she thought suddenly.

There had been too much to do, too much to think about, above all too much to feel; and now she longed for only one thing—sleep, a deep dreamless sleep which would make her forget herself and everyone else.

Perversely she had not been able to sleep during these past three weeks and had lain awake night after night until she could bear it no longer, so that she had sent for the old Doctor who had looked after her and the twins since they first came into the world.

"Not sleeping, eh?" he said, peering at Toria through the horn-rimmed spectacles which made him look like a wise old owl. "It is this ridiculous life you lead. Too much dancing, not enough fresh air, and not nearly enough food. You are far too skinny! If you go on like this, you will be losing your looks."

It was a joke rather than a threat and Toria smiled.

Nevertheless she knew he had spoken the truth. She was too thin. Her clothes were falling off her, but luckily her trousseau had been made to her new measurements.

Yet how she loathed the new clothes in which she had had to stand for hours, and about which she had had to endure endless consultations, long and animated discussions! But they, like everything else, were part of the price she must pay for marrying Charles.

She remembered with a wry smile how she had imagined they could slip off and get married quickly. Charles had believed it too and had gone off the very day they got engaged to buy a special licence.

How blind they had been to think such a thing was possible!

There had been two days, nearly three, when they had made their plans for a quiet wedding with no one there but their immediate families.

"I shan't even have a white wedding dress," Toria told the disappointed twins. "It is all such a waste of money."

"You could turn it into an evening dress afterwards," Xandra said practically.

"It would always have a smell of orange blossom about it," Toria protested. "And I have seen these so-called convertible wedding dresses. Whatever one does to them afterwards, they still look as if you have left your veil behind by mistake. No, I shall be married very simply, a nice comfortable travelling dress. Charles is talking about flying somewhere for our honeymoon."

She had been able to talk sanely and sensibly about it, even while all the time she was wondering if it was really possible for her to do what she intended to do. Was she or was she not helping Michael?

That was the question which presented itself over and over again.

Then on the third day everything was altered. The telephone rang when they were having luncheon. Olga went to answer it, for the twins usually took it in turns to answer the telephone as everyone else was too lazy to move.

"It is for you, Toria," Olga shouted through the door of the dining-room. "Somebody from the *Evening Standard*."

"The *Evening Standard*," Toria repeated. "I wonder what they want."

She went to the telephone.

"Is it true," a voice said, "that you are announcing your engagement to Air Vice-Marshal Charles Drayton?"

Toria hesitated. She hated lying, but at the same time she had no desire for the Press to get wind of their engagement before it was put in *The Times*.

She and Charles had arranged that they would announce their engagement and their marriage at the same time. It would be simpler that way.

"I may tell you," the voice at the other end of the telephone went on, "that we have contacted the Air Vice-Marshal at the Air Ministry and, while he did not deny the engagement, he asked us to telephone you."

It seemed useless to prevaricate after that, and Toria capitulated.

"Actually we are engaged, but we don't want it announced yet."

"And you will be married soon?" the voice asked.

"We shall be married very quietly. We have not yet decided on the date," Toria said.

Five minutes later she put the telephone down wearily.

"That's done it," she told the family in the dining-room. "How do you think the Press got to hear we were engaged? They are certain to put a paragraph in to-night, and then we shall be inundated with all sorts of relations asking if they can be invited to the Church."

"I can't afford a reception," Lord Lynbrooke said suddenly.

It was always difficult to know if he was listening to what was going on. He appeared to move permanently in a world of his own, but now for once he had over-heard what the girls were chattering about.

"I know that, Daddy," Toria said. "We reckon at the outside that there won't be more than twenty or thirty people. Charles says he will bring down a case of cham-pagne and that ought to be enough for everyone."

How little they had thought then what bomb was going to burst upon them!

The *Evening Standard* carried the news of their en-gagement that evening.

There was a picture of Toria looking ravishingly lovely in a Hartnell dress which she had modelled the previous season, and there was a photograph of Charles coming from the last Investiture at Buckingham Palace.

There were paragraphs and paragraphs about them both, and that was only the beginning.

The morning papers took up the story with rapidity. For the first time Toria realised that she was marrying a national hero, a man whose war exploits had carried him into the first rank of those who were almost wor-shipped for their daring brilliance.

She herself had been the darling of the gossip writers ever since she "came out". It was gratifying to read how beautiful and glamorous she was, but it was not so grat-ifying to realise that the newspapers had set an ava-lanche in motion which she and Charles were complete-ly powerless to stop.

The Castle was besieged by photographers, newspa-per reporters and fans.

There was always a crowd of sightseers hanging about the gates, and the twins even declared that some of them slept there in the hope of being first in the morning queue.

Charles found it impossible to leave the Air Ministry without having to pass through a crowd of young people who wanted his autograph.

After twenty-four hours of attempting to answer the telephone Toria left the receiver off. But nothing could stop their being the focus of attention.

One of the most famous dress-makers in London, for whom Toria had posed on several occasions, offered to give her her wedding dress and the main part of her trousseau.

A milliner whose original creations inevitably produced headlines and photographs at the beginning of the Season insisted on providing her with all her hats.

There were other contributions from a dozen other firms and, as Toria said finally, she felt they ought to have acknowledgements printed at the end of the marriage service as was done in a theatre programme.

It was obvious from then on that there was no chance of having a quiet ceremony.

Toria's Godfather, whose existence she had forgotten for many years, but who happened to be a Bishop, wrote saying that he would like to marry them.

Charles' mother, who until then had remained very much in the background, telephoned to say that under the circumstances it was impossible for her not to invite at least a hundred or so friends and relatives to be present.

More than once Toria felt like running away and disappearing, but she knew that that was impossible.

One person leaving the family was quite enough. Michael had disappeared and no one knew where he had gone, and that, combined with everything else, had made the Castle almost unbearable.

It was bad enough to have to endure such a commotion, so much comment and so many sincere and heartfelt congratulations and good wishes, without being beset with anxiety the whole time as to what had happened to Michael.

It was so like him, Toria thought bitterly, to add to everyone else's worries by going away without a word of explanation and without even sending a postcard to say that he was all right.

Susan Butler had come to the Castle, asked to see Lettice, and when she had learned from her that Michael had vanished, had burst into a flood of extremely unbecoming tears.

Toria had come unexpectedly into the room in the middle of this and had been forced to listen to Susan's bitter tale of misery.

Michael had come over to her home, she said, and asked her to marry him. She had accepted with alacrity because she had always loved him. He had left after luncheon, leaving her to tell her parents the news.

They were not particularly pleased, for they were well aware that Michael was penniless and without a job of any sort. But they were not going to stand in the way of their only child's happiness, and there was no doubt at all that Susan was happy, ecstatically so.

After a few feeble objections they agreed to the engagement, and Susan had rung Michael up at the Castle, elated and excited at having got her own way; but Michael had been curt to the point of rudeness.

She had realised that something had upset him, but he would not tell her what it was.

"It seemed," she said pathetically, "as if he was not interested in me any more."

She ended by saying that he had put down the receiver before she had finished what she was saying, and the very next morning she had got a scribbled note from him saying that the engagement was off.

She could hardly believe that her short-lived happiness had come to an end so quickly.

She thought there must be some mistake and had rung up Michael, only to learn that he had left the Castle and no one knew where he had gone.

Lettice was as puzzled by his disappearance and almost as hysterical as Susan herself, but Toria said very little. She had told no one what had happened when she went to meet Michael the day she had become engaged to Charles.

She could see his face now as he had stopped sudden-

68

ly and, gripping her by the shoulders, had swung her round to face him.

"Don't be a little fool," he said. "You don't mean what you are saying?"

"But I do," Toria replied. "I have promised to marry Charles."

He had stared at her and then his face seemed to grow pale as if she had dealt him a sudden blow.

"But Michael, don't you understand?" Toria said hastily. "It is the only thing to do. You said you would go away, but that is ridiculous. You have nowhere to go. I like Charles, and he is terribly rich. He will help you, he will help us all."

Her voice died away. Somehow it was impossible to go on talking with Michael looking at her like that.

After a moment he released her shoulder.

"You damned idiot," he said. "I told you that I would get engaged. Why do you want to interfere?"

"I am not interfering," Toria said with a pathetic effort at dignity. "You can't possibly marry Susan and you know you can't. She is everything you most dislike. You will make her miserable and you will be utterly miserable yourself."

"Do you think you will be any happier with a smug ass like Drayton?" Michael asked.

Toria was silent for a moment. She knew that Michael resented what he thought was Charles' superiority.

She wanted to champion Charles, but she also wanted to choose her words so as not to make Michael more angry than he was already. But he did not give her time.

"Very well then," he said furiously. "Go ahead and sacrifice yourself if that is what you want. You like being a martyr, that's the truth. Anyway, you will have money if nothing else, but count me out."

Again she did not know how to answer him, and while she hesitated for words, conscious that her eyes were pricking with tears and there was a sudden lump in her throat, Michael strode away from her, walking swiftly and with very long strides towards the Castle.

"Michael, wait for me," she called after him, but he did not look back.

Because of the tears which suddenly overflowed, blinding her completely, she had been unable to catch him up.

After a few minutes she had given up the chase and sitting down on a fallen tree, had cried her eyes out.

It was an hour or so later before she went back to the Castle, to find that Michael had gone and no one had seen him go. It was only eventually that they discovered that an odd pair of pyjamas and a tweed jacket were missing from his bedroom.

At first only Toria was disturbed by Michael's disappearance, but she said very little about it.

The others were used to Michael's moods and, when he did not appear for dinner, they thought he must be either working or sulking.

But at breakfast next morning Xandra informed them all that Michael's bed had not been slept in, and it was then that Lettice began to get worried.

It was two days before Lord Lynbrooke realised that his nephew had left the house, and it was Mrs. Fergusson who took it most prosaically.

"Now don't you worry your head," she said to Lettice. "Mr. Michael won't go far unless he's got a chance of getting plenty to eat. He doesn't often miss his meals! Men are all the same, it's their stomachs as guides them eventually. If he's hungry, he'll come home; and if he don't, you may be certain he has found a good table somewhere on which to rest his elbows."

Toria felt that everyone would have been more perturbed if there had not been so much excitement over her wedding. As it was, it seemed to her by the end of the week that she was the only person longing and aching for news of Michael.

Every morning she looked through the envelopes as the postman brought them, hoping against hope that he would send her a line to say that he was all right.

But there was nothing, only hundreds of letters of congratulations and even more communications from shops, manufacturers and travel agencies.

"I am sorry all this should have happened," Charles said more than once, as he found Toria with a pile of unopened letters in her lap and a stock of parcels all containing wedding presents which they neither of them wanted.

"I don't think either of us can blame the other," Toria said. "We seem to be running neck and neck for the popular vote. Charles, how I dislike the great British public when it turns sentimental!"

She gave him a bundle of fan letters to read which, she said, made her "perfectly sick". He took them away and handed them to his Secretary.

"Let us go up to London and dine," he suggested a week later when a Secretary had been established at the Castle and Toria had given up all hope of coping personally with the daily correspondence.

Toria shook her head.

"What is the point?" she asked. "The last time we went out in London we were unable to eat and unable to speak. It was nothing but people talking to us. It was more tiring than staying here."

"We ought to have run away," Charles said, "but it seems so pointless unless it is because of disapproving parents."

"And no one can say that either of our parents are that," Toria said.

Toria was right. There was certainly no disapproval. Lord Lynbrooke, when he realised how rich his future son-in-law was, was more than delighted at the prospect of giving his daughter away.

Charles' mother, although a restrained, unemotional person as a rule, had told Toria with a note of deep sincerity in her voice that she had always hoped she would like her prospective daughter-in-law and she could not be more delighted with her son's choice.

If only she had had news of Michael, Toria thought, she might even have been able to be happy! But somehow the thought of him hovered over her like a cloud, spoiling everything, even her pleasure in Charles' continual kindness to the family.

She managed to avoid thinking of Charles as anything but a kind, benevolent benefactor.

She kissed his cheek when he arrived and when he

left; but they seldom seemed to be alone together; and when they were, Toria felt far too tired to do anything but put her head on Charles' broad shoulder and close her eyes.

Only once had he been more possessive and that was one night when they were motoring back from London together.

Although she did not realise it, she was looking particularly lovely and very ethereal in a dress of black lace which seemed to make her seem as if she might float away into the shadows at any moment.

Charles put his arms round her and his mouth sought hers hungrily and possessively.

"Toria!" he whispered. "I love you! Please love me a little!"

Toria had heard the urgency in his voice and she told herself that this was the moment when she must make some response, must be kind to him, must show her gratitude for all he had done, for all he had given the family.

But her own weariness seemed to keep her spellbound. It was not the thought of Michael which kept her from responding then, it was just an utter physical fatigue.

She could not kiss Charles back, could do nothing but turn her face away from him and hide it against his shoulder.

With a perception which was surprising he had understood how tired she was.

He said nothing more, just held her closely in his arms until, long before they had left the lights of London behind, Toria was asleep.

She had wakened as they arrived at the Castle door.

"Have I been asleep?" she asked. "Oh, Charles, I am so sorry. I am afraid I have been very boring tonight, but I am terribly tired."

"I know you are," he replied. "Go to bed, darling, and sleep well. I will telephone you in the morning."

He made no attempt to come in. He did not try to kiss her again in front of the chauffeur.

He just raised her hand to his lips and watched her

72

open and shut the front door before he turned away and was driven back to London.

But Toria had been unable to sleep. She lay awake, accusing herself of failing Charles even as she had failed Michael.

"I am a failure too," she told herself aloud.

The words seemed to echo round and round in her brain. She thought that she could hear Michael saying it first of all, and then herself.

Surely, she thought, Michael would come back for the wedding?

There was no question of his not knowing when it was, for every newspaper had reported the date and many of them even carried a picture of Lynbrooke Parish Church.

There was something delightfully simple, the public were told, in the fact that Charles and Toria had chosen to be married in the small, grey stone edifice which had once been built on the Lynbrooke Estate, rather than in one of the fashionable Churches of Mayfair.

"I don't know what they think is so simple about it," Lettice said as she read aloud from the newspapers on the day before the wedding. "There will be so many Bishops and Clergy in the chancel that they will hardly be able to move. The Church will be packed with everyone from Mayfair, and if you had to pay for your dress it would cost you at least two hundred pounds."

"To crown everything—and that's the right word," Toria replied, "my great aunt, who I thought was dead years ago, insists on my wearing her tiara. She says she has left it to me in her Will, but I might as well have the pleasure of appearing in it on my wedding day. Just a quiet and simple wedding, Lettice, with three thousand pounds' worth of diamonds glistening on my head!"

"How Michael would laugh!" Lettice said suddenly.

Toria felt a pang of misery go through her.

Yes, Michael would laugh, she thought now as she stared at herself in the mirror, and she longed for him now as she had never longed for him before.

It would somehow have been familiar and comforting to have Michael sneering at all the elaborate prepara-

73

tions, at the army of florists downstairs, transforming the shabby old sitting-rooms into bowers of flowers so that no one should see how dilapidated and poverty-stricken the Castle really was.

The pantry and kitchen had been taken over by the caterers, who looked down their noses at Mrs. Fergusson's none too clean stove and inadequate scullery.

There was a red carpet outside the front door and dozens of waiters in attendance, all looking more pontifical than any Bishop.

Yes, Michael would laugh, Toria thought. He would laugh, too, at her sophisticated, yet simple dress of white satin with its pearl and diamond embroidery.

Charles had suggested that she should carry lilies; she looked at her bouquet now lying on a chair and even as she did so she saw Michael's eyes and heard him say mockingly:

"Sweetly traditional, my dear."

"It is not fair," Toria thought suddenly.

Why should she be haunted by Michael? Yet by his very absence he had managed to create an atmosphere from which she could not escape.

There was his empty chair at the dining-room table, the passage which led down to his workshop, the door to his bedroom, his old battered felt hat which still hung in the hall.

They were all there, haunting and taunting her so that she could not escape from them or him, however much she tried.

"It is time I dressed," Toria told herself.

She rose from the dressing table and as she did so caught sight of her new dressing case, one of the many presents that Charles had given her. It was fitted with gold fittings, her monogram emblazoned on them in tiny diamonds.

"So rich!" Michael would have sneered.

At the same time he would have liked them.

"They were in good taste," Toria thought.

Wearily she moved across the room and picked up her wedding dress. As she did so, Lettice came into the room.

She was wearing a new dress and coat of coral red which was extremely becoming to her dark prettiness; but although the clothes were new, they had not been expensive.

Toria realised with a sudden tightness of the heart how badly they showed up against her ultra-smart and ultra-expensive clothes. But then her trousseau had been given to her, whereas they had had to scrape together enough money to buy Lettice and the twins new clothes to appear in at the wedding.

The twins had wanted to be bridesmaids, but Toria had said no when she was at first trying to keep the wedding small and quiet; and afterwards it seemed madness to add to the preparations which grew more elaborate and more fantastic day by day.

She had even left the choosing of the twins' dresses to Lettice, and now, when they came bursting into the room for her approval, she stared at them in astonishment.

They both wore coats of periwinkle blue velvet and on their heads they had tiny berets made also of velvet and each trimmed with a bunch of ermine tails.

Toria had not modelled at the best houses for years without knowing expensive clothes when she saw them; and the moment she looked at the twins' clothes, she knew perfectly well that they had not been purchased with the very small sum she had allotted to Lettice for the purpose.

"Where did you get these coats?" she asked, "and who paid for them?"

The twins both gave a shriek of delight.

"They are a surprise," they said. "They are lovely, aren't they? Oh, Toria, say you are pleased with them."

"How did you pay for them?" Toria asked, but the twins shrieked again almost in unison.

"We will give you three guesses."

"It was Charles, of course," Toria said quickly.

She knew she had guessed right before the chorus of voices told her so.

It seemed to her that she heard Michael's voice again.

"Bought the lot of you, hasn't he? It won't be your family any longer, but his."

It was then she saw the fur that Lettice carried over her arm. It was a sable tie, just what Lettice had always wanted to set off her dark beauty. Charles too! Was there no end to what he would spend?

Toria asked herself the question and suddenly hated her dressing case, the mink coat that was hanging up on the wardrobe, the diamond wrist-watch that was waiting in its case on the dressing-table for her to clasp it round her wrist.

Money, money, money! And Michael had lost her because of it, Michael whom she loved and who loved her.

She felt as if she were stifling, but neither Lettice nor the twins seemed to notice.

They were all talking about Charles, what he had given them, what he had promised. Charles, Charles! His name came so easily to their lips.

Toria had a sudden desire to scream, to ask them if they had forgotten Michael, if he had vanished from their minds overnight, if all the years in which he had lived with them could be wiped out so easily.

Lettice had adored him, she was sure of that, yet now she was preening herself in the glass, Charles' present draped across her shoulders.

"It is so soft," she was saying. "I think sable is the loveliest fur of all, don't you, Toria?"

Toria did not answer.

Instead, she slipped her arms into her shabby woollen dressing gown, which was worn and threadbare and yet in its very familiarity somehow comforting.

It was an old friend. She had worn it at home for years, keeping her more elaborate wrap for when she stayed away.

The twins and Lettice were paying no attention to her, so she opened the bedroom door and went down the passage.

There was a green baize door at the end of it which led to the nursery quarters. Michael's room was beyond it.

Toria walked down the passage and pushed open the door of his room.

It was a narrow little room with a wooden bedstead shoved into one corner, a dilapidated chest-of-drawers taking up most of the space.

There were framed photographs on the wall, school photographs, groups which included Michael when he was at school. There were several war-time snapshots of Air crews grinning into the sunshine with their machines behind them, and the photograph of a German fighter going down in flames.

The room was bare and austere, and suddenly it seemed to Toria so pathetic that she longed to sit down on the hard, narrow little bed and cry.

This room was Michael's room. In it he kept the only things he really possessed. This was the room to which he had come back at the beginning of every holidays, which he had left at the end of them to go back to school.

This was his, and his possessions were so few that one could almost count them on one hand.

The riding crop standing in one corner of the room, a tennis racquet beside it. They had been presents, Toria remembered, from her father.

There was a bookcase in the corner which contained a few well-bound books which had been Michael's prizes at school, and a collection of tattered detective novels which he had always assured them was the only reading he really enjoyed.

It was untrue, of course. Michael was well-read.

He was the only person in the family who had managed to read quite a number of the books in the big Library downstairs. But he had wanted to simplify his life in everything.

Because he could not afford to buy books, he had pretended, as he had pretended over so many things, that he liked what was mediocre rather than that anyone should think that he was yearning for what was good and too expensive.

"Poor Michael!" Toria whispered aloud.

Suddenly she thought he was laughing at her.

It would have been easy to make fun of her, standing there in her old blue dressing gown, being sentimental over the man who had walked out of her life. Yet had he done that?

She was marrying Charles for one reason and for one reason only; because she believed it would help Michael, and now he was not even here to see her do it.

She felt as if she wanted to scream, to cry out for him, to let the whole world know that Michael was missing and must be found.

How could she be married if he was not there to see her?

How could anything be altered or arranged in her life without Michael's approval or disapproval?

"I am being hysterical," Toria told herself.

She went from the room, slamming the door behind her.

She came back through the baize door on to the front landing to hear the twins shouting for her.

"Toria, Toria, where are you? You will be late for the wedding if you don't hurry."

She went slowly back to her room. Her feet felt as if she must drag them forward.

"I won't be late," she said mechanically.

Lettice looked at her and stopped preening herself in the glass.

"I say, you do look white, Toria. Would you like some brandy or something?"

"I am all right," Toria answered.

"Mrs. Fergusson said you never touched your breakfast," Xandra said. "But she said all brides are like that. It's the excitement. There are the most delicious sandwiches on the buffet. Olga and I ate half a dozen, didn't we, Olga? And then a waiter said we were not to have any more. I thought it was rather a cheek myself as Charles is paying for them, but the waiter was so grand we really could not argue with him."

"I don't want anything to eat," Toria said.

"Can we get you a cup of tea?" Olga suggested. "You mustn't faint, Toria. They would make an awful fuss in the papers if you fainted at the wedding."

Toria smiled at Olga. Despite being much quieter than Xandra, Olga was often the more practical of the two.

"I think a cup of tea would be very nice," she said.

More from the idea of pleasing the twins than because she really wanted it.

"We will go and get it at once," Xandra said, "and do you think it would matter if we said you wanted some sandwiches? Because, if you don't, then we could eat them ourselves."

"I don't think it would matter a bit," Toria said.

"Then that is what we will do," Xandra said. "Come on, Olga."

They ran from the room, looking incredibly pretty in their smart blue coats and berets. Toria turned to Lettice.

"You must keep an eye on Olga," she said. "She will injure her health if she isn't careful. Did I tell you I found her sleeping on an old sack the other night because she thought it was the nearest thing she could find to a hair shirt?"

"What on earth was Olga doing penance for?" Lettice asked.

Toria shrugged her shoulders.

"She is an expert at finding sin in the most unlikely places," she said. "She will doubtless want to kneel in prayer all tonight because she has over-eaten herself at the wedding. You mustn't laugh at her, but you can reason with her."

"I will do my best," Lettice said, "but the twins don't pay much attention to me, as you well know."

"I shan't be away for long," Toria said.

She wished she wasn't going away at all. She wanted to stay at home, for life to go on as it always had.

She wanted time to go backwards, so that everything might be as it was before Michael said he loved her and Charles came into her life.

Lettice interrupted her thoughts.

"You must dress, Toria. We have only got another ten minutes before we leave for the Church."

Toria sighed.

"Very well then. Help me with the dress, will you? It does up at the back."

Actually she was only a few minutes late, and as she came down the stairs with the full skirts of her satin dress billowing out around her and the diamond tiara shining above the misty frailty of the family lace veil, she felt as if she was taking part in a play—an unrehearsed play and she did not know how it ended.

Her father was waiting for her in the hall. Lord Lynbrooke of the whole household had refused to have any new clothes for the occasion.

His coat, which he had bought for his own wedding, was, he said firmly, perfectly good enough for Toria's.

There were, it was true, a number of moth holes in it, and as the Earl had got thinner as the years passed by, it hung loosely from his shoulders; but at the same time with his grey cravat, pearl tie-pin and double-breasted waistcoat he looked quite smart.

Only Brandy and Soda eyed him with jaundiced eyes as they lay miserable in their baskets, having been told firmly and in no uncertain terms that they were not wanted.

Nothing was more of a penalty to them than to be left at home, and now mournfully, as they watched their master leave the house, they rested their noses on their paws and their ears and tails drooped miserably in unison.

The drive had not been improved by the amount of traffic which had travelled up and down it in the past three weeks.

Toria found herself jerked from side to side as the car travelled over the bumps; and when finally they reached the lodge gates and turned on to the main road, she was forced to straighten her tiara in the looking glass which was fitted into the side of the car.

"One day we shall have to get the road mended, Daddy, or someone will break his neck when he visits the Castle."

"Charles has already spoken to me about it," Lord Lynbrooke replied. "He knows of a new substance which they are putting down on drives."

80

"I suppose he will pay for it?" Toria asked.

"Well, if he doesn't, we can't have it done," Lord Lynbrooke remarked.

Toria opened her mouth to say she thought in that case it had better remain undone, then changed her mind. What was the point of arguing, and anyway there was no time for an argument just now.

The Church was only a few yards further down the road.

Already she could see the crowds outside the Church, the cars parked for nearly a mile, the hundreds of sightseers standing on the low wall surrounding the Churchyard, straining their necks for a first sight of her as the big car drew up at the gate.

"You would think some of these people would have something better to do," Lord Lynbrooke remarked tersely as the chauffeur got out to open the door.

"Don't think about it, Daddy, it will only annoy you," Toria said, knowing full well that, when her father expanded the theory that the nation was going to the dogs because nobody worked hard enough, it always sent up his blood pressure.

Lord Lynbrooke muttered some response to this, but she did not hear it.

Instead she was blinded by the flashes for the press cameras, and she only hoped that her smile would not come out in the photographs as forced as it felt on her stiff lips.

It was hard work to get through the surging crowds to the Church door and then there was a wait while someone signalled to the organist that she was there and the Choir shuffled to their feet and opened their books.

At last the organ began. Everyone turned round to look at her. The Church was packed to suffocation. There had never been such a parade of feathered hats, mink coats and white carnations.

There were at least a dozen ushers, all friends of Charles', who, he had explained to Toria apologetically, had insisted on giving him a hand as they had either served with him in the war or been at school with him.

Tall, good-looking young men in morning coats,

there seemed to be an unending array of them until at last Toria had passed them and she saw ahead the Bishop waiting.

It was then that she became aware that Charles was at her side. She had an insane impulse to slip her arm through his, to hold on to him, to ask him to send all these people away.

He had managed so many things, perhaps he could manage this too. And then she realised that the Service had started.

She felt Charles take her hand, and his fingers were warm and strong, as comforting as they had been that day in the window seat when she had been crying over Michael and he had asked her to marry him.

She was making her responses; the ring was on her finger; and they were moving forward to kneel at the altar.

It was all over. She was married.

A great number of people she had never seen before were kissing her in the vestry, and then she was walking down the aisle on Charles' arm, with Mendelssohn's Wedding March booming through the Church.

There was a shout of good wishes from the crowd outside, more photographs, someone thrust a bunch of white heather into her hand, and then they were driving away from the Church back towards the Castle.

Charles had said nothing, but Toria was aware that he was holding her hand tightly.

They turned in at the lodge gates, and Toria took her hand away from Charles so that she could hold on to her tiara.

"Are you all right, darling?" he asked.

"Daddy says you are going to have the drive mended," Toria said.

Even as she said it she felt it was not the right thing to say to one's husband immediately after they were married, but the words were out and there was nothing she could do about it.

She felt suddenly lost and afraid.

"I was never a very good sailor," Charles remarked drily.

Toria laughed. It was only Charles after all. Why had she been frightened? Why did everything seem so unreal?

"I shall look a complete wreck by the time I arrive," she said, as another bump threw her against Charles.

He put his arm round her to steady her, and as he did so he said:

"You look lovely, just as I dreamt you would look."

His voice was rather deep and rather low.

"Fine feathers make fine birds," Toria said. "You know I meant to be married in my travelling tweeds."

"I am glad you weren't," Charles said. "I wanted you to look like this on our wedding day."

"Well, there is one thing, we shall have plenty of photographs to remind us of it in our old age," Toria said.

She felt that the conversation was forced.

Thank goodness, they had reached the Castle and a hired butler was hurrying forward to open the door.

She crossed the hall, Charles following.

"We are to receive everyone in the sitting-room," she said. "They can then pass through the Library and back into the dining-room."

There was a huge bank of flowers where she and Charles were to stand. Lilacs, carnations, and white tulips which had been flown specially from Holland for the occasion.

Toria arranged her dress and pulled her veil over her shoulders.

"Now we are ready," she said. "They are taking a long time to follow us."

"I expect the drive is acting as a kind of anti-barrage," Charles said.

At that moment there was the sound of a very noisy engine spluttering to a standstill outside.

"Here is someone at any rate," Toria said.

"It is a motor-cycle," Charles answered.

"It must be a press photographer," Toria replied. "I wonder why Daddy and the twins are taking so long to get away from the Church."

Even as she spoke, she heard a voice in the hall. She

could not hear what was said, but at the sound of it she felt her heart stand still.

Her eyes were fixed on the door. She felt as if she could not breathe while she waited.

There was a heavy footstep and then, as she had expected, Michael stood there.

He was wearing a very old and tattered mackintosh, his hair was streaked across his forehead and his face was dirty. It seemed to her that he was breathless.

He stood looking at her for a long moment and then he came forward, his eyes on hers, seeing her and her alone.

"Toria," he said, "I have won a football pool. Fifty-five thousand pounds!"

It seemed to Toria then as if something struck her. She felt Michael fade away into the darkness and she knew she was falling.

She put out her hands to save herself, but she could touch nothing.

Only as she fell she heard her own voice cry out desperately and recklessly.

"But Michael . . . it is too late . . . too late."

5

"Too late! Oh Michael, it is too late!"

Toria could hear a strange, broken voice which was somehow her own speaking, as she came out of the darkness into which she had fallen. Then she heard Lettice remark:

"She does not know what she is saying."

Toria opened her eyes.

She was lying on the sofa, and a number of people were standing round her. She saw Lettice first, then the twins, her father and lastly Charles, standing a little aloof from the others, his eyes fixed on her face.

She put her hand up to her forehead.

"What has happened?" she asked.

"You fainted," Lettice replied. "I told you you were crazy not to have something to eat before you went to the Church."

"Don't talk! Give the girl some brandy," Lord Lynbrooke said sharply.

Lettice slipped her arm round Toria's shoulder and lifted a glass to her lips. Toria took the glass from her.

"I am all right now," she said and drank quickly.

She felt the fiery liquid run down her throat and almost instantly the cloud which had seemed to hover just above her eyes lifted.

She sat up, choking a little, and took another drink.

"Now I shall be drunk," she said. "Raw spirit on an empty tummy is a thing one is always warned against."

"Would you like to lie down or shall I get you something to eat?" Lettice asked.

"Neither," Toria replied.

She looked across the room and saw that the door into the hall was closed, but through it she could hear the murmur of voices.

"Charles and I have got to receive our guests," she said.

She got unsteadily to her feet and crossed to the mantelpiece so that she could look in the mirror above it. Her tiara was slightly awry on her head and her veil was crumpled.

"Quick, Lettice, arrange my veil again," she said. "People will wonder what has been happening to me."

"Are you all right, Toria?" Xandra asked anxiously. "You looked terribly white just now. We thought you were dead."

"Did you come in and find me lying on the floor?" Toria asked. "How upsetting!"

"It was terrifying," Lettice said. "We did not know what had happened."

"She has been doing too much."

Charles spoke at last.

Toria glanced at him and then looked quickly away again. Would nobody, she wondered, make any reference to Michael? She glanced at her own reflection in

85

the looking-glass. The brandy had brought the blood to her cheeks.

She looked lovely, a glowing, radiant and happy bride.

"Come on," she said impatiently. "We can't keep the people standing outside the door all night."

"Don't you think you ought to see the Doctor?" Lettice asked. "I saw him in the Church. He must be here by now."

"Leave the girl alone. She's all right!" Lord Lynbrooke said. "If you keep on fussing, we shall have some of those damned reporters in here asking questions."

Toria glanced at her father gratefully.

He understood, if the others did not, that the less said about this the better. She wondered what he was thinking, what Lettice and the twins thought.

They too must have heard that agonised outburst which had come unconsciously from her lips. And Charles!

What did Charles think? She glanced at him again and had a sudden sense of panic. What did she know of this strange, calm-faced man who stood beside her?

Yet she was married to him and bore his name.

There was no time for retrospection, no time to do anything but take up their positions in front of the bower of flowers and let the stream of congratulations and good wishes flow over them like an encroaching tide.

"You look lovely, darling."

"It was an absolutely perfect wedding!"

"I do congratulate you, Charles!"

"All possible good wishes to you both!"

After all, there was nothing original one could say, Toria reflected, as for the hundredth time she replied:

"Thank you so much. I'm so glad you could come."

She smiled mechanically, turned, raising her cheek for another kiss from the next person. She could hear Charles' voice, calm and unhurried, almost like an undercurrent to her own higher tones. Occasionally he said:

"Toria, this is a very old friend. He was with me in Burma." Or "Toria, this is my Aunt. You remember she sent us that lovely glass bowl."

Toria would smile, thank Charles' aunt profusely for a present which was exactly what they wanted, although she had no idea which it was among the hundreds of parcels which were piled together in the schoolroom.

Charles' secretary, Miss Miller, had unpacked them, sorted them out, and sent letters of acknowledgement, explaining that the recipients would write later when they were less rushed.

"It is extraordinary," Toria remarked to her once, "how few things one receives that one really wants."

"And what do you really want, Lady Toria?" Miss Miller had asked, looking up at her through her horn-rimmed spectacles.

Toria thought for a moment.

"Now that you ask me, I am not sure what I do want. I suppose the answer is nothing that one could receive from comparative strangers." She looked down at the miscellaneous collection of Pyrex dishes, salad bowls, vases and book ends.

"Does anyone really think that one can start a home with things like that?"

Miss Miller looked shocked.

"Oh, but Lady Toria, they will be ever so useful," she said. "After all, the Air Vice-Marshal cannot have had everything as a bachelor, can he?"

"No, of course not. We ought to be very grateful," Toria said, feeling that she had not only been ungracious but had shown herself in a bad light in front of Charles' secretary.

"And things do cost so much nowadays! It means a real sacrifice to give someone even the smallest present," Miss Miller rebuked her.

"Yes, yes, of course," Toria agreed.

She wished she felt more grateful; but somehow, looking at the guests as they filed past, she was certain that very few of them had made any sacrifice whatsoever to give her and Charles a present.

In many cases it was just vulgar curiosity which had

made them send a present at all. They had wanted to come to the wedding, and the easiest way was to buy themselves an invitation, so to speak.

It was cheaper than taking a ticket for a theatre or even a cinema, and to some people far more entertaining.

What was it about weddings, Toria wondered, which excited people in a way that nothing else seemed to do? Shaking hands now, she thought she had never seen so many strangers.

They could not all be Charles' friends, and they certainly were not hers. She could not even identify them by their names as they were boomed out by an announcer who for three guineas had been engaged from the firm of caterers.

He was bending now towards a small, middle-aged woman wearing a white hat trimmed with purple feathers, a coquettish tulle bow round her neck.

"Mrs. Hagar-Bassett," he announced, and she came forward.

"Such a lovely wedding, and you both have my very best wishes."

"Thank you," Toria said.

"So very many congratulations," Mrs. Hagar-Bassett said to Charles. "I have never seen a lovelier bride."

"Thank you so much," Charles said.

So Lord Lynbrooke had invited Mrs. Hagar-Bassett to the Castle after all these years! She must have been very insistent, Toria thought.

Perhaps it was more than she could bear to miss the excitement of a big social wedding which had received so much publicity in the newspapers.

Toria watched the white and purple hat disappear into the crowd and felt suddenly that it was infinitely pathetic.

They had laughed at Mrs. Hagar-Bassett so often; but what did she feel, peeping out at the family room behind her lace curtains? Did she get any happiness out of her association with Lord Lynbrooke?

Were there many compensations in having a friendship which was conducted in such a secret and almost surreptitious manner?

It was strange to think they were real people, her father and this woman, suffering real emotions, torn within themselves perhaps as she was torn about Michael. No, they could not be!

It was impossible to think of anyone feeling as she felt now, receiving congratulations, being kissed, saying the right thing over and over again.

The perfect bride! Yet all the time she felt wild, unconstrained and desperate.

Where was Michael? Where had he gone? Why had he come in like that and shouted at her that he had won a football pool, and then vanished?

Had Charles turned him out or had he just gone of his own free will when she had collapsed at his feet? Why didn't anybody tell her? Why wasn't Michael there now?

"Thank you so much!"

"It is so sweet of you!"

"I am so glad you could come!"

The same words were repeated over and over again. She must sound like a gramophone record, Toria thought, and yet she must go on saying them.

More people and still more people were crowding through the doorway, the noise sounding like the roar of an engine.

Michael had come on a motor-cycle. Where had he got that from? And where had he been these past three weeks?

It was unbelievable that this should have happened. Perhaps it was not true and she had dreamt the whole thing. Perhaps it had been just a nightmare.

"Thank you so much!"

"I am so glad you like my dress!"

"It was lovely you could come."

"This is my cousin, Toria. Lady Sanderson. She lives in Yorkshire and has come all the way down for the wedding."

"How kind of you! I am so glad you could come."

Another name was announced in stentorian tones, another and yet another.

She must have swayed for a moment, for she felt herself brush against Charles' shoulder. He looked down at her quickly.

"Are you quite sure you are all right?"

"I am rather tired."

"Then we will stop shaking hands, and I will go and find you something to eat. We have got to cut the cake anyway."

"Can we stop?" Toria asked.

Her outstretched hand had already been taken by someone else, and a voice was saying in gushing insincerity:

"I do hope you will both be terribly happy; it has been such a lovely wedding."

"Thank you so much. It was so kind of you to come."

And then in some magical manner of his own, Charles had taken command. He lifted her veil and slipped it over her arm, then he was guiding her through the crowd, making people move backwards as if they were an approaching bulldozer.

"Yes, we want to get to the dining-room. I think it is time we cut the cake."

A path was cleared for them and they moved forward, greeting a friend here and there, until eventually Toria found herself opposite the buffet on which reposed a huge three-tiered white cake surmounted by a great bunch of orange blossom.

Somebody gave her a glass of champagne and she sipped it slowly.

"Try and eat something," she heard Charles suggest, but her throat seemed closed and parched, and she knew it would be utterly impossible for her to swallow anything in the way of food.

"I am all right," she answered.

They cut the cake and had their health proposed by a distinguished looking man in Air Force uniform who Toria vaguely remembered was Charles' Chief.

They were toasted in a hundred raised glasses of

champagne, and Toria found herself thinking it was fortunate that her father was not paying for it.

She looked at the sea of faces in front of them. There was only one whose face she wanted to see and he was not there. She was certain he would not be, and yet she could not help looking.

Where was Michael? Was he sulking in his workroom, or had he shut himself in that austere little bedroom which had been his since he was a little boy.

Where had he gone? Why wasn't he there?

She felt a hand slipped into hers and looked down to find Xandra beside her.

"Are you going up to dress soon?" the child asked. "I will come and help you if you like. Olga and I have eaten six ices each, and now we feel sick. At least Olga does. She says it is a direct punishment from Heaven for being greedy."

"I will be going up in a few minutes," Toria replied, "and I would like both you and Olga to come up and help me."

"I will go and tell her," Xandra said, and slipped through the crowd like a small eel.

Charles glanced at his watch.

"We have got half an hour," he said to Toria, "if we are to keep to our schedule."

"I will go and change."

He cleared a way for her to the door. It took some time, for there were so many people who wanted just one more word with the bride.

Most of them, Toria thought, were the type of people who always had to be seen speaking to the most important person on every possible occasion. She singled out three or four less pushing guests who were watching her but not intruding themselves.

Her old Nannie; the retired governess in the village who gave lessons to the twins; Mrs. Fergusson's sister, who had journeyed all the way from the Isle of Wight to give a hand in the house.

There were other friends too whom she was determined to single out; girls with whom she had been to school; the fitter at one of the big dressmakers whose

91

dresses she wore continually for photographs and never could afford herself.

At length they reached the staircase.

"I am afraid we shall be late getting off," Toria said to Charles.

He looked at his watch and smiled.

"It doesn't matter," he replied. "I have arranged for us to have a private aeroplane and it won't go without us."

"That is all right then."

Toria turned away and started to climb the stairs. As she went, she heard Michael's voice from the past, sneering:

"They are the type of people who always have a fleet of private aeroplanes to take them everywhere and a Rolls-Royce waiting at the Airport."

She could not remember to whom he had been referring, now it might be her. They had laughed at people who were rich enough to travel *de luxe*.

Toria ran up the last six steps. She had got to find Michael—she must see him. She turned towards the baize door which led to the old Nursery quarters; but even as she did so, she heard his voice.

"Toria!"

He was standing in the doorway of her own bedroom. He had taken off his mackintosh, but his hair was still untidy and his face dirty. She ran down the passage towards him.

"Michael, what has happened? Where have you been?"

He drew her into her bedroom and shut the door. She heard the key turn in the lock.

"So I am too late!" he said.

"Have you really won some money or is that a joke?" Toria asked.

His eyes seemed suddenly to blaze at her.

"If you think it is a joke to ride two hundred miles on a motor-cycle you are much mistaken. The damned thing broke down twice or I should have been here before you were married."

"But, Michael, why didn't you telephone me? When did you know about this?"

"Do you think I didn't try to telephone?" Michael asked. "They said the line was out of order."

"Somebody must have taken the receiver off again," Toria said. "We left it off the first week after the engagement got into the papers."

"I heard this morning," Michael said. "Fifty-five thousand pounds, Toria."

"Where were you?"

"In Manchester, working in the docks."

"In the docks!"

"Yes, it is the sort of job anyone who has some muscles can do. As long as I had my health and strength, I couldn't be a failure at that. I made ten pounds last week and eight the week before that."

He was boasting, Toria thought, rather like a small boy who has managed to outjump the other children in his class.

"Michael! Michael!" she said helplessly.

He put his hand in his pocket and looked her up and down.

"Well, you make a lovely bride."

"Don't laugh at me, I can't bear it," Toria cried.

"Do you think I can bear it?" he asked, his voice hoarse with emotion. "I only had one idea when I knew I had won, and that was to get to you quickly. I borrowed the motor-cycle from the chap I was living with. It was the first thing I could lay my hands on. Where I was living there aren't any garages that would hire out fast cars. I tried to telephone you three times on the way down, and that is what delayed me. Then when I arrived and saw that blasted car covered with white ribbons outside the front door, I knew I was too late. But I had to come in and make sure.

"I told myself all the way down that I could just do it, could just get here before you went to the Church. I imagined I might take you away with me. I don't know quite how, for you wouldn't be able to get on the back of a motor-cycle in that rig-out."

His voice cracked suddenly.

"Don't, Michael, don't," Toria begged. "This is not something that we can joke about."

"I am not joking," Michael replied. "Good-bye, Toria."

He walked towards the door and Toria gave a cry.

"Michael, where are you going?"

"To hell would be the dramatic answer," Michael replied, "but actually I am going downstairs to get drunk."

"And after that?"

"After that I shall go and collect my fifty-five thousand pounds and get very drunk indeed. Don't worry, Toria, no man blows his brains out with fifty-five thousand pounds in his pocket."

He turned the key in the lock.

"But Michael, Michael," Toria said frantically, her hands going out towards him. "You can't go like this, you can't!"

"And how do you want me to go?" Michael asked. "Would you prefer it this way?"

He swept her into his arms, crushing her dress and pulling her veil back from off her head with the roughness of his embrace. She felt his mouth, hard and brutal against her lips.

His violence was frightening and the passion behind his kiss seemed almost to devour her.

Then just as she felt she could not breathe, but must be suffocated by his very strength, and her hands fluttered against him in a futile effort to escape, he flung her away from him.

She fell against the table at the side of the bed. She clutched at it to steady herself, but it toppled over and the china lamp which stood on it fell to the floor and smashed in a thousand pieces.

"Michael!" Toria cried. "Michael!"

But he was gone. The door slammed behind him, leaving her half sprawled across the bed, but she made no attempt to move.

Instead she lay there, closing her eyes as if she would shut out her sense of utter desolation.

94

Michael's teeth had cut her lip and she could taste blood.

Though she was not fainting, she felt dazed and almost half conscious, as if everything else had slipped away from her save the pain on her lips and the feeling that she was bruised all over.

The door was opened.

"Toria, are you there?" It was the twins. "Oh, Toria, what has happened?"

It was Olga who asked the last question, and she was perhaps the only person for whom Toria would make an effort, even if she were dying.

She forced herself to sit up and smile.

"My dress caught against the table, and look, I have broken my lamp. Isn't it a pity?"

"Oh, Toria, how could you have been so clumsy," Xandra cried. "You have not torn your dress, have you?"

Toria shook her head.

"No, it is quite all right," she said. "Don't bother about the broken china. We will get someone to sweep it up."

"You might have cut yourself on it," Olga said. "Are you quite sure you haven't hurt yourself?"

"I am quite all right," Toria replied.

"You look pale again," Xandra remarked. "You had better have some of the wedding cake. We managed to take away two large pieces."

She produced them from her coat pocket wrapped in a rather dirty handkerchief.

"Olga and I were going to sleep on them tonight. If you do, they say you will dream about the man you are going to marry. But you can eat some if you are hungry. There will be enough for us."

"It is very kind of you, darling," Toria said, "but really I am not hungry."

Olga looked up from the floor where she was kneeling to collect the broken china.

"I hope I dream of someone as nice as Charles," she said. "He is nice, Toria, very nice."

Her voice was serious, and Toria was sure there was

95

a special meaning for her in those quietly spoken words.

"Yes, he is nice," she repeated. "Too nice!"

"What do you mean by too nice?" Xandra asked curiously. "Can anyone be too nice?"

"Did I say too nice?" Toria asked hastily. "I mean too kind. Look at those lovely coats he has given you, and all that champagne he has paid for downstairs."

"We tried some," Xandra said. "It is horrible! Bubbles went up our noses and tickled. I much prefer ginger beer."

Olga got up from the bedside and walked over to the dressing-table where Toria was lifting the tiara from her head.

"Why did Michael come back?" Olga asked. "He came rushing out of the sitting-room just as we got back from the Church and when we went in we found you lying on the floor."

Toria did not answer for a moment. She was thinking, as she had often done before, that Olga was much more perceptive than Xandra.

She was so quiet and serious and most people paid more attention to Xandra, but Olga was the thoughtful one and very little escaped her notice.

"I think Michael was upset at having missed the wedding," she replied truthfully. "He had come all the way down from Manchester on a motor-cycle."

"Is he going to stay here now?" Olga asked.

"I don't know," Toria answered. "But if he does, be kind to him, twins."

Olga nodded her head.

"He isn't a very happy person, is he?" she said.

Toria gave a little sigh and then, before she could reply, the door opened and Lettice came in. She was carrying a tray in her hands.

"I brought you a cup of tea and some bread and butter," she said.

"How dull," Xandra exclaimed, "when there are all these lovely things to eat downstairs!"

"Actually I think it is just the thing I want," Toria said. "It was sweet of you to think of it."

"Actually I didn't," Lettice replied. "Charles told me

to find Mrs. Fergusson and get her to make it for you. He says you are not to come downstairs until you have eaten all the bread and butter."

It was like Charles, Toria thought, as she sipped the tea and felt its warmth somehow comforting. He always managed to think of the little things which made all the difference to one's comfort.

If it suited Michael, he would drag one from Land's End to John o' Groats without a drink of water; but Charles was different. How perfect it would be, Toria thought suddenly, if Charles and Michael were amalgamated into one person!

Lettice was chattering excitingly although Toria was not listening to her.

"It has been the most wonderful wedding!" she exclaimed. "Everyone says it is the prettiest they have ever seen."

"I wish it had been a London one," Xandra said, "and then Olga and I could have been bridesmaids. Lots of people said what a pity it was Toria had no attendants. I didn't realise until now what fun it would have been to be bridesmaid."

Toria said nothing.

She was thinking that if the wedding had been postponed for just another day it would not have taken place; yet somehow she could not imagine herself marrying Michael, going away with him, as he intended when he had come rushing down from Manchester.

Could she have done it?

Could she have just walked out on Charles and the crowds of people waiting at the Church, on the caterers and florists, on the dressmakers who had presented her with her trousseau and her wedding dress, on the friends who had sent those stacks of unwanted presents in the old School room?

Could she have done that?

She wondered what story the evening newspapers would have carried. "Society beauty runs away on the eve of her wedding." "War Hero's bride deserts him at the Church door."

There would have been long descriptions of Charles'

exploits once again, photographs of herself, of the Castle, of the Church and perhaps even of Brandy and Soda.

Then there would have been comments made by their friends and relations. Perhaps even Mrs. Hagar-Bassett would be asked to say what she thought of "the runaway bride".

Toria felt laughter rising in her throat almost hysterically. She went on eating the bread and butter, as if her very life depended on it, until the plate was empty. Lettice lifted the tray from the dressing-table.

"Charles will be pleased," she said, and looked at Toria meaningly as she said it.

"I feel quite hungry myself now," Xandra said. "Shall we eat some of the wedding cake, Olga?"

"Go and get something to eat," Lettice said. "If anyone tries to stop you, say it is for the bride. They will give you anything you ask for then."

"That's a jolly good idea," Xandra said.

The twins rushed from the room, leaving the door open behind them. Lettice crossed the room to shut it, then she turned and looked at Toria.

"So it was because of money that Michael went away," she said.

The statement was made accusingly, and Toria let her wedding dress fall to the floor before she answered:

"Have you spoken to Michael?" she asked at length.

"I did not have a chance," Lettice replied. "Where has he gone to?"

"I have no idea," Toria answered.

She took her going-away dress from its hangar and put it over her head. Lettice crossed the room to stand beside her.

"I don't understand," she said. "Why is Michael behaving like this?"

There was something in her voice which told Toria all too clearly that for the first time she suspected her brother of being in love, but not quite brave enough to put it into words. Toria glanced at the clock on the mantelpiece.

"I am late for Charles," she said. "Do help me, Lettice. We shall never get to the Aerodrome at this rate."

It was a deliberate attempt to avoid confidences. For the first time in their lives since they had become close friends Toria had deliberately turned away from her cousin and refused to be frank and honest with her.

She knew by Lettice's face and the troubled expression in her eyes that her cousin was aware what was being avoided, but there was nothing Toria could do about it.

Breaking point had been reached and if she talked of Michael much more, she would reveal all too clearly her feelings and her own anxiety about him.

Hurriedly she buttoned her dress, slipped the little blue hat with its jaunty quills on the side of her head, and took her new mink coat—one of Charles' wedding presents to her—from the wardrobe.

"Help me into this," she said.

Lettice slipped it over her shoulders, and she took up her bag and gloves from the dressing-table.

"I suppose I have remembered everything," she remarked reflectively.

She knew without looking round that Lettice was staring at her.

"Toria," Lettice said suddenly in a strangled voice. "Does Michael love you?"

Toria turned towards the door. To do so she stepped over her wedding dress, leaving it lying there, a white pool of gleaming, expensive satin on the worn carpet.

"I don't know, Lettice," she lied. "I don't think that Michael really loves anyone except himself."

She had opened the door when she found Lettice's arm linked in hers.

"It was a silly question really," Lettice whispered. "I was just somehow afraid for the moment, but I see now I was being silly. Michael is in one of his moods, but he will get over it."

"Yes, of course. I am sure he will get over it," Toria answered, lying again and hating herself for it.

Charles was waiting for her halfway up the stairs.

There was a group of ushers with him, laughing and

joking, yet managing to convey an attitude of deference in the manner in which they addressed him.

Charles moved away from them and walked a few steps up towards Toria as she descended the stairs towards him.

"I am sorry if I am late," she said.

"It does not matter," Charles replied, "and, as I told you, the aeroplane will wait for us."

"Where are you off to?" one of the ushers asked, "or is it a closely guarded secret?"

"I have no secrets," Charles answered blithely.

Several of the men laughed as if at some tremendous joke.

"We are going to Monte Carlo as it happens," he continued. "We are flying to Nice and motoring on from there."

"Well, if you get bored, there is always the Casino," someone said.

Charles slipped his arm through Toria's and led her down the stairs.

"Have you had anything to eat?" he asked in a voice that she alone could hear.

"I ate everything you sent up to me," she replied.

"Good girl!"

His approval was warm and friendly; then they entered the hurly-burly of the crowd that was waiting to see them off. There were dozens of people to be kissed; there were good wishes to be thanked for once again; and then at last they were in the car and the twins were running alongside it waving.

There was the last shower of rice and confetti being thrown through the windows, and then they were away, bumping down the drive, being thrown against each other as the driver accelerated a little quicker to get away from the crowds.

There were still a number of sightseers hanging about the lodge gates. They waved and cheered as Toria and Charles passed them.

Toria waved back, then leant back wearily against the padded seat.

"It is impossible for me to smile at anyone again

ever," she said. "Fashionable weddings ought to be forbidden by law. It is absolute cruelty for the bride and bridegroom."

"It is all over now," Charles said soothingly.

He looked up in surprise as the chauffeur brought the car to a standstill and opened the door.

"I have stopped, Sir, to take off the shoes and notices that have been put on the back," he said.

"Oh, are there some there?" Charles asked in surprise.

The chauffeur grinned.

"Two old boots, three slippers, and a placard saying 'JUST MARRIED'."

"I am sure the twins are responsible for all that," Toria said. "They were determined we should not miss one of the traditional horrors. I have got rice all down my back, and I could feel them stuffing it into the pockets of my coat."

"Well, at least everybody enjoyed themselves," Charles said.

She glanced at him quickly, but he was not looking at her. As the car started again, Charles settled himself in the other corner and stretched out his legs in front of him. Toria closed her eyes.

"I am going away from home," she thought. "I am leaving the Castle behind, the twins, Daddy and . . . and Michael."

Where was Michael? Was he mixing with the guests downstairs in the dining-room or had he procured a bottle of champagne for himself and taken it along to his workshop?

He had done that once before for a New Year's Party when Toria had brought some friends down from London. He had taken a dislike to them or had been annoyed at their turning up unexpectedly.

Toria had found him, some time after they had brought in the New Year, sitting by himself in the darkness, his feet resting on the table, an empty bottle beside him on the floor.

"Michael, why are you here alone?" she asked.

"I am enjoying myself," he answered. "I feel pleasantly drunk and being exceedingly well entertained by my own company."

She switched on the light and crossed the room to stand looking down at him.

"Come and dance, Michael," she begged. "We are having such fun, and I don't want you to miss it."

"Why this sudden solicitation?" Michael asked mockingly. "Go and play with your fancy friends. They don't want me and I don't want them."

"Oh, Michael, don't be difficult," Toria pleaded. "Let us at least start the New Year by being happy."

"I am happy," Michael insisted. "Haven't I just told you I am very pleasantly drunk?"

She had left him then and gone back to the others. But somehow, she remembered now, he had spoilt the evening. It had not been the same without him.

She had been conscious all the time of a feeling of emptiness.

"I suppose that was because I loved him," Toria thought. "I did not know it, but it must have been inside me all the time."

She wondered if Michael would ever remember that evening now that she had gone away.

It was one of so many occasions when they might have been together but he had refused her company and had gone off on his own, leaving her with other people or even by herself.

She had always thought that, when she fell in love with someone, she would be with him all the time. She believed that one of the things love meant was being with the person one loved.

She had never believed it possible to be in love with someone like Michael with whom one was always at cross purposes, who always contrived somehow to make one unhappy even in the moments when one should be supremely happy.

"He has spoilt my wedding day at any rate," Toria thought.

She wondered, if she had married Michael, whether he would have been as difficult as a bridegroom as he was when an uninvited guest. He had a habit of making difficulties even where there appeared to be no possible reason for them.

And yet because he was there, everything seemed so different, so vital and alive.

"We are just arriving at the Aerodrome," Charles said quietly.

Toria opened her eyes. It did not seem long since they left the Castle. She had been thinking of Michael and had forgotten where she was or where she was going.

"Oh, the Aerodrome," she said a little stupidly, and added: "How long will it take us to get to Nice?"

"Not more than two hours," Charles replied. "A little more if the wind is against us. Would you like a drink or anything before we start?"

"No, thank you," Toria answered.

There were various officials to be seen before they left. There were more congratulations to be accepted, more handshakes and then at last they were off. Toria felt relieved that conversation was impossible.

The aeroplane made too much noise, and besides, the pilot was within hearing. She settled herself comfortably in her seat, hoping that she would sleep. Charles, she noticed, had the evening papers on his lap.

On the front page there was a picture of herself coming from the Church, but she felt too weary to want to have a look at it.

Her lip was sore where Michael had kissed her, and she imagined she could still feel his arms, hard and painful, around her shoulders.

It was the second time they had kissed. She wondered why kissing Michael was quite unlike kissing anyone else.

There was hardly any pleasure in it, only a fierce agonising pain which seemed to stab at her heart, and a physical discomfort which seemed, she thought ruefully, to continue long after Michael had gone.

She thought of him working at the Docks. It was so like him to do something like that. She could imagine him lifting heavy bales, queueing, when the week's work was over, for his pay-packet, which would give him almost a fierce satisfaction because he had earned it without influence, without help from anyone. Why, why was he so touchy?

She could remember once, when she was particularly hard-up, being offered a quite substantial sum of money by a middle-aged man who had been paying attention to her for some time.

She had refused him nicely, thanking him for the offer and saying it was quite impossible for her to accept money from anyone.

"I wonder why you say that," he questioned and continued, "People make such an unnecessary fuss about money. If I sent you twenty pounds' worth of flowers, you would accept them without question; if I gave you a very handsome Christmas present, it would not worry you in the slightest; but because I offer you cash, which doubtless you need for something really essential like your Dentist's bill or a new pair of shoes to keep the damp out, you are forced by convention to refuse it. I, personally, can see no difference in my giving you cash or a bottle of scent."

Toria smiled.

"A cheque is what no nice girl accepts from a man," she said.

"In principle, yes; but in practice no. Personally I think it is rather vulgar to make such a fuss about money, either because one has or one has not got it; and if you personally know you are doing nothing wrong in accepting it, why not do the sensible thing and let me give you what I shall otherwise spend on chocolates?"

Toria had thanked him and refused; but she had often thought there was a good deal of common-sense in what he had said.

Sometimes she thought that Michael made an unnecessary and vulgar fuss about not having any money. She wondered how he would feel now with a huge Bank balance. Would it alter him?

Would so many of his moods, which came directly from envying other people or being annoyed at his own inefficiency, vanish because they were no longer necessary?

Perhaps he would become fat, pompous and quite unemotional because there was no longer poverty and failure to upset him.

Toria smiled at the thought, and found herself drifting away into an uneasy sleep. She dreamed that she was walking up the aisle to be married.

She could see the Bishop waiting for her, but he was Michael, Michael with his hair untidy and his face dirty shouting at her that she was too late, too late to be married.

She awoke with a start, feeling suddenly very cold. Charles was asleep in the other seat. He slept quietly, breathing evenly and easily.

She watched him for a moment, realising that in his own way he was extremely good-looking. He had not the spectacular, flamboyant good looks of Michael, but a clear-cut English face, square forehead and a determined chin.

He looks clever, she thought, and realised for the first time that he must have brains to be the youngest Air Vice-Marshal in the R.A.F.

He, too, was an inventor but a successful one. Somehow it was difficult to remember how important Charles was in his own work. He never talked about it, never thrust his knowledge upon you. He was always ready to listen.

"He is a very nice person," Toria thought.

She remembered the quiet seriousness of Olga as she had said those very words just a few hours ago.

"The children know that I shall be safe with Charles," Toria thought.

Inevitably the question came to her mind, safe from what? Did she mean poverty, the ordinary daily difficulties which had not seemed very important in the past, or did she mean safe from Michael?

But how could anyone want security from someone one loved?

Toria shivered under her mink coat. She was cold and tired. It was too much that Michael must come with her on her honeymoon, haunting her continually.

Charles opened his eyes.

"Have I been asleep?" he asked, and looked at his watch. "We ought to be there in a moment."

Toria looked out of the window. Below them she could see the sea, the smooth, calm Mediterranean.

Dusk was falling and the lights were coming out all along the coast, yellow twinkling lights which seemed somehow to have a gaiety as well as a brilliance about them.

"The wind was behind us," Charles said. "We shall be in on time if not a few minutes early."

Toria smiled at him. It was too much effort to try and shout above the roar of the engines. Charles bent over her to fasten her safety belt as they landed.

She smelt the fragrance of his hair oil and was suddenly aware of his hands, strong and purposeful, fastening her safely into her seat.

The aeroplane began to descend. Toria waited for her ears to pop and the sudden roar which always succeeded it, and then at last there was a slight bump and they were running across the ground.

There was a car waiting for them at the aerodrome and their luggage was stowed away in the back. They were soon driving away from the glittering crowded streets of Nice along the coast road which would carry them to Monte Carlo.

"You must be tired," Charles said, "but I am glad it was not rough."

"I am never air-sick," Toria replied.

"You are lucky then," Charles said. "They tell me it is one of the worst sensations there is."

"I am also a good sailor," Toria remarked.

Even as she spoke, she thought what an extraordinary conversation it was for two people going on their honeymoon. Charles might have been someone she had picked up in a train.

Why were they talking in this stilted manner? She had a sudden impulse to ask him what he was thinking, and then knew she could not say the words.

At the back of her mind was a question which she dared not ask even of herself, but it was there. She had the horrible feeling that sooner or later she had got to face up to it.

It was coming nearer and nearer to her, that moment when Charles was going to ask her about Michael.

6

The suite into which Toria and Charles were shown at the Hotel de Paris was ablaze with flowers. There were big bowls of pink carnations and sweet-scented hyacinths on every table.

"How lovely!" Toria exclaimed, and the receptionist who had shown them upstairs smiled appreciatively.

"We did our best to carry out Monsieur's instructions," he said.

Toria looked at Charles.

"Did you order all these?" she said. "How nice of you!"

He did not smile at her and she felt that he deliberately avoided her eyes. She passed through the sitting-room into the bedroom.

It had a small balcony overlooking a garden beyond which was the sea. Toria stood for a moment looking at the lights in the harbour and at the great rock of Monaco towering above it.

It was all very beautiful. The stars were shining, and carried on the night breeze was the fragrance of mimosa.

"It is lovely!"

Toria said the words aloud, then looked round to find she was still alone.

She wondered why Charles was being so long in joining her; then she heard the sound of a door being unlocked and the voice of the receptionist saying:

"It is fortunate, Monsieur, that the room is empty. We did not anticipate that you would require two bedrooms."

So that was what Charles was doing! Toria, looking through the open door into the sitting-room, saw him pass with the receptionist into a room on the other side.

She felt suddenly cold and a little afraid, and with a gesture of utter weariness she pulled her close-fitting, feather-trimmed hat from her head.

There was a knock on the door of the sitting-room. The porters had arrived with the luggage.

She heard Charles in surprisingly good French tell them which baggage to bring into each room. A few minutes later everything was arranged, and the porters departed with a *"Merci beaucoup, Monsieur"*, which meant that Charles had tipped them generously.

Now they were alone.

Toria felt as if she could not move, could not even begin to open the suitcases arranged neatly round the walls of her room on the low wooden stands which were so convenient for unpacking.

She could only stand holding on to the back of the chair by the dressing-table, waiting.

She felt her heart miss a beat in sheer panic when Charles came to the door.

"You must be famished and I know I am," he said. "I suggest we have a bath, change and go down to dinner as soon as possible."

His voice sounded friendly and pleasant. Toria felt her tension ebb away from her.

"I am longing for a bath," she managed to say. "But I shall be a long time. I have got to unpack and I have no idea where anything is."

"Why not ring for the maid?" Charles suggested.

"I had not thought of that," Toria replied.

"I will do it for you," he said.

He pressed the bell-push marked *"Femme de Chambre"* on the bedside table, then he strolled across the sitting-room into his own room.

Toria remembered how on her previous visits to France and elsewhere abroad she had always had to save money, counting her francs, wondering if she could afford another meal, let alone unessential luxuries.

It would have been impossible for her on those occasions to have contemplated asking the maid to unpack for her. Such a request would have meant a big tip and she had never had sufficient money for that sort of thing.

But now she was married to a rich man and everything was changed.

She took off her travelling coat. The light caught the wedding ring on her third finger, a thin platinum band.

What had it done to her, what did it mean? Already the ceremony in the Church seemed far away as if it had happened a long time ago.

She remembered the dream-like quality which had pervaded the whole ceremony. She felt now as if she had been half unconscious the whole time, moving mechanically while her thoughts and feelings were elsewhere.

And then, when they got back to the Castle, Michael appeared. She could see his face so clearly as he had stood in the doorway. Toria shivered.

She did not want to remember any more, to recall her own voice crying out those revealing words which must have betrayed a secret—hers and Michael's—all too clearly.

If only she were not so tired, she thought to herself, it might be easy to make light of the whole thing, to bring up the subject before Charles did, to invent some fantastic lie that she had not been referring to herself but to someone quite different.

But she felt as if her brain was refusing to function.

She could not think, could not plan, could not make a coherent picture of the odd pieces of memory, emotions, unhappiness, which seemed to lie about in her mind like an intricate and quite unsolvable jig-saw puzzle.

Only her bath was comforting. Toria felt a little of her fatigue slipping away from her as she lay up to the neck in the warm water which she had scented with Gardenia bath essence.

She could understand why people liked to die in their bath, she thought, and felt it would not be too terrible to cut one's arteries and know that one's life blood was ebbing away.

She could almost imagine herself drifting into oblivion in such a manner; and then she sat up abruptly, ashamed of her own morbid thoughts.

"I am not going to die," she said out loud. "I am going to live and be happy. I have got to be happy."

Her tone was defiant but she heard the words hiss back at her from the tiled bathroom walls as if they were simply an expression of fear. She got out of the bath and wrapped herself in the big bath towel.

She knew she was trying to make herself think calmly, trying to infuse some vitality into her tired mind and into her even more exhausted body.

Resolutely she put the thought of Michael from her.

If she kept remembering all that had happened this day, she felt she would go mad. It was enough that she could not move her lips without knowing they were bruised and recalling the roughness of his kisses, the brutality of his mouth on hers.

When she was dressed, she looked at herself in the long mirror on the big polished wardrobe and told herself that she had got to forget Michael, at least for some hours.

It was Charles' wedding night as well as her own, she thought, and there was no point in both of them being unhappy. Charles must not be made to suffer because of Michael. It was enough that she should be miserable.

She seemed to endure a physical pain between her breasts at the very thought of him. Charles had married her because he loved her. He had asked very little in return and that little was surely within her power to give.

"I will make him happy," Toria said aloud.

There was some satisfaction in knowing that she was beautiful. Charles at least could be proud of his wife. She was wearing a dinner frock made for her by one of the leading dress-designers in England.

It was beautiful in itself, yet managed to be a frame to accentuate and portray her own personal loveliness.

The dress was of smoke-blue chiffon, spangled with tiny mother of pearl sequins and trimmed round the shoulders with sprays of tiny roses also ornamented with sequins.

It made Toria's skin dazzlingly white, and her hair

110

was the colour of budding mimosa as it fell softly on either side of her little face.

She picked up the velvet wrap which her maid had laid for her on the bed and went towards the sitting-room. For one moment she paused, then taking a deep breath she opened the door and passed into the other room.

Charles was waiting for her. He was sitting in an armchair reading a newspaper. He rose to his feet at her entrance.

"You have been very quick," he said. "I was expecting to wait much longer."

"Are you usually so patient?" Toria asked. "Most men shout and roar when they are ready, and hate being kept waiting, especially for a meal."

"It depends very much for whom they are waiting," Charles replied.

There was something in his voice which made Toria feel shy. She glanced down at her frock and as if she called his attention to it, Charles said:

"This is a very lovely dress."

"I am glad you like it," Toria said. "It is almost worth the discomfort of the fittings to know that one's clothes are a success when eventually one is able to wear them."

"Let us go down and dazzle the dining-room," Charles suggested.

He opened the door for her and she preceded him down the passage.

Toria had been to Monte Carlo before, but she had never stayed at the Hotel de Paris. The enormous dining-room with its gilt-encrusted walls, its yellow satin hangings and huge Edwardian murals surprised and amused her.

"It is so perfectly in keeping with the place," she said to Charles. "Monte Carlo could be nothing but rococo. The Casino is like a wedding cake, the formal gardens look as if they were painted on a drop scene, and now this—it is quite perfect."

"I don't know whether I admire it myself," Charles said, concentrating on the menu.

Toria looked around her and thought how much Michael would like it.

He adored ornamentation, the rich sensuous luxury of satin and velvet, of gilt and crystal. That was another side to his revolution against all that was poverty-stricken, dull and economical.

"I want everything to be bizarre," he had said more than once. "I want the world filled with the fantastic and the beautiful. Tables should be loaded with gold plate and orchids. Houses should be filled with marble statues and flunkeys in knee breeches and gold-laced livery. Women should be be-feathered and be-jewelled."

Toria had laughed at his outburst. Somehow she had understood that Michael was always trying to escape from the ugly harsh outline of his own penury.

Yes, he would like this, she thought, and looking around, she recognised some of the other diners and felt herself smile as she realised what an appropriate setting it was for some of them.

At a table by the door sat the old Comtesse Yvonne de Farlante. She had once been a great beauty. Now at over seventy she had not forgotten the years in which she had been fêted and acclaimed, and she refused to bow to old age.

When she was very young, she had married a Duc and left him because she said he was a bore. Now she still wanted lovers and when they grew scarce, she found gigolos to take their place.

She was amusing, witty and had an ageless fascination. Tonight she sat alone, wearing a little black skullcap on her hair, which was set in a thousand tiny curls, while round her neck she wore five rows of magnificent pearls reported to have been given to her by one of the Grand Dukes of Russia.

There was no setting more appropriate to the Comtesse than Monte Carlo, Toria thought, and she recognised at the next table a contemporary of hers who had not weathered the years nearly so well.

One of the last survivors of a family of world-famous financiers, he looked exactly like a tortoise. His clothes hung on him loosely; his neck seemed almost to emerge

112

from his collar, the wrinkled folds of his chin falling from a curiously unlined face.

He had once been one of the most dashing young men of his generation, and it was said that no woman was safe when alone with him, while to drive with him in a hansom was to court disaster.

Now in his old age he travelled about with a woman nearly as old as himself who had been his *chere amie* for nearly thirty-five years. But his interest no longer lay in women.

It was food which excited him, not the rich, delicious, appetising food which he had enjoyed in his youth, but the vitaminised, medically recommended food which he believed prolonged his life.

When he travelled, it was with a retinue of people to care for that last and most treasured possession.

He had arrived in Monte Carlo with four cars, a Doctor, a nurse, his chemist, two valets and last but by no means least his own refrigerator, which he considered it was essential to take with him wherever he went.

He and the Comtesse were almost the last of the glamorous, exciting aristocracy which had once flooded Monte Carlo every spring in search of amusement.

"Do you see anybody you know?" Charles asked, and his voice interrupted Toria's thoughts.

"Quite a number," she replied.

It was true. She knew a large number of people in the great crowded dining-room.

She had no particular affection for them, nor they for her, yet Toria knew that, as soon as they realised that she was present, they would rush up to her with gushing greetings of affected pleasure, and would expect her instantly to join their parties and to spend her time drinking and gambling with them.

She wondered what Charles would think of them, these acquaintances with whom she had passed a great deal of time one way or another in the years when she had been drifting around London, accepting hospitality from anyone who was prepared to pay for it.

She knew only too well what the reputations of such people were, the majority of them being wasters and ne'er-do-wells; and yet they had two virtues—they were both amusing and generous. They, too, like the Comtesse and the old financier were the remnants of a lost and forgotten era.

They had come into being in the years that existed between the two wars. "Café Society" America called them, and like butterflies who could only live in the sunshine they disappeared when there was work to be done and sacrifices to be endured, only to reappear just as gay but maybe a little older when the war had ended and peace descended again on Europe.

"I can't think why they want to travel," someone said once. "You will always find them in the Ritz bar of every city; and if one didn't look out of the window, one would never have any idea of which city."

They were unstable parasites in a world which could ill-afford such people, and yet Toria felt that one could hardly help liking them.

The men all had a charm about them. They were well dressed, and there was something dashing and jaunty about their carnation buttonholes and fat cigars.

They drove fast, expensive, streamlined cars, and they always appeared to have an enormous amount of money, though no one ever knew from where it came.

The women were lovely, there was no disputing that. They were groomed into being the last word in fashion. Their clothes were all by couturiers with famous names, and their jewellery came from the Rue de la Paix.

They seldom said anything that one could remember, yet their laughter could be heard tinkling gaily above the soft rhythm of the bands which played in any night club that was the *dernier cri*.

Mutation mink was now draped over their shoulders, where a few years ago they were wearing sable and chinchilla, and Dior's fantastic creations had now supplanted Chanel and Schiaparelli who had been their favourites before the war.

They contrived in some extraordinary manner of their own always to be a little smarter than every other woman in the room, however much money she might have, however important she might be socially.

114

There was something about them which made them so up-to-date that everyone else was out-dated.

"Who are your friends?" Charles asked, as a waiter came hurrying to his side with a folded note on a plate.

"Darling, it is divine to see you again! Do join us after dinner. We long to hear all about the wedding. Bébé."

Toria handed the note to Charles.

"Do you want to go and join them?" she asked. "It is the party of four in the corner."

Charles glanced towards them—the sun-tanned, over-polished men and their chic, over-jewelled women.

"I expect you are too tired tonight," he said quietly; "but if you want to go, I am of course agreeable."

Toria shook her head.

"I am much too tired," she said. "We shall see them tomorrow and every other day we are here. We won't be able to escape them even if we wanted to."

"I see no reason why we should be with anyone we don't want to be with," Charles said.

Toria smiled.

"You don't know Bébé!" she said. "She is very persistent, and you forget that we are celebrities for the moment."

Charles looked at her in surprise.

"I have never heard you sound bitter about it before," he exclaimed.

"But I am not," Toria replied quickly. "I am only laughing a little at ourselves."

"The nine-days' wonder will soon be over," Charles assured her gravely. "There will doubtless be another wedding next week twice as exciting as ours and everyone will have forgotten our very existence."

"I am not even certain that I should like that," Toria retorted.

She pencilled a note to Bébé and sent it back to the table, saying that she and Charles had just arrived and they were far too tired to join any party that night.

She felt sure Bébé and her friends would understand.

When the note had gone with the waiter, she wondered if she had been wise. The conversation she and Charles were making to each other was an effort.

There was something stilted in the sentences they spoke, as if not for one moment did they reveal their minds or their real feelings.

Charles had ordered a delicious dinner and, as course succeeded course, Toria found her mind wandering away from what they were saying. It was somehow impossible to concentrate on the trivialities of the conversation.

More than once Toria thought that time was going very slowly.

"I wonder what the twins are doing tonight," she said suddenly.

"They will be at the theatre," Charles replied. "I arranged with three of my friends who were Ushers to take them and Lettice to see a show at the Hippodrome. I felt it would be very depressing for them after you had gone. They will miss you, you know."

"But it won't be for long," Toria replied.

Charles glanced at her reflectively.

"I want to talk to you about the twins one day," he said. "Don't you think it would be a good idea if they were sent to a really good school, somewhere where they would not only learn something but would make nice friends?"

Toria looked at him in surprise.

"But they are so happy at home, and they do lessons in the village. There is a very nice woman there. She was a governess and now has retired. She teaches them every morning."

"It does not sound to me to be an adequate education," Charles said.

"They know about as much as I did at the same age," Toria replied a little defiantly.

"I think they would be happier at school," Charles persisted, "especially now that you have left home and there is nobody to look after them."

"There is Lettice," Toria said. "I was thinking, of course, that they could come to us when we have decided where we are going to live."

"That is already decided," Charles replied. "I have bought a house in Chesterfield Hill. It was to have been a surprise when we got home. Perhaps I ought to have consulted you about it before. It is a small house, easy to run, and quite frankly I do not think there will be room for the twins to live there permanently. For the holidays, yes, and they can also come down to my home in Worcestershire, but I think they ought to go to school."

Toria suddenly felt angry. For the first time since she had known him Charles seemed to be interfering.

"I will think about it," she said a little stiffly. "I have, of course, always decided these matters as we have no mother."

"And now I hope you will let me help you with your decisions," Charles said.

"Why should I do that?"

She knew her question was truculent, but she could not prevent herself from asking it.

"Because I am very fond indeed of the twins," Charles answered, "and I want to do what is best for them."

"Home is the best place for all children," Toria said.

"Where there is a mother and a father, I agree with you," Charles replied.

Toria was suddenly silent. She was thinking of Mrs. Hagar-Bassett and wondering if Charles knew about her. She thought too of Michael with his moods and difficult moments.

She was not dishonest enough to pretend to herself that such an atmosphere was good for children of Xandra's and Olga's age. Perhaps Charles was right. Now that they could afford it, a really good boarding-school might be the happiest and the best place for the twins.

And yet how she would hate to lose them! She felt suddenly as if someone was taking her own children away from her. There would be long months when she would not see them. She could almost feel the loneliness creeping into her bones.

"I hate schools," she said a little petulantly.

"Did you ever go to one?" he enquired.

"Only for six months," Toria replied. "A so-called finishing school."

She remembered how she loathed leaving the Castle; but somehow, when she got there, it was not so bad. It had been rather fun to be so busy, having so many friends, having so many interests, so much to talk about.

Yes, she did not regret her time at school; but the twins were much younger, and it seemed awful, somehow, to condemn them to be disciplined, to be stuffed with instruction for the next five years.

"I will think about it," Toria repeated.

Again she felt angry with Charles for having presented her with this problem tonight of all nights.

Charles was quite unaware that he had upset her in any way.

"I know it will be best for the twins," he said, as if the issue had now been settled. "And now, if you are finished, shall we walk across to the Casino?"

"Yes, let us do that," Toria agreed.

A number of people had already left the dining-room, but even so it took Toria and Charles some time to reach the door. There were at least half a dozen old friends holding out their hands and saying with a meaning smirk:

"Aren't you going to introduce me to your husband?"

Charles was courteous and polite, but somehow detached, Toria thought.

She found herself being drawn into the old vortex of insincere expressions of affection, cries of delight at another woman's dress, the slightly catty manner with which one spoke of old acquaintances.

It was all so familiar and easy, and Toria slipped into the part required of her as if it fitted her like a glove, but all the time she was acutely conscious that it was a part.

Charles had never seen her like this. He had only seen her at the Castle, when she was natural and ordinary, just herself.

Yet was that any more herself than this sparkling, amusing creature who called everyone she met "Dar-

118

ling", and who talked a lot of nonsense in an exaggeratedly social manner which made even the most banal remarks seem amusing?

She had somehow not expected to notice this difference in her behaviour when she was with Charles. With Michael she had always been absurdly self-conscious because he laughed and taunted her with it.

Also he would mimic her and her friends; and afterwards she could never, having listened to him, be quite natural when he was there.

But it was only Michael who made her feel like that.

Now it was disconcerting to find that all the time she was talking and laughing and glittering like a little firework she was aware of Charles standing a little in the background and watching her.

At last they were free to walk through the marble pillared hall alone for a few minutes until they reached the Casino.

Toria slipped her velvet wrap round her shoulders.

"We need not go out of doors unless we want to," she said. "There is a passage from the Hotel to the Casino."

"If it is not too cold for you, I would like a breath of air," Charles said.

"And I would like it too."

She wondered what Charles was thinking as they walked down the steps and crossed the road into the Casino.

There was the usual impression of sparkling glitter in big rooms lit by crystal and gold chandeliers. There were the monotonous voices of the croupiers, the chatter and movement of the onlookers, the tense alertness of the gamblers.

"Let us go into the *Salle Privé*," Charles suggested.

They pushed their way through the crowds, thronging the outer rooms of the Casino into the comparative quiet of the *Salle Privé*.

There was almost a hush in these rooms despite the fact that there were several hundred people gathered round the green-baized tables, playing *chemin de fer, trente-et-quarante* or roulette.

"Do you want to gamble?" Charles asked.

119

"I might as well try my luck," Toria replied.

He changed some money into two hundred franc plaques. He gave a pile of them to Toria, and she went up to a roulette table. She put a plaque on number 17 and, as she did so, remembered that it was Michael's lucky number.

"If anything is going to happen, it will happen on the 17th."

How often she had heard him say that and had laughed at him for being superstitious! How much Michael would have enjoyed being in her place tonight!

He loved gambling. He would wager his last shilling on a horse, supremely confident that it would come in first and unreasonably angry when it did not.

More than once Toria had lectured him for wasting the little money he had on games of chance. She had always laughed at him for doing his football pools.

"You are just like the servants," she said more than once, "believing that one day you will make a hundred thousand and be able to retire."

"I shall make it all right," Michael had answered, "but I shan't retire. You wait and see."

His confidence had been justified, Toria thought. He had won a fortune. Now she was not there to see what he would do with it.

"Zero," she heard the croupier call out.

She had lost her money, and wandered away to another table. Soon she had lost every plaque she had and turned round to find Charles beside her.

"Have you won?" he asked.

She shook her head. It was a moment or two before she added:

"Have you?"

She heard him rattle together some plaques in his pocket.

"I have made a little," he said. "I am usually lucky."

"I should not have thought you were a gambler somehow," Toria remarked.

"I am not," he replied. "That is why, when I do take a chance, it usually turns up trumps."

"I am tired," Toria said suddenly. "Is it too early to go to bed?"

"It is nearly twelve o'clock," Charles said. "Early for Monte Carlo, but not for people who have done as much as we have today."

They walked through the rooms in silence.

As they came out on to the steps of the Casino, Toria stood looking at the floodlit gardens. The flower beds, stiff and formal, were ablaze with colour. The palm trees stood out theatrically against the darkness of the star-spangled night.

Even the statues on the Hotel de Paris, huge naked goddesses emerging from a modest foam of white marble, had an air of mystery and seduction about them.

One had the feeling that something thrilling was just about to happen—that the curtain was rising.

"Monte Carlo is a perfect stage setting," Toria said softly.

"For what?" Charles asked.

"For . . . for . . ." Toria hesitated.

She had been about to say "for love", and then she checked herself.

"For . . . cosmopolitans," she finished lamely, and wondered if Charles had noticed her hesitation.

The lift took them up to their floor. Charles opened the door of the suite with the key and Toria, passing in front of him, switched on the lights.

She heard him close the door behind them, and to conceal a sudden sense of embarrassment she went to smell a bowl of carnations.

"They are lovely," she said.

Charles did not answer her and after a moment she was forced to look up at him. He was standing looking at her gravely.

"Is it too late for us to talk for a little?" he asked.

"I should say much too late," Toria replied quietly. "Can't whatever you have to say wait until tomorrow?"

She managed to speak lightly, but at the same time she felt her mouth go dry.

"That depends on what you feel about it," Charles

answered. "I wanted to ask you, of course, about your cousin Michael."

Toria felt suddenly as if her legs would not hold her any more. She sat down on the sofa, her full skirt billowing out around her.

"What about Michael?" she asked, and knew that her voice had an unnatural ring in it.

"You are in love with him," Charles said.

She had been waiting for the blow all the evening, but now that it had come she flinched from it.

"What . . . what do you mean?"

"I think you know what I mean," Charles replied. "I knew you were not in love with me, but I did not know until today that you were in love with anyone else."

"You did not ask me," Toria retorted a little defiantly.

"It never entered my head that you would marry me if you were fond of someone else," Charles said.

"I might have reasons for that."

"It is money, of course."

Charles' voice was sharp and for the first time very bitter.

"No, it was not money."

Toria almost shouted the words at him.

"I am sorry. Will you give me a reason then?"

Toria twisted her fingers together. This was being even more unbearable than she had expected.

She tried to think of all the things she had planned to say, but it seemed as if her brain was stuffed with cotton wool.

Charles walked across the room and back again.

"If you would only confide in me," he said, "and let me help."

"I've told you it was not money," Toria replied. "There were other reasons. I wanted to get away from Michael."

"He apparently had the same idea."

"He went away without telling me."

"And if he had arrived the day before we were married, would you have thrown me over?" Charles asked. asked.

There was a long pause before Toria answered him.

122

"I don't know," she said at last. "That is the truth, Charles! I don't know."

"You asked me to marry you as quickly as possible," Charles said. "If you had not been in such a hurry, you could have married Michael now that he has won some money."

Toria suddenly jumped to her feet.

"What is the point of all this?" she asked, "and why are you saying all these things? What good does it do? We are married, aren't we?"

"I want to know exactly where I stand," Charles replied.

"You are my husband," Toria said, and her voice was a little hysterical.

"As you say, I am your husband," Charles remarked drily, "but it is not particularly gratifying to find on your wedding day that your wife is very much in love with someone else."

"How do you know? Why do you assume that?" Toria asked wildly.

"You forget that I saw your face when Michael arrived at the reception," Charles replied. "I heard what you said as you fainted."

"I heard it too," Toria muttered as if she spoke to herself. "I did not mean to say it, it slipped out."

"I realised that," Charles replied. "I don't particularly relish being deceived, you know."

"There was no question of deceit," Toria protested. "You asked me to marry you and I said yes. You did not ask me if I loved you or if I loved anyone else."

"I suppose I was a fool," Charles answered, "but I somehow imagined you would be too honest to give your hand where there was no chance of giving your heart."

He smiled, but his eyes and lips were cynical.

"That sounds like a line from a Victorian novel, doesn't it? I suppose I am old-fashioned and dull; but when I was listening to you talking to these people downstairs tonight, I realised that I knew nothing about you or the world you have lived in."

"I am sorry, Charles."

Toria's eyes were raised to his.

"There is no need for you to be sorry," Charles said. "I have merely been extremely foolish. Like a large number of men before me, I expected too much."

"Oh, please don't be so hurt about it," Toria pleaded. "You have been kind, terribly kind. I like you very much, I trust you. I feel safe with you, but I can't help it . . . I do not love you."

"And you do love your cousin Michael?" Charles insisted.

It seemed as if he would force an admission from her.

"I suppose so," Toria agreed. "But what good does it do to talk about it? Can't we forget it?"

"Can we?"

She wanted to lie then; but even as she tried to force the words to her lips, she knew it was impossible. She was too tired to prevaricate, or even to pretend.

There was something, too, about Charles which prevented her from doing any of these things. She did not answer, and after a moment he made a little gesture with his hands.

"You see," she said. "Well, what are you going to do about it?"

Toria flung back her head and looked him straight in the eyes as she asked the question.

"Nothing!"

His voice was very final. He walked across to the window, opened it and looked out into the night. His back was very uncompromising, his shoulders were so broad.

He seemed bigger and a little overpowering, Toria thought. He stood there without moving and after a moment or two she felt she could bear it no longer.

"Charles!" she said, and when he did not turn she repeated, "Charles, I am terribly sorry about all this, but . . . I . . . I am your wife."

She did not know how else to put it into words. She wanted to tell him that, as far as she was concerned, she was ready to go through with their marriage.

She could hear her voice quiver away into silence; then Charles turned round.

His face was contorted almost out of recognition, his eyes narrowed as he looked at her.

"Do you think I want you on those terms?" he asked furiously.

His eyes seemed to burn their way over her white face; then he walked from the room into his own bedroom.

He shut the door behind him, and what made it infinitely more frightening was the fact that he did not slam it.

He closed it quietly with what seemed to Toria an absolute finality.

7

Having spent a night of unhappy self-accusation and regret, Toria awoke in a very different mood.

She had felt ashamed and humbled in the dark hours of the night, when she lay sleepless, feeling sorry for Charles and for herself and even at moments angry with Michael.

It was all such a sorry muddle, and now their lives were tangled and twisted so that no one was happy and no one had gained anything out of what had at one moment seemed a sensible and unselfish action on her part.

Now she thought she must have been mad.

In marrying Charles she had solved nothing, neither Michael's future nor her own; and yet she had believed that she was making the sacrifice for his sake, ensuring him at least of a roof over his head in the house that had been his only home since his parents died.

Now that he was rich he could go where he wanted, do what he wanted, and all she had managed to do was to make herself unhappy, and Charles too.

There was nothing she could reproach Charles with.

He had married her believing her heart-whole if not in love with him; and the deception, if that was the right word for it, was all on her side, and she was now forced into the miserable position of knowing that she had behaved badly.

Tossing and turning on the soft bed, Toria thought herself a very despicable person until the sunlight, glinting through the shutters, awoke her to the realisation that the night was past and another day, gloriously sunny and invigorating, was waiting for her.

She opened the shutters and stood at the window in her nightgown.

She could feel the golden sunshine warming her body, blinding her eyes and making her feel as if it embraced and comforted her, smoothing away the very wrinkles of unhappiness.

It was then that pride came to her rescue and as if it raised her from her knees she felt it strengthen and invigorate her so that instinctively she squared her shoulders and threw back her head.

After all, she asked herself, of what had she to be ashamed?

She had not lied to Charles. He had asked her to marry him and she had accepted. She had not told him that he was the only man in her life.

If he liked to assume such a thing, it was surely an unwarranted assumption on his part. He might be famous and a hero to the masses, but she was after all not without a following of her own.

She was young, she was pretty, and above all she was alive in a world that was meant to be lived in and enjoyed. Who could be unhappy and retrospective on a morning like this?

Toria shaded her eyes from the sun and looked below her. The sea was vividly blue as the Madonna's robe, the ships in the harbour were gay with flags, the garden below her window was a riot of bougainvillaea, its luxurious purple blossoms sprawling in sensuous abandon over the white walls.

The oranges on the trees were like balls of gold and there was a soft whispering rustle as of silken skirts among the leaves of the palm trees. It was all so lovely, so gay.

"Why should I be so unhappy?" Toria asked herself, going back to bed.

She rang the bell for breakfast; and lying back against her pillows, she ate the delicious crisp rolls which had been baked that morning and drank the fragrant coffee which was so very different from the beverage which bore the same name in England.

She wondered what Charles was doing.

There was no sign or sound of him from the other bedroom across the sitting-room. When breakfast was finished and Toria had eaten all that had been brought to her, including a tiny pot of local honey which tasted and smelt of mimosa blossom, she got out of bed and went into the bathroom.

Determined to enjoy every moment of her day, she lingered for some time in the scented water and then dried herself in the sunshine, feeling once again that no one could be unhappy when the sun was so golden, warm and seductive.

Dry and half dressed, she went to the wardrobe to choose what to wear. Toria knew enough of the climate in the South of France to know that, however warm the sunshine, there was always the chance of a treacherous wind rising to destroy the illusion that summer was really there.

Eventually she took from its hanger a dress of pale mauve jersey, the exact colour of parma violets, which had a short coat trimmed with sable tails to wear over it.

When she was ready, Toria looked at herself in the mirror and smiled. She looked like a bride and a very attractive one, whatever Charles might feel about it.

Jauntily, and with a little air of defiance, she opened the door of her bedroom. She half expected Charles to be waiting for her in the sitting-room, but the room was empty and she saw that the door into his bedroom was open.

"Charles!"

She called his name, but there was no answer. Then she saw that there was a piece of writing-paper lying on the table in the centre of the room. She picked it up and

127

recognised Charles' neat, rather precise writing, which was somehow characteristic of him.

"I have gone for a walk. I shall be waiting for you on the terrace about 11.30, if you will meet me there.

Charles."

Toria read it twice and made a little grimace. It annoyed her that Charles should have sauntered off, and she felt also that he was being rather ridiculous.

Why couldn't he have knocked at her bedroom door and told her what he was doing?

This aloof attitude was not only irritating, but it made her feel like a child who was being rebuked unnecessarily.

She crumpled the piece of paper up in her hand and threw it into the waste paper basket.

How did Charles know that she was not worrying about him, how did he know that she was not feeling miserable and unhappy after what had occurred last night?

Although Toria had never been in love herself, she had, of course, had a great number of men in love with her. She had to admit that Charles was different from most of them.

He said little and he had been very undemanding during the time they had been engaged to each other.

But that was not to say that he was entitled to behave entirely differently from every other man she knew. If he loved her, he should be considerate of her feelings before fussing about his own.

Besides, Toria thought, it was all very well for Charles to be hurt and upset by Michael, but she was still married to him; he could still be a man in possession if he wished it.

As she stood there, she began to feel resentful about the whole thing. Had she been in Charles' place, she thought, she would have ignored the whole episode.

She would just have behaved as if the drama at the wedding had not happened; and after they were man and wife in the fullest sense of the word, he could have afforded to snap his fingers at Michael.

As it was, he was erecting endless barriers which would be difficult to demolish and, once raised, would make things very uncomfortable.

Toria shrugged her shoulders. Oh well, let him play the game his own way, she thought, but she would play it hers.

She was well aware of her own attractions. There had been many men with whom she had flirted and in whose company she had enjoyed herself.

She could not bring herself to marry any of them. But—it was strange now she thought of it—she had not minded marrying Charles even while she knew she loved Michael.

It was Charles' sense of solidarity and the feeling he gave her of security which had made her like him so much.

Now he was being unpredictable and she thought to herself that in that way he was likely to lose all that he might have gained.

There was something about having exquisite, expensive clothes and knowing that not only was she young and beautiful, but that the sun was shining, which made it impossible for her to go on suffering and being self-abased.

Toria went downstairs and walked from the Hotel, looking for someone or something to amuse her.

It was not yet half past eleven and she had every intention of keeping Charles waiting. At the same time she did not want to sit upstairs in the suite or even in the pompous, over-luxurious atmosphere of the lounge.

She thought she would take a stroll in the gardens which climbed the hill outside the hotel to the main street.

In them there were deep rock pools filled with goldfish and bordered by strange exotic plants, and there were seats where one could sit underneath the shady trees and listen to the pigeons cooing or watch them swoop down to pick up crumbs which children and softhearted old ladies brought them daily.

There was a little donkey cart which took the children for a ride for fifty francs a time, and everywhere there were flowers, purple, crimson, magenta, rose, yellow and orange.

Flowers that were breathtaking in their vivid loveliness and seemed to make the gardens as unreal and theatrical as the Casino itself with its stucco goddesses and its pointed roofs silhouetted against an azure sky.

Toria, however, had not gone very far towards the gardens when she heard someone call her name.

She turned round and saw a man in a big Hispano Suiza drawing up outside the Hotel.

"Toria," he repeated. "Is it really you?"

She smiled and walked towards the car, reaching it just as the driver sprang out on to the pavement, holding out both hands to her in a gesture of almost exaggerated welcome.

"Angel Face, what a surprise!" he exclaimed.

"I shan't say 'fancy seeing you here', Billy," Toria said. "I was quite certain I should."

"And I might have expected to see you when I read about your wedding," Billy Grantly replied. "Where else should anyone honeymoon at this time of year?"

"We had to do the right thing, of course," Toria said with mock solemnity.

Billy laughed.

"Come and have a drink," he suggested. "Where is the lucky bridegroom?"

"He has gone for a walk," Toria replied. "I am meeting him later. At the moment I am quite alone."

"Not while I am about," Billy replied.

He slipped his arm through Toria's and they walked across the road to the Café de Paris and sat down at a table in the sunshine.

"Tell me about yourself," Billy said after he had ordered two cocktails from the waiter.

"There is nothing I can tell you that you haven't already read in every paper in the country," Toria said. "I am sick to death of myself. But tell me what you have been doing."

She looked at her companion as she spoke and

thought how refreshing it would be if Billy really told one the truth about himself.

He was one of those mysterious cosmopolitan men who turned up at every playground of the world at the right time and in the right season.

He seemed to know everyone, and that included not only smart society people but financiers, industrialists, bankers, gamblers and even more shady individuals.

When Billy Grantly entered a cocktail bar, everyone seemed anxious to talk to him and to stand him a drink. And yet, Toria thought, no one seemed to know anything about him except what he chose to tell them, and that was really nothing.

To begin with, no one was certain what was his real nationality.

There were stories that his father had been a Greek and his mother a Russian, and that he had been educated in France. There were other people who swore that he came from Egyptian stock, and others who were quite certain that he was the only Armenian left alive after their frequent and invariably bloody massacres.

Toria had heard people repeat over and over again that they knew for a fact that Billy Grantly's name ended in -ovski or -azu or -nerof, but none of the stories coincided one with the other, and only one thing was quite certain at the end of them all, that Billy's name was too simple and too unassuming for it to be the one he had inherited at his birth.

Where did his money come from? That was another cause for speculation.

Even the big financiers with whom Billy seemed to be on such easy terms of familiarity were unable to provide a clue to the mystery.

From their point of view Billy was able to tell them a great many things they wanted to know; and if they were able occasionally to do him a good turn, it was a part of the day's work; but that by no means could be his only source of income.

His suites at the Ritz in Paris, the Dorchester in London, the Simirimus in Cairo and the Waldorf-Astoria in

New York were always the most luxurious and expensive in the place.

His cars attracted attention wherever he went and his yacht, large and extremely comfortable, was guaranteed to provide amusing parties for a host of guests whenever it was in the harbours of Cannes and Monte Carlo or turning up unexpectedly in Tunis or Gibraltar.

"Billy the enigma," Toria had heard him nicknamed.

Looking at him now, she thought, as many women had thought before, that his enigmatic aura added to his attractions. He was good looking in an unobtrusive manner.

Clean shaven, his dark hair was always as neatly and correctly brushed as if he had just come from the hairdresser.

He dressed well with the easy elegance of an Englishman, and yet there was just something about him which made one quite certain that, although his English was perfect and his name impeccably British, he was in fact not of British nationality.

It was difficult to know what it was that made one so certain about this. Perhaps it was the green emerald in his signet ring, perhaps it was an unnatural alertness in his eyes, or perhaps it was nothing more than instinct which made all Englishmen certain that he was not one of them.

The French were equally emphatic that he was not French; and as far as anyone knew, other nations were all quite sure that Billy was not one of them.

But what did it matter? Billy usually managed to make himself the king of any place he frequented within a few hours of his arrival.

"I am giving a party tonight," he would say. "Do come!"

The words were an automatic invitation to an evening of gaiety and enjoyment.

There would be superlative wines and food, which had been ordered by Billy earlier in the day in a manner which made a Chef try to excel even his own excellence.

There would be amusing, witty conversation; there would be artistes of renowned ability to sing, dance and entertain the company of distinguished, famous and notorious guests.

What was the reason for so much munificence Toria had wondered more than once; but like all the other questions she asked about Billy there was no reply or explanation.

"I've just arrived from Scandinavia," Billy said now.

"You have always just arrived from somewhere," Toria teased. "Why Scandinavia?"

"Why not?" Billy parried. "One has to spend the winter somewhere. I went across to California for Christmas. I meant to make my way down to Mexico, but business brought me home sooner than I intended."

"What business?" Toria enquired, knowing quite well that he would not tell her.

"My dear, the world, as we know, is in a financial mess," he said solemnly, "but don't let us be gloomy. Tell me about your marriage. Are you happy?"

"That is hardly a question you ask of a bride the day after the ceremony," Toria replied.

Billy grinned at her.

"All right, let it pass! You have certainly picked a winner by all account, Toria. I want to meet your husband."

"Do you mean to say you don't know him already?" Toria questioned. "I thought you knew everybody in the world."

"Everybody but him," Billy replied. "That is why I am so anxious to make his acquaintance."

"I am not certain he will appreciate you," Toria said. "He has always led a sensible, steady life."

Billy raised his eyebrows.

"It does not sound as dull as all that," he said. "Recommended for the V.C., holder of the D.F.C. and two Bars, the youngest Air Vice-Marshal in the Force, and the inventor of some of the most useful little gadgets the Air Ministry have ever had on their lists."

"How do you know all this?" Toria asked.

"My dear, I read the papers," he replied, "and when I saw that my old friend and quite the loveliest girl I have ever known in my life was getting married, do you think I wasn't curious enough to find out a little about the bridegroom? In my opinion he is one of the luckiest men in the world today."

"Billy! Billy! What a lovely speech!" Toria laughed. "Thank you."

"Let us go and find that young man of yours," Billy suggested, "and I will make it all over again. If he does not like me after that, I shall go and lie down in my cabin and have a good cry."

"Have you got your yacht here?" Toria asked.

"Sleeping in it as a matter of fact," Billy replied. "I really prefer being at the hotel, but the crew have got rather slack. I have not been using it for six months and I thought it was time they had some hard work to do. Will you come out for a cruise some day?"

"I would love it," Toria said.

"We will fix it then. It looks as if the weather is going to be good. Are you a good sailor, I can't remember?"

"About seventy-five per cent," Toria said; "but I have a preference for the sea being like a mill-pond."

"Well, we will have it all arranged," Billy smiled. "I would like your husband to see my yacht. I have got some inventions of my own there which I believe he would find extremely interesting."

As they strolled towards the terrace, Toria thought how strange it was that she had never discussed Charles' work with him. She had no idea what inventions he had made or indeed what they were about.

She tried to remember if there had been anything about them in the papers, and failed. She made a mental note that it would be the first thing she would ask him as soon as he stopped being silly over Michael and became friendly and pleasant again.

There were crowds of people on the Terrace, sitting under orange umbrellas, sipping cocktails and listening to the soft strains of a band. Toria and Billy stood looking around them.

"I wonder where Charles can be," Toria said, and then she saw him.

He was standing with his hands in his pockets with his back to the cocktail drinkers, looking out to sea. He

134

looked very tall, stolid and English, and Toria had a sudden impulse to run to him and slip her arm into his.

But instead she walked slowly towards him, Billy at her side. They had almost reached Charles before he realised they were approaching. Toria saw his eyes go speculatively towards Billy.

"Hullo, Charles."

"Hullo, Toria. I was wondering when you would turn up."

"I met an old friend who delayed me," Toria explained. "He says you have never met each other. Charles, this is Billy Grantly."

"How do you do?"

Charles was conventionally polite, but somehow without being sure why it was so, Toria was sure that he was not pleased to meet Billy.

The latter obviously had no doubt as to his welcome where Charles was concerned.

Genial, amusing and in a subtle way extremely flattering, he led them to three comfortable seats under an orange umbrella and ordered drinks.

"Look here, you must let me pay for these," Charles said, but Billy waved his offer to one side.

"Certainly not! I must drink your health now as I was not invited to the wedding yesterday. What do you want as a wedding present?"

"I can tell you a number of things we do not want," Toria said. "But if you ask me like that, I can't think of a single thing I want in the whole world."

"Lucky girl," Billy laughed. "As an old friend I think it will have to be something really nice. I will slip into Cartier's this afternoon and see if I can find something as lovely as your eyes. That is, if your husband won't object to your receiving presents from an old friend?"

He spoke as if he insinuated that he and Toria had been far more friendly than was obvious on the surface. Toria, however, was equally determined that Charles should not misunderstand her friendship with Billy of all people.

"If you do give me a present, Billy, it will be the first I have ever had from you. I remember you saying that you would give me a Christmas present once, but it never materialised."

She was amused to see that for once Billy looked a little nonplussed.

"I shall sack my Secretary," he said at length rather feebly.

Toria laughed.

"I didn't really expect it. You made the promise during one of your very good parties, and there were at least six other girls besides myself who watched for the postman during the next three weeks."

Billy turned towards Charles.

"What does one do when covered with confusion?" he asked.

"I have no idea," Charles replied briefly.

"I suppose it has never happened to you," Billy said. "But let us talk seriously for a moment. I do want to congratulate you on that last gadget of yours, the anti-freeze adjuster. It was absolutely brilliant."

Charles looked surprised.

"How do you know about it?" he asked. "It has not yet been released from the secret list."

Billy made a little gesture with his hands.

"Toria will tell you that I know a lot of things and a lot of people," he said significantly. "As a matter of fact I have done a little work myself for your department one way or another."

"Really?"

Charles made it a question, and Billy replied:

"Yes, really. In fact I shall not be indiscreet when I tell you that your Air Ministry is extremely grateful to me for a great deal of information I have been able to convey to them. Do I make myself clear?"

He looked directly at Charles as he spoke, but Charles seemed to be wilfully stupid.

"Not quite," he replied. "Are you suggesting that you are Secret Service or something like that?"

"My dear fellow!"

Billy glanced over his shoulder.

"You cannot be too careful, especially in a place like this. Let us talk of other things now; but when you come and dine on my yacht, as I hope you are going to soon, we will discuss it then."

He glanced at his watch and got to his feet.

"Will you forgive me if I leave you? I have got a very lovely lady waiting for me at the Hotel de Paris. We are motoring over to the Château Madrid for luncheon. Now let me see, when can you dine? Tomorrow night or the night after?"

Toria was just going to ask Charles which day would suit him, when she saw his expression and realised to her surprise that he was disliking Billy.

She was not certain how she knew this because at a second glance Charles' face looked incalculable and with his usual impeccable politeness he was standing up to shake hands with Billy as he left.

And yet there was something in the stiffness of his bearing and the look in his eyes, the slightly tightened line of his lips, which told her that he was not amused.

Quite suddenly she was annoyed. What right had Charles to criticise her friends? Billy had been charming, generous and had done his very best to be pleasant.

If Charles was going to be difficult at the very outset of their marriage, it did not augur well for the future.

Quickly, because she was angry, Toria accepted Billy's invitation without any more being said.

"We will dine with you tomorrow."

"That will be lovely, and I am so looking forward to it."

He took her hand and pressed it with both of his.

"I will send the car to the Hotel at eight o'clock." He hesitated and then added, as if the thought had only just struck him. "No, I won't! What about that cruise? We had better take advantage of the weather while we can. Come on board at luncheon time and bring enough things with you for one night. We might run across to Capri. I am told there is the most wonderful night club there. It would be too much of a bore to come back after dinner, so you can both stay on board and I will bring you back in the morning. How is that for an idea?"

Charles said nothing, but Toria could feel him bris-

tling beside her. His silence made her accept as gushing-
ly as she had accepted the invitation to dinner.

"Oh, Billy, that will be too divine. We shall both
adore it."

"Twelve o'clock then," Billy said, "and bring a warm
coat. You never know at this time of year what it will be
like when one gets out to sea."

"I won't forget," Toria promised, "and thank you
very much."

"I shall be counting the hours," Billy smiled. "Anyway, I expect I shall see you tonight in the Casino."

He waved his hand and strolled away. Charles sat
down again at the table. Toria looked across at him.

"That will be fun, won't it?" she asked, apparently
oblivious of the fact that he was frowning.

"What do you know about this man Grantly?"
Charles enquired.

"I have known him for years," Toria answered. "One
meets him everywhere."

"What do you mean by everywhere?" Charles asked.

"Oh, here and in Paris, and London."

"In private houses or in nightclubs?" Charles asked.

"Let me think!" Toria rested her chin on her hand.
"I'm sure I've met him at private dances. Yes, I remember one which somebody gave at Claridge's. . . ."

"I don't call that meeting him in a private house,"
Charles interrupted. "He might have been brought in a
party."

"What are you trying to suggest?" Toria said. "That
he is an undesirable acquaintance? Are you afraid he
will upset my morals or yours?"

"I was not thinking about either of our morals as it
happens," Charles replied. "I seem to have heard about
this Mr. . . . Mr. Grantly, but I can't remember what
was said about him. Did he ask you about me?"

Toria laughed.

"Really, Charles, I can't make out whether you are
being a crushing snob or very conceited. Billy, as it happens, said very charming things about you. He did not
question me as to who you were or where you came
from, if that is what you are trying to find out."

"Did he ask you about my work?" Charles enquired.

"No, of course not," Toria replied. "And if he had, it would not have been much use. I was just thinking, as we walked down here, that I know nothing about what you have done, about all these inventions people are always referring to."

"Who are referring to them?" Charles asked sharply.

"Well, Billy for one person," Toria replied.

"That is just what I have asked you," Charles said. "What did he say?"

"But you were here," Toria said. "You heard him."

"Oh, I don't mean that," Charles replied. "You said that, as you came down here, you were thinking that you knew nothing about my inventions. What brought that to mind?"

"Only something Billy said."

"And what did he say?"

There was a pause while Toria tried to remember.

"Oh, I know," she exclaimed at length. "He said he would like you to see the yacht as he said he had some inventions of his own there which he thought would interest you."

"Is that all?"

"Yes, I am quite certain that is all. Why all the fuss?"

"I don't know," Charles said. "Tell me everything you know about this Mr. Grantly."

"The trouble is I really know nothing," Toria said. "Everyone I have ever met has speculated as to who Billy is, where he comes from, and how he manages to be so rich; but no one knows."

Charles looked thoughtful.

"I think we will find out a bit about him before we accept his hospitality," he said.

Toria sat up in her chair.

"I have never heard such nonsense!" she cried. "Really, Charles, if you are going to be so stuffy and peculiar about my friends, it will make life quite intolerable. Billy is a very amusing and very charming person. He knows everyone and goes everywhere. It is really too ridiculous that you should start querying his position and thinking that he is not good enough to know us. Personally, I have always known him and been delighted to do so."

Her voice was quite sharp for a moment, but Charles did not look apologetic.

"I get the inference," he said. "What is good enough for Lady Toria Gale is certainly good enough for Mr. Drayton."

"I didn't say that," Toria ejaculated, "but if the cap fits. . . ."

"It does, as it happens," Charles said. "But with all due apologies to the smart social position of the Gale family I personally am not very keen on knowing Mr. Billy Grantly, if that is indeed his name."

"I had no idea you were so smug," Toria accused him angrily.

She was so angry that she had a wild desire to hurt Charles and wound him in some way. She sought for words.

"I shall begin to think soon," she went on after a moment's pause, "that the publicity of these last three weeks has turned your head. If you are going to set yourself up as a judge as to whom we shall know and whom we shall not know, our acquaintances will be very limited."

"Not necessarily," Charles replied.

"Let us make this very clear from the beginning," Toria said. "I have no intention of giving up my friends just because I have got married. They have been loyal and kind to me when I hadn't a penny; they have gone out of their way to help me and to give me a good time when they knew I could do nothing in return, when I was so poverty-stricken that often, when I went away to stay, I would have to borrow money from my host to tip his own servants. Granted, my friends are not all Dukes and Duchesses, and many of them are not exactly what your mother would call highly respectable; but they are my friends and I love them. They have never let me down, and if you think that just because I have married a rich man I am going to drop them, you are very much mistaken."

Toria was trembling with rage as she finished speaking, but Charles appeared quite unperturbed. He took a cigarette out of his cigarette case and put it to his mouth, then he took his lighter from his pocket and lit it.

"Now we know," he said at length. "You are determined, I suppose, to go on the yacht tomorrow?"

"Quite determined," Toria answered. "You, of course, can do as you like; but I have accepted Billy's invitation and I shall not go back on my word."

"Very well!"

Charles spoke very quietly. Toria felt her anger ebbing away from her. Neither of them spoke, and after a few minutes she said in a low voice.

"I am sorry if I was rude."

"I am sorry if I annoyed you," Charles replied.

Toria suddenly felt lonely and deflated. She had always hated quarrels.

There was something very degrading about quarrelling here in the South of France with a man she hardly knew and yet whose name she had taken as her own.

"Don't let us quarrel, Charles," she pleaded.

His face lit up immediately in response.

"I don't want to quarrel, Toria," he said. "I think I am making rather a mess of the whole thing. Perhaps it is because I am inexperienced. I have never been married before."

There was something young and rather whimsical in his voice. Toria smiled back at him.

"Neither have I," she replied, "and I always did dislike amateur theatricals."

"Shall I tell you what I have been thinking?" Charles said.

Toria nodded. Charles looked down at the table.

"I came to the conclusion last night," he began, "that we have both been in too much of a hurry. We got married before we got to know each other. You know very little about me, and I know very little about you. Marriage ought to be based on more than just thinking someone is the loveliest person one has seen in one's life."

"It was my fault," Toria said in a low voice. "I asked you to marry me quickly."

141

"I don't think we want to go into the question of whose fault it is," Charles went on in a sensible, matter-of-fact tone. "What is past is past. We married for better or for worse. It seems to me that if we look at the position sensibly and think it over, we might become friends."

Toria was silent. She felt a little piqued that Charles should infer also in a roundabout way that, though he had fallen in love with her looks, he was now not certain that she was as lovely inside as outside.

But even as she formulated such a thought, she felt ashamed. Charles was trying to be nice and constructive, and she was being rather beastly about it.

Impulsively she put out her hand across the table.

"Let us get to know each other, Charles," she smiled. "There are a lot of things I want to know about you."

His fingers closed over hers with a sudden intensity which was painful.

"I don't want you to forget one thing," he said in a low voice.

"What is that?" Toria asked.

"That I love you."

"And yet . . . yet last night. . . ."

Toria stopped. She was not certain how to put into words the fact that they had both slept alone on the first night of their marriage.

"I know," Charles said as if he could read her thoughts. "But I am going to try and make you love me. I am not suggesting that it will be easy. I am not conceited enough to think that I shall succeed; but I am going to try, and try damned hard."

He squeezed her fingers again and this time she gave a little cry of pain. He opened his fingers and looked at hers lying white and bloodless on his palm.

"Sometimes I forget how small you are," he said. "When you frighten me, you seem immeasurably bigger and stronger than I am."

Toria gave a little laugh.

"Do I frighten you?" she asked. "Are you ever frightened of me?"

"Terrified," Charles said, and she was not certain if he was joking or not.

"But that is ridiculous," she expostulated.

"Not really, when you come to think of it," Charles said in an unemotional tone. "And now what about luncheon?"

She felt as if he deliberately ended the conversation. She got to her feet, and as she did so, the glittering flags of the yachts down in the harbour caught her eyes.

"I should like to go out on the sea tomorrow," she said. "It will be fun if the weather is as nice as this."

She spoke deliberately, determined that Charles should not think that her agreeableness was a sign of weakness and that she was retracting anything she had said about being loyal to her friends.

"It should be nice," he said without a moment's hesitation. "It is a pity it is too cold to swim."

He had capitulated completely, and Toria was well aware that she had won the first round of the contest. And yet, now that she had got her own way, she knew with a sudden irritating reversion of feeling that she was sorry she had accepted Billy's invitation.

It would be a bore to pack their things for one night so soon after they had arrived. For one moment Toria thought she would tell Charles that after all she had changed her mind; that she did not really care if they went with Billy or not; and if he preferred it, they would stay where they were in Monte Carlo.

She had almost parted her lips to say the words when an old hackneyed adage of Mrs. Fergusson's came to her mind: "Begin as you mean to go on."

How often she had heard Mrs. Fergusson say that when a new girl came to help in the house or a fresh woman from the village took over the cleaning! "Begin as you mean to go on!"

If she gave in to Charles now, he might expect her to do so on every other occasion. She had made her stand, she had fought her duel and won.

It would be stupid to retract just as she had made Charles amenable to what, after all, must be one of the fundamental principles of their married life.

"We must not forget to take warm coats," Toria said. "It is very difficult, when the sun is out, to realise how cold it can be in the evening."

The die was cast. She had made it clear that they would go with Billy tomorrow. She glanced up at Charles. His face appeared unclouded and he was no longer frowning.

There was nothing to worry about. She had got her own way; yet she wished she did not have an uneasy feeling at the back of her mind that she had done the wrong thing.

8

The big Hispano Suiza, which carried on its bonnet the badges of the Automobile Clubs of practically every country in the world, was waiting for them when Toria and Charles came down the steps of the Hotel de Paris.

Their suitcases were stowed away in the boot and they sat down on the back seats, which were upholstered in red leather.

"Did you ever see anything so luxurious?" Toria asked. "Billy certainly knows how to do himself well."

"He must have a lot of money to spend, too," Charles said a little grimly.

Toria glanced at him, wondering from the tone of his voice if he was still slightly resentful at her having accepted this invitation.

"He is in the enviable position of having pounds in England, dollars in America, francs in France," she answered lightly, "and I expect liras and piastres and marks in all the other countries he wants to visit. Why aren't we clever enough to do that?"

"Do you mean us personally or us as a race?" Charles asked.

"I was generalising about the British as a whole," Toria replied; "but have you got a personal pull on the Treasury? If so, let us travel, for I adore it."

"I might be able to wangle a few dollars if you want to go to America," Charles said.

"Oh, I do," Toria explained. "I have never been to New York and I should love to go there. Can you find a good excuse?"

"I daresay I could," Charles said a little guardedly.

"It is really rather shocking how little I know about you," Toria replied. "One day, when you have time, we will have to sit down and you will have to tell me the story of your life. I want to know everything, really everything."

"I am rather flattered," Charles said, "but I am afraid you would be bored."

"Now you are asking for compliments," Toria smiled, then added in a different tone: "But seriously, Charles, I do want to know everything about you. I was thinking last night about what you had said about getting to know each other. You are right. We have been in too much of a hurry."

"At the same time I am fully aware," Charles said, "that if we had not been in a hurry, you would not have been sitting beside me at this moment. You would have been planning your marriage to your cousin Michael."

Toria felt for a moment as if he had slapped her in the face. She felt that she had been charming, striving to put out a friendly hand, but Charles had abruptly repulsed her.

For a moment she hated him; and then she realised that he was not being vindictive or nasty, he was merely in his usual manner stating a fact.

All the same, it seemed to bring the conversation to an end, and they sat in silence until the car drew up at the harbour.

The yacht was berthed only a little way from where they alighted. It was very large and white and decorated with flags which fluttered in the slight breeze blowing in from the sea.

No sooner had they alighted than two or three sailors came running up the gangway to take their luggage from the back of the car and bring it aboard.

Charles looked the yacht over with an appraising eye.

145

"She is a very nice ship," he said at length, and Toria felt that he was impressed. She was childish enough to be glad that at least he could not be disparaging about the yacht.

As they walked down the gangway, she was surprised to hear no sounds of laughter. She had been expecting a big party and had warned Charles there was certain to be a crowd.

"I shall take a rather elaborate dress for the evening," she said. "It is always the same when people say 'bring anything, it doesn't matter what you wear'. Every other woman there turns up in the most marvellous creation and makes one feel a fool."

Now, as she stepped on to the deck, there were no glamorous young creatures in exotic clothes lying about on the red and white striped cushions; and when they entered the big many-windowed saloon, that also was empty.

"Perhaps we are early," Charles suggested, seeing Toria's look of surprise.

"I expect that is it," Toria replied; but there was no time to say more before Billy entered.

He came into the room holding out his arms in welcome, his smile as well as his words assuring them of his delight at seeing them.

"It is going to be a wonderful afternoon," he said. "I can't tell you how delighted I am that you have both come."

"It is sweet of you to ask us," Toria said. "I have been telling Charles what fun your parties always are."

Billy had crossed the room and opened the cocktail cabinet which was fitted into the wall and decorated in front with false backs of books, so that at first sight it appeared to be nothing more than a book-case.

"What are you going to drink?" he asked.

Then as both Toria and Charles hesitated, he added:

"I hope you are not going to be very disappointed, but I have not asked a party to meet you. I thought that, as you are on your honeymoon, you would like to be by yourselves, and I am extremely good at playing goose-berry."

"But we should not want you to be anything of the sort," Toria said.

At the same time her heart sank. She had been sure that Billy would have asked a party, and now she felt that it would have been much easier if he had.

She was well aware that Charles had taken a dislike to Billy from the moment he first saw him, but she had consoled herself with the thought that at least the two men need not see much of each other during the time they were on board.

She had been on one of Billy's yachting parties once before. There had been a whole crowd of young, gay people who had danced, played bridge or slept in the sun just as the fancy took them.

There had never been a moment when one must be serious or bored.

She had never imagined that Billy would be so stupid as to ask Charles and her alone, and himself as the third. There was, she thought, nothing she could do about it now.

She wished she had not been so quick in accepting Billy's invitation. Charles was not like Michael, who made scenes and was extremely voluble when he was upset or annoyed; but Charles could, when he did not like something, create an atmosphere which made Toria feel uncomfortable even if he said very little.

She glanced at him now as Billy handed him a skilfully mixed cocktail.

He was being polite, talking in quite an ordinary tone, yet Toria fancied there was something clipped about his voice, as if he were being careful not to reveal his true feelings.

She thought perhaps she was being fanciful, or perhaps it was merely that Michael had made her acutely sensitive to other people's reactions.

She had often wished that she did not mind what everybody thought or felt; yet, however much she tried, she could feel herself being depressed or elated, cast down or stimulated just because of what someone else was feeling.

Now, because she was worried and even a little depressed, she quickly drank from the cocktail which Billy gave her and held out her glass for another one.

"Tell me what you have been doing," Billy said, "besides being happy, of course."

"Well, we gambled a little last night," Toria answered. "Charles won about ten mille, but I lost. I always do. Then we went down to the night club and danced until the early hours of the morning. I had no idea that Charles was such a good dancer."

"Another accomplishment," Billy said. "What a list you have to your credit, Drayton! By the way, I really must call you Charles, for Drayton sounds so formal and I have known Toria ever since she first burst upon an astonished world."

"Yes, we met at my first dance in London," Toria said. "Do you remember? It was at the Savoy and so boring that you collected a big party and took us all on to the 400. I remember being terribly thrilled, for it was my first visit to a night club."

"You were the prettiest débutante I had ever seen," Billy said, "and, may I add, you have grown more beautiful year by year."

"Thank you kindly, Sir," she said. Toria laughed. "Another cocktail and I shall believe everything you say."

"Why not, if it is the truth?" Billy asked.

He tried to fill up Charles' glass; but when the latter refused, he said:

"Would you like to look round the ship? As I was telling Toria, I have a few inventions of my own which I think will amuse you. Press a button or pull a switch and all sorts of exciting things happen."

'That is the sort of thing I really enjoy," Toria said. "Don't you, Charles?"

"It depends," he said in a cold, non-committal voice.

Toria turned her shoulder petulantly towards him, feeling that he was not quite playing the game and was making things more difficult than they might be.

The yacht was magnificent, there was no doubt about it. Every inch of space had been utilised to its best advantage. The decorations were superb, the curtains had all been woven specially to designs made by a well-known French artist. The State rooms were furnished with beds, not bunks; and from a woman's point of view nothing was lacking which could add to her comfort and ease.

There were ordinary lights, specially seductive lights and bright clear lights which enabled one to make up without flattery. There was indeed everything one could desire, Toria thought.

A wardrobe cunningly concealed in the wall, drawers which pulled out from all sorts of unexpected places, and the bathroom tiled in green glass which made one feel as if one was at the bottom of the sea.

For Toria and Charles Billy had arranged that they should have two cabins communicating with each other, and each had a separate bathroom.

So skilfully was the ship designed that there was even a small place attached to each cabin where a passenger could put his own luggage.

"I have never seen anything so clever," Toria exclaimed over and over again; and when at length they returned to the cocktail bar and Billy mixed them another drink, he said:

"I am glad you like her. Her engines are smooth and quiet. You will hardly believe we are moving, once we get under way."

"I see you have a very powerful engine," Charles remarked.

Billy shook his head.

"No bigger than is usually put in the boats of this size," he replied.

"I should have thought it was," Charles remarked. "Do you use this ship for cruising about in the summer months?"

"I cannot answer that question yet," Billy replied. "It was only delivered six months ago."

"Oh, then she isn't the one you had two years ago?" Toria exclaimed. "I thought it seemed bigger."

"I like to change my boats as often as I change my cars," Billy said briefly. "Luncheon should be ready soon."

It was announced a few minutes later, and they went down below.

The dining-room was panelled in striped pine and over the sideboard there was one really lovely picture, painted by a very famous artist who specialised in marine subjects. The curtains were of red velvet and so were the cushions on the chairs.

Apart from the fact that the chairs and the table could be screwed down during rough weather, they might have been stepping into an expensively decorated flat in London or Paris.

"We are moving!" Toria exclaimed suddenly as she glanced through the port hole just before sitting down at the table.

"I told my Captain to get off about one o'clock," Billy said.

"I have never seen the sea so blue," Toria said. "I wish I had a camera which would take colour films. I have always wanted a view of the coast from the sea."

"I will show you some I have taken, if you like," Billy replied.

"But I am speaking of a Cine Camera," Toria said. "Can you take colour photographs?"

"Yes, of course, but one has to get them developed in America. It is a good process, don't you think, Charles?"

"Very good," Charles replied.

"What do you think of that camera, Z.22, that you are using on your scientific surveys?" Billy enquired.

Charles raised his eyebrows a little.

"I thought it was definitely too hush-hush to be discussed," he said a little frigidly.

Billy smiled.

"Not when we are all among friends," he said. "And I would like your opinion of it."

Charles looked down at the roll he was crumbling between his fingers.

"I really don't feel in a position to offer an opinion," he replied.

Toria could feel the atmosphere was tense.

"Oh, Charles, don't be stuffy," she exclaimed. "Tell

us about this wonderful camera. I would love to know about it."

"Actually your husband is quite right," Billy said. "As he says, this camera is very hush-hush, and after all, he knows nothing about me. I might be a spy in disguise."

"Nonsense, Billy, you don't look like one," Toria laughed. "I feel they always wear long beards and need a hair-cut."

"You never know," Billy said. "I remember in the war the most unlikely people turned out to be spies, while the women who wore decollete evening dresses and looked like Mata Hari were invariably Parsons' wives out on the spree for the first time in their lives."

"The only spies I have ever known," Toria said, "are dear old gentlemen who have long since retired and who after half a dozen gins say in a hissing whisper: 'I wish I could tell you about the days when I was in M.I.5.' "

"I know the type only too well," Billy laughed. "Now, Charles, what is your experience of spies?"

"I don't know that I have ever met any," Charles replied. "I am not particularly interested in them, for there is no reason why they should be interested in me."

Billy threw back his head and laughed.

"Now you are being either extremely modest or a hypocrite. You know as well as I do that in your job there are a great number of things which would be of the utmost value to the enemy."

Charles' eyebrows went up if possible a little further.

"Have we got one?"

Billy laughed again.

"I was only trying to pull your leg. I am a good-tempered chap and I shall refuse to be drawn."

Toria felt that Charles was behaving badly. She gave him a meaning glance across the table.

"I don't think Charles is being cautious at all," she said to Billy. "It is just that he knows nothing and does not want to say so."

"Perhaps he knows too much," Billy answered.

"Anyway, I stand rebuked. What shall we talk about now?"

It was obvious, Toria thought, that Charles was being unnecessarily wary and Billy was trying to smooth over an awkward moment. She flung herself into the breach and started to talk as gaily as she knew how.

She was soon rewarded by hearing Billy laugh heartily, and even Charles joined in and seemed likely to forget to be awkward and aggressive.

Luncheon became quite an amusing meal, and when the coffee had been brought and the men had each poured themselves a glass of port, Toria got to her feet.

"I am going to sit on deck," she said. "It is too lovely an afternoon to be spending the time down below. I saw the most comfortable looking cushions as I came aboard and I am going to lie on them and hope that you both will join me as soon as possible."

"We won't be long," Billy assured her. "Ask the steward for anything you want, won't you?"

"Thank you."

Toria smiled at him.

She went from the dining-room and started to walk down the companion way. She had almost reached the steps which led to the upper deck when she found that she had left her handbag behind.

She had put it down beside her chair while they had luncheon and had forgotten to pick it up again. It contained amongst many other things her sun-glasses, which she knew she would require if she were lying in the sun.

She retraced her steps, not hurrying herself, but pausing to look at the prints which decorated the companion way. They were French and exceedingly decorative, if slightly risqué. She paused at the last one, which was just outside the door of the dining saloon.

It showed a ravishingly lovely French woman taking a bath while a young man peeped round the door and her maid tried ineffectively to obscure his view.

It was then she heard Charles' voice say:

"Would you like to be more explicit?"

There was something in his tone which held Toria's attention. Charles was being truculent.

She could hear that, and she felt dismayed as she listened for Billy's reply.

"Most certainly! As I have just said, I want to know the details of your experiments with the atom-propelled jet aeroplane engine."

"Who told you about this?"

Charles' voice was curt.

"That is not important," Billy replied. "I just want you to tell me what you know about it and also to tell me how you intend to use the atomic energy."

"I think you must be mad if you imagine that I should discuss such matters with a comparative stranger," Charles answered.

"I think you would find it wiser and far more comfortable, my dear Drayton, to answer my questions."

There appeared to Toria to be quite a threat in Billy's voice and she felt herself stiffen as she listened.

"And if I refuse?"

"There are other people who may not question you in such a pleasant manner or in such comfortable circumstances," Billy said.

There was a little pause.

"Do you have them here with you in this yacht?"

"No, but they are not very far away," Billy replied. "We are taking a cruise down the coast, Drayton. It would be unfortunate if you were forced to go ashore."

"So that is your game!"

Charles spoke quite quietly and every word seemed charged with meaning.

"We have been trying for some time to get this information," Billy said. "It would have been easy if anyone in your department could have been forced to talk, and we should not have been forced to take such extreme measures."

"May I ask exactly what these measures will be?"

"Certainly," Billy replied. "By the way, your cigar appears to be going out."

Toria heard a sudden movement as if Charles had

153

thrust his chair back from the table, and then Billy's voice, suave and slightly mocking.

"Before you go any further, Drayton, there is just one thing I would like to say to you. I carry a revolver in my pocket. If you attack me, I should not hesitate to shoot."

"I have no intention of attacking you," Charles said. "I am merely waiting for you to inform me of your whole plan. You were, I gather, not expecting me to give you the information—gratuitously."

"I anticipated that you might be difficult," Billy said. "You have quite a reputation for being tough."

"I am flattered," Charles said, and his tone was grim.

"This, briefly, is the position," Billy said. "We have been trying in every way we could to learn what we want to know about your experiments. We know that they have progressed very far and may shortly be put into operation. That means, of course, that the British Air Force would be immeasurably ahead of every European Force.

"It is therefore essential that we should know how far your experiments have got and what is the particular method you are using to harness atomic energy. You have, as I expected, refused to tell me this.

"Very well! We are cruising down the coast. By to-morrow morning we shall be anchored in a bay which is very charming and very beautiful. It would be sad, to say the least of it, if you and your charming wife should wish to go ashore and that, once there, an unfortunate accident should happen to you."

"Do you think you can get away with that?" Charles asked.

"Why not? There are various ways in which an accident can happen. The car in which you are driving along the cliff side can get out of control, and your bodies will be picked up on the beach, battered almost, I may say, out of recognition.

"Or you can choose to go climbing on the mountain and be found a week later, having fallen into a deep crevasse from which it was impossible to rescue you. Or you may choose to go fishing in this way we have spoken of, and the tides are very treacherous.

"Toria would fall overboard and get into difficulties. You would go to her rescue, but unfortunately it would be impossible to save either of you and you would die a hero's death, which is just what your British public will expect of one of their most famous airmen."

"I see!" Charles' voice was very cool and slow. "And while these bodies, battered out of recognition, are being wept over by our friends and relatives, would it be indiscreet to ask what would happen to me? And of course to Toria?"

"You would be the guests of a certain power whose name there is no reason to mention," Billy said. "You would be well treated provided you divulged the information they wanted. They might even persuade you to work for them. At any rate, if you are reasonable, there is no reason why you should not live, for a while at any rate, in comfort and security."

"Behind the Iron Curtain?"

Charles' voice was incredulous.

"Quite a number of people do live there," Billy said. "But why discuss these matters? My dear Drayton, it is all so easily avoided. If you give me the information I require—nothing in writing, nothing to say that you have in any way been indiscreet—we will go to Capri tonight as we have planned, and tomorrow I deposit you and the lovely Toria back at Monte Carlo. You can then forget the whole episode."

"Does one forget when one is a traitor and betrays one's own people?" Charles asked. "You, of course, would be in the right position to answer that question?"

There was a moment's pause, then Billy replied in a voice that was infinitely menacing.

"I advise you not to over-estimate my good nature, Drayton."

"Then, I apologise," Charles said. "I had no idea you were so touchy. But then, even the worst of us have an Achilles heel somewhere."

There was a sudden crash as if Billy had overturned a glass.

"You know, Drayton," he said after a moment, "the trouble with you is that you have a very small sense of humour, or are stupid enough not to know when you are beaten. The British characteristic, I may add."

"As we seldom have any experience of the latter," Charles remarked, "you can hardly expect our behaviour to be other than traditional."

"What is your answer?"

Billy's question was very curt.

"It is only a question of a few words to me and then you can return to Monte Carlo. We can go back tonight if you like. You can say you are not feeling well, or I can make the excuse that I have forgotten some extremely important appointment. We have a wireless operator on board. Just a few words, Drayton. You won't have to repeat them, for I have an extremely retentive memory."

Still Charles did not speak and after a moment Billy continued:

"You know, the days when Britain protected her subjects are gone for ever. In those days, if the most obscure Mr. Brown of Battersea was put in prison or detained for disobeying some slight by-law, the sight of a battleship in the harbour was enough to ensure an immediate and abject apology. Now notes between Governments take a very long time. They would not be expedited even to rescue such a distinguished person as yourself."

"Do you think such methods will do you any good?" Charles asked.

"My dear fellow, results are what count in the world today. We shall get from you exactly what we want to know. If you refuse to tell us, you may die a martyr to your public school code of morals, but you won't die with your secret intact. You know that as well as I do.

"Modern methods of imprisonment, modern drugs and indeed modern tortures make it impossible for a man to die with his lips sealed. I am not telling you anything you don't know already, I am merely reminding you."

"I have to grant that the whole thing is very cleverly

156

thought out," Charles said. "Was the plot spontaneous or have you been hatching it for some time?"

"You have been in our thoughts, my dear Drayton, for a long time. The difficulty was how to approach you. We had thought of more ordinary methods, but unfortunately they were not likely to appeal to you. Your taste in women was impeccable, and you are unfortunately a very rich man."

"I see!"

There was a long pause and then Charles said:

"I am just beginning to realise what must have happened to other men who were working with me when they had an accident or suddenly became very well off."

Billy smiled.

"Oh yes, there are many methods of approach. We do not resort to this sort of thing unless it is absolutely necessary."

"One thing you seem to have overlooked," Charles said. "Supposing I accept your first suggestion, tell you what you want to know, and return to Monte Carlo. Do you imagine that I shan't inform the authorities about you? It would be difficult for you to visit Britain or America again after what I have told has been recorded on your dossier!"

"My dear Drayton, how you under-estimate us," Billy said. "You will return to Monte Carlo if you tell me exactly what I want to know. You will see a certain amount of me during the remainder of your visit there. In the course of the next day or so Toria will receive a wedding present. You remember I have already asked her what she requires?

"The present will take the form of something really superb. An emerald necklace perhaps, or some rubies and diamonds from Cartier's. At any rate, it will be very costly and an outstanding gift, and one which, should there be questions raised about it later, would be very difficult to explain away as being the usual little present of an old friend to the wife of Charles Drayton."

"I see!" Charles said. "Another case of bribery."

"It would be difficult for you to explain in open court why you should allow your wife to accept a present costing over ten thousand pounds," Billy said. "You could, of course, leave the onus on her; and it could always be assumed, should the need arise, which it won't, that she had quite innocently conveyed to me the information I wanted, not knowing the true meaning of what she had procured and quite prepared to accept the very handsome present I offered in exchange."

"I understand," Charles said. "Yes, you have got it all tied up. But the fairy story doesn't ring true."

There was a little pause.

"Then what is your answer?" Billy asked, a shade too eagerly, Toria thought.

"You must give me time to think it over," Charles replied. "I cannot make up my mind as quickly as all that. You say that we arrive at this place some time tonight."

"About dawn, I think," Billy replied. "If you require it, I can give you all the time in the world in which to make up your mind. There is no hurry. I am only too delighted for you to remain on board as my guest. There is only one thing I must warn you of once again. I am always armed. If you are thinking of cutting my throat while I sleep or hitting me over the head with a bottle while I look the other way, you will find I am very good at defending myself and that when I shoot, I shoot to kill."

"But of course," Charles said. "I hardly expected anything else of you."

"There is only one thing which surprises me."

"And what is that?" Billy asked.

"Why in taking an English name you thought for a moment it would deceive anyone into thinking you were English."

"On the contrary, a great number of people found it very comforting to know that my sympathies, like those of my ancestors, were all with that obstinate, unimaginative race who have managed through some of the most extraordinary mischances in history to rule a quarter of the earth's globe. But their day is finished. I don't want to depress you, Drayton, but their day is finished."

"I wonder!" Charles said.

"We will see," Billy replied confidently. "Another glass of port?"

"No, thank you."

Toria suddenly realised that at any moment the men might be leaving the dining room saloon.

It was essential that she should not be found eavesdropping outside the door. She turned swiftly and sped up the companion-way.

Fortunately not only was the floor carpeted, but she was wearing rubber-soled shoes.

When Charles and Billy came on deck a few minutes later, she was lying outstretched in the sun, her eyes closed against the brilliance of the skies.

She raised herself on one elbow as the men approached.

"I am so glad you have come up," she said. "Charles, I have left my bag downstairs. I left it by my chair at luncheon. Will you be an angel and fetch it?"

"No, I will go," Billy said instantly. "Besides, my being useful will be a good excuse to leave the honeymooners together for a few minutes. Make the most of them, my children."

He was smiling and for a moment Toria thought that what she had overheard must have been a trick of her imagination, a nightmare she had dreamt.

Could this really be happening? She could hardly credit her own senses.

Things didn't happen like this, not to ordinary people like them, not when the world was supposed to be at peace and the rumbles and grumbles of war in the newspapers were so dull that nobody bothered to read them.

It could not be true, it could not; and yet she had stood outside the dining saloon a long time and overheard all that had been said.

Even now the full meaning of it could hardly percolate into her mind. It was all too dramatic, too much like a cheaply acted film.

Was it possible that Billy Grantly, whom she had known all these years, the man who had always appeared to be the perfect host, was this obnoxious creature who was prepared to go to any length, even to that of murder, to suit his own ends?

This was the explanation of his yachts and cars, his big suites in luxury hotels, the parties he could give to all those who enjoyed a party.

Beneath the laughter, the gaiety there lurked a menacing evil. And now she and Charles were in desperate and terrible danger.

She felt her brain racing, she felt every nerve in her body straining as if to meet a sudden attack. There must be something they could do, some way in which they could escape unscathed from this horrible and fearful position.

First of all she must tell Charles what she knew. She looked up at him and then, just as she was about to speak, she saw a steward approaching.

He was bringing out a comfortable deck chair and arranging it in a sheltered position. It was made of red linen and it had an awning to put up over the head and a comfortable rest for the feet.

Charles sank down into it. His expression seemed very much as usual save that it appeared to Toria that his eyes were dark and grave.

"He is thinking," she thought, and then added with a sudden fluttering of her heart, "We have both got to think. We have got so very little time, so very little."

"Charles," she called to him in a low voice.

Even as she spoke his name, Billy appeared with her handbag.

"It was exactly where you said it was," he said gaily. "You are the only woman I have ever met who could describe really accurately where she had left something. It is usually in an entirely different place."

"Thank you so much," Toria said.

She forced herself to smile at Billy, determined for the moment at any rate that he should not know what she had learned.

It was not true, it was not true, she kept thinking to herself. It could not be true.

There was the warmth of the sunshine, the rhythmic throb of the engine only a very little beneath them, the comfort of a soft cushion under her head, and Billy in his white flannels and blue blazer smiling down at her.

She thought that perhaps she was going mad. How could he have said the things she had overheard just a moment or two ago? How could he have suggested the ghastly diabolical fate which would await them if Charles refused the information he required?

She felt panic grip her throat and knew that, whatever happened, she must keep calm. Somehow there must be a way out of it, somehow a solution would present itself. But what, what was it?

"Are you comfortable, Toria?" she heard Billy ask. "Would you like another cushion?"

"No, no, everything is perfect," she heard her own voice reply.

Not by even a tremor did she betray the fear that was mounting within her breast.

9

Toria lay for a long time, her eyes closed against the sunshine, her body apparently relaxed while her brain raced.

The more she reiterated to herself word by word the conversation she had overheard between Charles and Billy, the more she was certain of one thing—that, whatever happened, Charles would never get away alive.

If he gave Billy the information that he wanted now and they returned to Monte Carlo, some "accident" would happen to him before he had the chance to inform the authorities as to what had happened.

A man in Billy's position was not likely to take risks; and however much he might try to trap and implicate Charles, he was bound to be afraid that Charles would make a clean breast of the whole affair and that, even if there were no dire consequences this time, he would be a marked man in the future.

With a sinking heart Toria was convinced that Charles' life was forfeit whether he turned informer now or whether the information was extracted from him later on by people who would doubtless be more skilled at the job than Billy Grantly.

In a palpitating consternation she remembered all the things she had read about interrogation of that sort—the questioning that went on hour by hour, day and night under relentlessly bright lights; the way in which the person questioned was never allowed to sleep until he was crazed with a desire for it; the physical violence which would often accompany the questioning; and more horrifying than anything else, the use of drugs which enfeebled the mind and made the strongest will weak and pliable.

Lying on the soft cushions on deck Toria suddenly wanted to scream aloud, plunge overboard and swim for the shore.

She felt a terror possess her such as she had never known in the whole of her soft, sheltered life, a terror of pain and of seeing someone she was fond of tortured and maimed.

Then even as she felt fear stampede within her, she opened her eyes and saw Charles lying back in a deck chair apparently at his ease, a cigarette held quite steadily between his fingers.

He was calm, but Toria knew that his brain was racing too, trying to find a way out, trying to think what could be done; and she remembered that he would have a far greater grasp of the implications of what all this meant and what lay before them.

She had only the vaguest ideas on the subject, ideas culled from magazine stories, articles in the paper and the chatter of her friends.

"My dear, you must meet Ivan. He escaped from behind the Iron Curtain and can tell one of the most gruesome and hair-raising stories of what happened there."

How well she could hear the light, lilting voices expressing superficial horror and understanding very little of it!

Once again Toria felt that the whole thing was fantastic. This could not be true, this could not be really happening.

She looked at Billy. He too was apparently relaxed and half asleep in the sunshine, but his hand was in the pocket of his blazer and Toria knew that, if Charles were to make the slightest hostile movement, it would be easy for Billy to deal with him.

"It isn't true, it isn't true!"

It seemed to her as if the soft hum of the engine was repeating the words over and over again.

She thought of home, of the stalwart solidness of the Castle against the March sky. Perhaps it would be raining and the twins would be in the sitting-room playing the gramophone.

She could see their faces very clearly. Xandra's alert and gay, her lips always half curved in a smile, her repose as transitory as that of a butterfly which alights for a second on a flower and is always ready to rise again and wing its way onwards.

Olga was so different. Quiet and reserved, her features were identical with Xandra's, but her expression was very different. Unusual in so young a child, she had a look of spirituality which was the reflection of her gentle, serious little soul.

Toria felt herself aching for her sisters. She wanted to feel their arms round her neck, to know herself safe at home.

A fragment of a conversation came back to her. It had taken place a year ago, perhaps more. They had been talking about bravery; it may have been Michael's war record which had brought up the subject. Toria could not remember the context, she could only recall Xandra's saying:

"I wonder if we should be brave if we got into terrible difficulties or if we knew that we were going to die violently and unpleasantly."

Toria remembered shivering. She was thinking of the bombs which had fallen so near the Castle in the war.

"I always hope I shall behave with courage whatever happens," she said.

163

"What would you do if you were told you were going to be martyred?" Olga asked.

"Like the saints?" Toria enquired with a smile.

"I should scream and scream, I know I should!" Xandra cried.

"What would you do, Toria?" Olga asked.

"Don't let us talk about it," Toria replied. "It is a horrible subject. I hope, when the time comes, that I shall die bravely, but one can't be certain of one's reactions in exceptional circumstances."

"You haven't told us what you would do, Olga, if you were sent to the guillotine or the stake," Xandra asked curiously.

"I should pray," Olga said very quietly.

Toria could hear her voice now, very soft, the words hardly spoken above a whisper, yet somehow they had been like a clarion call. Olga was such a child in some ways and yet her love of God made her curiously mature in others.

"I should pray."

The words were echoing in Toria's mind, and then suddenly she found herself praying—praying for help and guidance—praying that they might be rescued. She could not bear to think that Charles should die.

She thought, looking at him now from under her eyelashes, that she had never appreciated how good-looking he was. Always he had been overshadowed by Michael's flamboyant, spectacular good looks.

Charles' face was distinctive in that unobtrusive English manner which told of good breeding and decent upbringing and which was somehow all mixed up in one's mind with the public school code of behaving like a gentleman.

That was what Charles was so outstandingly—an English gentleman.

Even as she thought of it, Toria realised how modern young people would laugh at the idea.

It was considered clever nowadays to make a mock of the old school tie, to sneer at men who had a certain code of decency and honour, at those who were still chivalrous and courteous both in their private and public lives.

It was at that moment that Toria saw the difference between Charles and many of the men whom she found amusing and whom she had quite erroneously considered her friends.

She knew now that the majority of them were cheap and nasty. They were akin with Billy Grantly even though he was especially poisonous.

They all lacked the essential qualities which in the past had distinguished not one Englishman but the majority. Well might historians write that the true wealth of Britain lay in the character of her people.

It was not only patriotism which had enabled the British people to conquer a quarter of the world's surface.

It was a nobility of both mind and soul, an integrity of brain and spirit and a faith which believed unswervingly in Christian principles.

Those were the foundations on which Britain built an Empire. And it would not have been possible unless those who fought, legislated and dispensed peace and justice in the nation's name had themselves been worthy of the trust with which the British people invested them.

Charles was an Englishman of the type which had existed all through the ages. Comparing him with the men she had met in night clubs or in the company of people like Billy, Toria saw the difference now that it was too late.

She stirred a little restlessly. Was it too late?

There must be something one could do. It seemed to her that her one point of advantage lay in the fact that Billy had no idea that she knew what was happening.

This was a pleasure cruise, a little trip out to sea, and unless she made him suspicious there was no reason for him to guess that her feelings had in any way changed towards him.

With an effort Toria forced herself to sit up and exclaim with the gushing insincerity of all Billy's acquaintances:

"But this is heaven! I had no idea it could be so warm and lovely at this time of year."

"Glad you are enjoying it," Billy smiled.

"Look at that divine little Italian village over there," Toria went on, pointing at the coast. "I suppose we could not land somewhere for a short while? You won't believe it, but I have never been in Italy."

"We might do it on our return journey tomorrow," Billy replied.

Toria forced herself to smile.

"That will be marvellous. You won't forget, will you?"

"No, I won't forget," Billy replied.

She saw him glance at Charles as he spoke, but Charles' face remained imperturbable. He finished his cigarette, lit another, and flicked the match overboard.

"We are going at a good speed," he remarked, his voice cool and unhurried.

"Yes, I told the Captain to put on all possible speed so that we could travel a decent distance down the coast. As Toria says, Italy is very beautiful. The little harbours and villages are well worth seeing."

"I must not go to sleep then and miss anything," Toria said, patting her cushions so that she could watch the land comfortably from where she sat.

"I wish we could go nearer still," she added. "Have you got any binoculars on board, Billy? Oh, do look at that fascinating Castle on the hill! I would like to have a nearer glimpse of it."

"I will get you a pair," Billy said.

He rose and walked away across the deck. Toria watched him go. This was the moment when she could speak to Charles, tell him what she knew. Then suddenly she was afraid.

Suppose someone could overhear them, suppose that with every other gadget Billy had installed on the yacht he had also put in a dictaphone.

She had heard of those things so often, and somehow it would be like him to wish to overhear what his guests said.

She might be only imagining things, she might be

166

only making things more terrible than they were already; but she dared not speak, not while there was a chance of being overheard.

She felt as if even the deck had ears. She saw a sailor moving towards the bridge and fancied that he too was watching.

It seemed as if Charles had the same idea. She fancied for a moment that he was going to speak to her; then he merely took a puff at his cigarette and remained silent. But at that moment she caught his eye and saw an expression of worry and anxiety in his face which she had never seen before.

She knew then, as if he had said so, that his anxiety was not for himself but for her.

She longed to say to him:

"It is all right. We will get through this somehow, don't be upset."

But even as she formulated the words in her mind, she thought how extraordinary it was for her to want to comfort Charles, for her to feel protective towards him.

Besides she had no grounds for thinking anything was all right. It was all wrong.

Now she bitterly reproached herself for having come on this ill-fated cruise. Charles had tried to warn her that Billy was not to be trusted.

He may have known something about him, or it may have been instinct. Whatever it was, he had been wise and she, as usual, had been foolish.

Toria shut her eyes for a moment. She could feel again her own anger, her sense of irritability when Charles had tried to prevent her being so friendly with Billy Grantly. Why couldn't she have listened to him?

Why had her ridiculous mistaken loyalties prompted her to defend Billy against Charles?

She knew the answer, of course, even while she asked herself the question.

She had been punishing Charles because she had known without his putting it into words that he did not like Michael. That was why she had been angry.

She had always known ever since the first day he had

come to Lynbrooke that he disliked Michael and that he had tried to hide the fact for her sake.

That perhaps made it worse, the feeling that Charles was pandering to her, trying to keep in her good graces by being hypocritical where Michael was concerned.

And yet now Toria knew that everything she had thought about him was unfair.

Charles had fallen in love with her on that very first day, during that ridiculous disjointed luncheon when Daisy had calved and they had all rushed out to help old Fergie, leaving Charles, astonished and bewildered, alone with her father.

Yes, he had fallen in love with her then, and his reasons for being pleasant and considerate to Michael were because he had wanted to see her again and grasped at an excuse to return to the Castle.

It was not fair to blame a man for falling in love, but she had held it against him, on the defensive, ready to resent his criticism of anyone or anything she liked.

What a fool she had been, especially about Billy Grantly!

"Some day I will tell Charles I am sorry I was so stupid," Toria thought.

Then with a sudden startling pang of terror she remembered there might not be the time to tell him.

She suddenly felt she could bear it no longer. Whatever lay ahead she must share it with Charles, she must know what he thought. She bent forward.

"Charles," she said in a low and urgent voice.

Even as she spoke she saw Billy Grantly returning.

He came strolling down the deck still with his right hand in his blazer pocket, in the other a large and very powerful pair of binoculars.

Because she was afraid he might have heard her voice and seen the expression on her face when she spoke to Charles, Toria managed a cry of delight.

"Oh, Billy, those are wonderful! Look, Charles, did you ever see such a gorgeous pair of glasses? They must have cost a fortune! Whatever do you use them for, Billy? To watch your girl friends bathing?"

Billy laughed.

"That's right. I watch people when they least expect it. You would be surprised at what I see."

"It is too unfair!" Toria said, focusing the glasses on the shore. "And these are 'out of this world'. Look at that woman walking with the donkey. I feel I could almost speak to her. You must look, Charles."

She handed Charles the glasses and watched him skim the coast. She knew that he was hoping to see something which would be of help.

She too had hoped for the same thing when she asked for the binoculars, but there were only flat-topped white houses, castles perched precariously on cliff or mountain side, and the black-garbed peasants working in the fields or moving slowly along the narrow winding roads.

Without a word Charles handed her back the glasses. Toria used them for a little while and then laid them down by her side.

The yacht was moving very fast and further away from the coast. It was carrying them to their doom and she could do nothing about it.

Toria felt her face would crack if she smiled at Billy any more. Slowly she got to her feet.

"I am going down to my cabin to powder my nose."

"Can you find your way?" Billy asked.

"Of course," Toria replied. "If I do get lost in the spacious corridors, I will shout for help."

She heard him laugh as she went down the companion way. Her cabin seemed very cool and dark after the brilliant glare outside.

Toria shut the door behind her. She sat down at the dressing-table and put her head in her hands. What were they to do?

She felt as if every nerve in her body was throbbing. She could feel her pulse beating quickly and was almost certain she could hear the thumping of her own heart.

Then she realised that it was the throbbing of the engines, the engines carrying them swiftly to that moment when Charles would be interrogated, when he would be forced to reveal the secrets which he alone knew.

Toria opened her eyes and saw her own reflection in the looking-glass.

It seemed to her for a moment as if her face had changed completely. She looked almost ugly, strained and white, her eyes wide and dilated. She thought of the accidents that Billy had described so vividly.

She had understood his plans all too clearly when he said that the accident which would be reported to England and to their families would not happen to them at all but two other people. Two poor dupes would have to take their place.

She and Charles would be kept alive until the latter had been forced to reveal the plans of the aeroplane.

After that they would die, perhaps not so cleanly and decently as being involved in a motor accident or being drowned at sea.

Toria shuddered. She felt as if the walls of the little cabin were closing in on her, coming nearer and nearer until they were suffocating her. She wondered what Charles was thinking.

Was he planning how he would pounce on Billy and catch him unawares. Toria knew it would be hopeless. Billy was shorter and not so broad-shouldered as Charles, but there was a wiry strength about him.

She felt he was very likely a brilliant exponent of ju-jitsu. Besides, the revolver he carried in his pocket was sure to be fully loaded and he was very likely armed in other ways.

There was no question of a man like him being caught napping. He was too clever for that. He must in a long life of crime and intrigue have been in a great many unpleasantly tight corners. He would know how to get out of them, and the odds were all in his favour.

Toria looked wildly round her cabin, thinking there might be some weapon which would help her. If only she had a revolver, she thought, but she had never possessed one in her life. She remembered once Michael had given her his gun to fire when they were out pigeon shooting in the woods.

She remembered that when the moment had come to pull the trigger she had shut her eyes and relaxed her grip with the result that it kicked her violently in the shoulder and also bruised the side of her cheek. Michael had laughed at her, but she had felt defeated and shaken for hours afterwards.

Looking round the cabin, she suddenly realised that all her things had been unpacked. Even if she had had a revolver with her, it would not be in her possession any more.

Her clothes were hung up in the wardrobe, the gold and diamond fittings of her dressing-table were spread out on the dressing-table. Toria got up and walked to the porthole.

Outside in the sunshine she could see the coast of Italy. It was growing fainter; they were moving away from it.

"Oh, God, if you are merciful, help us! Please, please help us!"

Toria whispered the prayer out loud, and even as she did so her eyes fell on something which lay beside her bed. She walked quickly across the cabin.

There were two bottles beside the bedside lamp. A bottle of aspirins which she took occasionally when she had a headache and another smaller bottle which contained her sleeping capsules.

She stared at the latter for a long moment and then she took them in her hand.

She was recalling what the Doctor had said to her when he made out the prescription.

"I will give you something to make you sleep," he said; "but remember, you are far too young to require sleeping draughts. However, I suppose getting engaged to be married does not happen every day of the week, so it won't do you any harm to take one of these capsules when you feel that you really must have a good night's sleep."

"I shall go mad if I don't!" Toria exclaimed.

The old man had laughed.

"Don't you believe it. People are a lot tougher than they think. If everybody died or went mad when they thought they were going to, there would be precious few people left in the world."

171

He signed his name to the prescription and handed it to her.

"I made it out for twenty-five tablets," he said, "but I am hoping you won't need more than two or three of them. Once you get married to your young man these nerves will all be forgotten. Swallow one with a little water when you go to bed, and I promise you you will sleep."

"I have only to take one?" Toria questioned.

"Only one," the Doctor repeated. "There are one and a half grains in each capsule and that is enough to put anyone to sleep, however active his brain may be."

One and a half grains in each!

Toria repeated the words in her mind, and then taking up the bottle she tipped the capsules into her hand. They were bright yellow and she counted them quickly. There were twenty of them. She had taken five.

She sat down for a moment on the bed with the capsules in her hand and thought hard. Twenty of them. How could she use them?

She sat for quite a long time staring at the bright yellow capsules; then she put them down on the bed and went to the drawer of the dressing-table.

She took out a box of face tissues. Made of paper they were as soft and pliable as a piece of lawn. She tore one in half, considered the size of it, and divided it again.

Then she laid it on the bed and started to open the capsules. She tipped the contents of each one into the small square of paper.

When she had finished emptying the whole twenty, their contents made only a small pile of white powder. Toria thought for a moment and then pressed the capsules together and replaced them in the bottle.

Everything in the room must be just as it was when she came in. She must not arouse suspicion by anything she had done.

She picked up the piece of paper containing the contents of the capsules, screwed the ends together and put it carefully into the pocket of her skirt.

172

She crossed to the mirror, combed her hair and stared at herself in the glass.

An idea was coming to her, a plan was taking form in her mind. She stared at her own reflection, at the white jumper she wore with her navy blue yachting skirt, at the two rows of pearls round her neck.

They had been her mother's pearls. She had meant to have them restrung just before she came away on her honeymoon, but there had been no time. She put up her hand to them, feeling them warm and almost alive beneath her fingers as if something protective encircled her, keeping her safe.

Even as she touched them she felt as if she were not alone.

Someone was near her, someone was taking care of her. She almost felt like turning her head to see who was there, yet she knew she would not see the person who was near her.

For a moment she fought against the tears that came to her eyes. They were not tears of misery but tears of relief. In these overwhelming moments of horror and fear she was not alone.

Toria tried to remember all she could about sleeping draughts. If you took an overdose, did they work quickly?

The difficulty, she knew, would be to obscure the taste. She had bitten a capsule by mistake and knew how sharp and bitter it was.

A drink was the obvious thing, but she had an idea that coffee was an antidote. She tried to remember how she knew that, but she could not recall how or where the subject had come up.

Yet she was sure somebody had told her once that a woman who had taken an overdose of sleeping tablets was given black coffee when she was taken to the hospital. It may have been untrue, yet the information remained in her mind.

What else would obscure the taste? Tea was hopeless, she was certain of that. It would have to be a strong drink of some sort.

She got up from the dressing-table and walked towards the door. She had been away long enough. If she remained in her cabin any longer, Billy might come in search of her.

She went back on deck. The men were just as she left them. Both of them outstretched in deck chairs, apparently the picture of peace and comfort.

They were not speaking when Toria came near to them, yet she had the feeling that they had been talking and that her name had been mentioned.

She had no reason to think that, and yet she was convinced of it. She sat down again on the red and white striped cushions.

"Anything happened while I have been away?" she asked gaily.

There was a moment's pause before Billy replied.

"What did you expect to happen?"

She sensed the alert curiosity in his tone.

"Oh, I thought a porpoise might have bobbed up or even a mermaid; but I believe you have both been asleep and haven't even been looking at the view. We seem to be moving very far away from Italy."

"The currents round here are rather difficult, I believe," Billy answered cautiously. "We will come inshore a little later on."

"I am glad of that," Toria lied.

Billy looked at his wrist watch.

"It is getting on for five o'clock," he said. "Would you like some tea, Toria?"

"I would love some," Toria replied.

"Let us go into the cabin and order tea," Billy said.

He was careful to let both Toria and Charles precede him; then he followed them into the big comfortable cabin with its damask covered chairs and vases of bright spring flowers.

"Tea for you, Toria?" he said, ringing the bell. "What about you, Charles? Tea or whisky and soda?"

"Whisky and soda, please," Charles replied.

Billy opened the door of the cocktail cabinet and Toria suddenly had an idea.

"What are you going to drink, Billy?" she asked.

"I haven't decided," he answered. "Why?"

"Because next time you have a cocktail," Toria answered, "I want to make you one. I know you are the best mixer in London, Paris and New York, but I was given a most delicious recipe the other day by a Mexican. You have simply got to try it. It is called 'The Serpent's Kiss'."

"What is in it?" Billy asked.

"I shan't tell you," Toria replied. "I will make it, you shall taste it, and then you shall guess the ingredients. If you are right, I will give you the exact proportions for your next party. It is a guarantee of success."

She spoke gaily, her red lips smiling, her eyes shining a little as if with eagerness as she added:

"Oh, do let me make it for you, Billy."

"All right," he said good humouredly.

The steward appeared and he gave him the order for tea.

"Go ahead, my sweet," he said to Toria: "one can only die once!"

"Wait a minute," Toria said. "First of all you have got to say what you will give me if you don't guess the ingredients. It is a bet, you see. I give you the recipe if you guess right, but what do I get if you fail?"

"What do you want?" Billy asked.

Toria appeared to consider.

"A pair of gloves from that shop next the Hermitage in Monte Carlo," she said at length. "And I warn you they are the most expensive French suède there is."

Billy threw back his head and laughed.

"You are becoming a gold digger!" he laughed. "All right, I will take you on. No one can say I'm not a sport."

"I don't know about that, I think you are betting on a certainty," Toria said. "Do you remember that night at Ciro's when you said you could tell not only the year of a vintage port, but also the ingredients of a cocktail? We tested you and you were right about them all. If I defeat you this time, it will be a feather in my cap and a very good story for me to tell the others."

"Well, I'll give you your chance," Billy said.

Toria knew she had acted well. He had no suspicion of her intentions.

"We must have another party like that," Toria sighed. "What fun it was! Billy was really marvellous, Charles, and of course we all had bets on every glass. You must have won a fortune, Billy."

"If I remember rightly my share of the bill that evening very much exceeded anything I had won," Billy replied.

Toria gave a little shriek of laughter.

"I never thought of that," she said. "Of course it must have."

The steward returned at that moment with her tea. He put it on the table.

There were jam sandwiches, Toria noticed, and a plate of tiny iced cakes. She wondered if she would be able to eat them or anything else ever again. She felt sick at the very thought, and knew it was fear which was closing her throat.

"Give Charles his whisky and soda," Toria said to Billy, "and I shall get to work. Billy, you are not to watch me. Charles, keep an eye on him. He has in all probability got eyes in the back of his head."

Charles said nothing, but Billy laughed again.

"I would not be surprised at that. People have found it wiser not to tackle me from behind."

There was a sinister meaning behind his words, and Toria, sitting on the arm of a chair, laughed as if she guessed that he was making a joke, but she was not certain of the point.

She watched Billy pour Charles out a generous whisky and soda and then sat himself down with his back towards the cocktail bar, facing Charles.

Toria picked up a bottle of gin. She poured a little into the glass, then she glanced round. Billy had his back to her and yet she was afraid.

She had not been joking when she said he might have eyes in the back of his head. He was the sort of person who would sense anything unusual and anything dangerous to himself.

She put her hands to her neck. She gave a little tug to

176

one string of her pearls. She was afraid that the clasp might give rather than the silken thread on which the pearls were strung, but the clasp was a strong one.

Another tug and the pearls broke.

Toria gave a little cry as they fell from her neck, pattering on to the floor.

"Oh, my precious pearls!" she exclaimed. "I ought to have had them restrung because I was afraid they might do this, but I didn't have a moment to take them to the jewellers before I got married."

Charles got down on his knees.

"They are real, aren't they?" he asked. "We must be careful not to lose any."

"They were my Mother's."

Toria undid the clasp and laid the other string on the table.

"Please find every one," she pleaded. "I can't quite remember how many there are, but we can look up the insurance policy when we get back."

Billy bent down too.

"You won't lose any here," he said. "There are no cracks in the floor for one thing."

Swiftly Toria transferred the small piece of paper from her pocket to her left hand. Billy's back was towards her, although he still faced Charles.

Very quickly she managed to tip the whole of the contents of the paper into the glass which contained a little gin.

"I am sorry to be such a nuisance," she apologised.

"I can't see any more," Charles said.

"I should think we have got the lot," Billy agreed.

Each man had a pile in his left hand.

"Count the string on the table," Toria suggested. "It is the top row that has gone, so there should be about four less than in the unbroken row."

Billy sat down in the seat he had occupied before and put the pearls in an ashtray. Charles added his collection and, leaving Billy to do the counting, picked up his whisky and soda.

"I will go on with my brewing," Toria said. "You will need a drink after all this exertion."

She looked carefully at the glass. The sleeping draught was dissolving. There was no doubt about it. She added a little more gin and stirred it quickly, then she began to add liqueurs, mixing several recipes together.

Toria had mixed enough cocktails to know how to make one well-balanced and with just the right degree of piquancy. When she had got what she thought was the right mixture, she was careful not to put ice in it.

Instead she laid the shaker containing the cocktail in the ice bucket and packed the ice round it.

"Now you have to wait a few minutes," she said to Billy. "My Mexican friend said the great secret was to make the cocktail ice-cold, but not to mix in the ice. I must say I agree with him. In London now you get nothing when you are offered a drink but some rather over-flavoured water."

Billy laughed.

"You are making me so thirsty," he said, "that I shall enjoy the drink when I do get it too much to be really critical."

"No one could be critical of 'The Serpent's Kiss'," Toria replied. "Are all my pearls there?"

"A hundred and two," Billy replied; "that is the same as the other row with the exception of four."

"Then that must be right," Toria said. "Thank you so much. Now let me see? What shall I put them in?"

She went to the writing table and picked up an envelope and handed it to Billy. "Put them in and seal them down. If they are missing when I get back to Monte Carlo, I shall accuse you of theft."

She was playing for time, but Billy was quite unaware of it.

"I shall count them in front of you as the shopkeepers do with change," he said, "and no one can accuse me of anything."

"You are too quick to be honest," Toria teased. "I don't believe anyone gets the better of you."

"You would be surprised how many people try."

"They must be very silly," Toria said.

There was no mistaking the admiration in her tone. Billy could not help preening himself a little.

"The nicest thing about you, Toria, is that you are never catty," he smiled.

"What you mean is that I think you are clever and I say so," Toria parried.

She poured herself out a cup of tea.

"I was telling Charles last night," she went on, "how clever you are, wasn't I, Charles?"

"You were," Charles replied a little heavily.

"As he thinks most of my friends are half-wits," Toria continued, "it was quite a relief to introduce him to someone of whom he approves."

"Do you really think he approves of me?" Billy asked with mock humility.

"But of course he does."

Toria took another sip of tea and put down her cup suddenly.

"Darling, your drink. I was almost forgetting it. It ought to be cool enough now."

She lifted it from the ice box and carried it over to Billy.

"Now," she said, "shut your eyes and guess. I only hope I have made it right."

Billy took a small sip.

"It isn't bad," he said. "A little bit sickly perhaps."

"Oh, don't be horrid," Toria pleaded. "I shall burst into tears if you don't like it."

He took a still larger sip as if to please her.

"Brandy, Cointreau . . . no . . . Kümmel and I believe there is also some gin. It is a very odd mixture, Toria."

"You are being much too good," she pouted. "I can see my gloves disappearing rapidly over the horizon."

Billy drank again.

"There is something I can't put a name to," he said. "I wonder what on earth it is. Have you used any lemon?"

"I am not going to answer any questions," Toria parried. "You have got to tell me definitely. Lemon or no lemon."

"Lemon," Billy said.

179

"A very little," Toria admitted.

"I thought so!"

"You are too good," Toria complained. "It isn't fair!"

"There is something else," Billy said. "I'm not quite sure what it is, but I think there is a touch of Kirsch."

"Yes or no," Toria teased.

"Yes."

"You are right. Oh, Billy, I hate you."

"Is that the lot?"

"I am afraid so."

He drank off the rest of the glass.

"Funny," he said reflectively, "but I could have sworn there was something else. But it is not a bad drink, although obviously feminine."

"I think you are meaning to be rude," Toria said, "but I shall refuse to be angry with you. I just have to think you are clever, however cross I am at losing my gloves."

Billy lit a cigarette.

"When you have finished your tea, I will make you a cocktail, a new one I invented. It is far less subtle than yours, but it is certainly very pleasant to taste."

"What is it called?" Toria asked.

"It is called 'the Enigma'," Billy said, "and incidentally, that is the name of the yacht. Did you realise that?"

"No, I didn't," Toria answered. "Why do you call it that?"

"Oh, for reasons of my own," Billy replied. "It is sometimes what I feel I am myself."

"An enigma?" Toria questioned. "Perhaps you are! What do you think, Charles?"

"I don't think I am qualified to express an opinion," Charles said.

Toria glanced at him quickly. He was looking strained, she thought, and she knew what he must be going through. He was waiting his opportunity, yet it never seemed to come. She looked at Billy. He yawned suddenly.

"Rather hot in here," he said. "Shall we go on deck again?"

"Oh, let me finish my tea," Toria protested. "I haven't sampled one of those delicious cakes yet."

She took one from the plate and cut it with a tiny, silver-handled knife.

"Did your chef make these?" she asked.

She wished Charles would help her with the conversation. The strain of talking was almost unbearable.

"Yes, I believe he does," Billy replied. "Would you like some music on the radiogram?"

He opened the shining cover and chose a number of records from the pile on the table nearby.

"Here is one of my favourites," he said.

The strains of a sentimental tune filled the cabin. Billy sat down again in his chair. Toria looked at him and realised he was watching her.

"I'm putting on weight—but who cares?" she smiled, forcing herself to put a piece of cake into her mouth.

She felt as if it would choke her, the sickly taste of pink icing was absolutely nauseating, and quickly she drank some tea so as to be able to swallow it.

"Tell us about the new American shows," she asked, her elbows on the table. "I hear there are some very good ones."

"Two were outstanding," Billy answered and yawned again. "I have got the records here if you want to hear them."

"Oh, I would adore that," Toria said. "Do put them on when these are finished."

"You know, when I am alone," Billy said, suddenly serious, "I sit for hours listening to the music. I have got all the operas and they soothe me more than anything else I know."

"How strange!" Toria exclaimed. "I had no idea you liked opera, Billy. I thought you only cared for boogy-woogy."

"How little we know about each other really!" Billy answered.

"That is true," Toria said, "but sometimes I think we hardly know ourselves."

"Perhaps we don't allow time for either."

Billy yawned again, a long yawn that seemed to come from the very depth of his being.

"It is . . . damned hot . . . in here," he muttered, and then suddenly heeled over.

He fell forward on the table, but his hands failed to grasp it and he slipped very slowly on to the floor. There he grunted, but his eyes did not open. Charles started to his feet.

"He is drugged," Toria said quickly. "I gave him twenty of my sleeping capsules."

It was then she saw a Charles she had never seen before—Charles in action.

Moving quicker than she had believed it possible, he transferred the revolver from Billy's pocket to his own, then he lifted the sleeping man and laid him on the sofa.

"If anyone comes in," he said swiftly, "pretend to be resting, too."

"What are you going to do?" Toria asked.

"No time to explain," Charles answered. "I will be back! Don't be frightened."

He looked down at her anxious face; and then before she realised what was happening, he had slipped his arm round her and had kissed her on the lips.

"Bless you, my darling," he said. "You are wonderful!"

Then he was gone.

Toria stood still, her heart beating fast for some minutes after Charles had left her.

She felt as if she was moving in a dream and her brain functioned in a queer dreamlike manner which made everything seem distorted and unreal.

She fancied that she might awake at any moment to find herself in her own bed at home, ready to resume her ordinary, everyday existence, in which the greatest excitement was a party in London or the offer of another job at modelling clothes.

It seemed to her in that moment that her whole life had been over-coloured, a kind of Technicolor film since that moment not two months ago when Michael told her he loved her and started a strange chain of events which had culminated in this.

She stared at Billy's inert form on the sofa.

He was breathing deeply, drawing his breath in the peculiar manner of someone who is either drunk or doped. Charles had set him down carelessly and his blazer was ruckled up and his tie was flopping loosely across one shoulder.

Toria crossed the room, straightened his tie and pulled down his coat. She looked round and saw a rug lying over the back of a chair. Taking it, she spread it over Billy's legs.

Immediately it made him look more natural, and she thought that, unless the steward was unduly perceptive, he would see nothing wrong when he came to clear away the tea.

She stood listening, but could hear nothing. They were steaming far away from land and at what seemed to Toria a very great speed.

She wondered what Charles was going to do.

Would he force the Captain to turn the ship round and carry them back to Monte Carlo, or had he other and different plans?

Toria tried to remember what she had seen of the ship's crew when they went round the yacht. She thought then that the men were mostly foreigners although of what nationality she was not sure.

They spoke very little, she remembered, smiling politely when spoken to, but volunteering very little information.

Now as she waited she became increasingly afraid. Getting rid of Billy was only the first step.

She reckoned there were at least twenty to twenty-five men on board. How would Charles contrive to deal with them, even armed as he was with Billy's revolver?

She thought she heard someone coming and sat down on a chair, putting her feet up on the stool opposite and resting her head on the satin cushion.

It was essential that whoever came into the cabin should think that there was nothing peculiar in Billy being asleep at this particular hour.

Her ears had not deceived her, for no sooner had she settled herself than the steward who had brought the tea came into the cabin. Toria opened her eyes, then closed them again as if he had disturbed her.

He said nothing, merely going to the table, piling the teapot, plates and cup and saucer on to his tray. He was a small, dark-skinned little man by no means young, and there was an oriental look about him. Toria judged him to be a half-breed of some sort.

At least physically he was not to be feared, for he was very thin and the bones of his wrists protruded in an almost emaciated manner.

She tried to think what sort of servants she would employ if she were in Billy's place.

She imagined he would trust very few people with his secrets; the enigma of his personality had been the one thing which had ensured the success he had achieved so far in hoodwinking those who should have been suspicious of him.

She imagined that very strong pressure must have been put on him to reveal as much as he had in kidnapping Charles and herself; and then she remembered that whatever they did, whatever they said, they would not live to betray Billy.

The steward left the cabin, and Toria opened her eyes and looked at the unconscious man whom she knew as Billy Grantly.

She wondered now why she had ever been fool enough to have called him a friend or to have trusted him. Now that he was off his guard and was neither smiling nor deliberately making himself agreeable he looked very different.

Yet Toria had to admit in all honesty that there was nothing really sinister in his face, nothing which would have made her suspicious of him had she seen him asleep in any other circumstances.

He had been well chosen for the part he had to play; he was enigmatic awake or asleep, conscious or unconscious.

How idiotic one was about people, Toria thought.

One took them at their face value, being easily gulled

by those who were voluble and effusive, who went out of their way to be flattering and complimentary. Billy had brought the art of making himself agreeable to a fine art.

It was almost impossible to resist him when he was determined to be friendly, almost impossible to refuse his apparent kindness and generosity.

Toria wondered how many people had been lulled into a false sense of security and then had found, as she and Charles had, that he was not what he seemed. How long had he played this game?

She thought now, as she looked at his face, that he was older than she had at first thought.

There was a fine network of wrinkles round his eyes, and when he was not smiling, the lines between his nose and eyes were very pronounced.

As she looked at him, she remembered how often she had danced with him, taken his hand, smiled up into his face. She felt sick and disgusted with herself.

She should have known, her instinct should have guided her more truly than this.

She found herself thinking of the twins. She had never known them make a mistake about people.

Often they liked the most unexpected individuals, but they were invariably right. If they disliked anyone, however much one might try to convince them at the time that they were wrong, sooner or later they were proved right.

She remembered then how much they had liked Charles the very first day he had come to the Castle.

"He is nice," she had heard Xandra say. "I feel sure he will take Michael's invention."

"He would still be nice even if he didn't," Olga replied.

"Yes, of course," Xandra's agreement was spontaneous and unhesitating.

The twins had known at once, yet she had been by no means sure that she liked Charles on that first day. She thought him dull and a trifle stiff. Pompous she had called it at the time; but now she saw it was a quiet reserve, an armour with which he protected himself when he met new people.

Now Toria thought he was wise enough to reserve his judgment on strangers, to give his instinct a chance to work, a thing she had never done herself.

He had disliked Billy. How right he had been, how right!

She felt as if she could sit still no longer. She must know what was happening.

Yet Charles had told her to remain where she was and she knew she would be foolish to disobey. He knew what he was doing.

Toria got to her feet and opened the door of the cabin, but she did not go outside. She began to imagine all the most terrible things that might be happening.

Had Charles been overpowered by the crew, disarmed, perhaps shot and flung overboard? She wondered what would happen to them if he did not effect their escape and Billy came back to consciousness.

How long would he remain doped? She had no idea. She knew that one tablet gave her about six hours sleep.

She tried to calculate how long twenty would be expected to work, but found she could not do the simplest sum in arithmetic. She was too tense, too agitated.

She listened from the door. There was nothing to be heard, only the strong, even throb of the engines. There was not even the sound of voices.

Toria walked across the cabin and looked out of the porthole. The vivid shining blue of the sea and sky was almost a mockery in itself. It was a day for happiness, for joy and laughter, yet she and Charles lay under the shadow of death.

She wondered what Michael would have done in the same circumstances. She could almost see the anger in his face, the expression in his eyes. He would never have remained quiet and calm if he had sat in Charles' place at the luncheon table.

He would have exploded with anger; he might even have rushed at Billy and have been shot down.

Toria felt thankful that Michael was not with them. The whole thing would somehow have been impossible.

186

She would never have been able to think out a way of rendering Billy incapable.

She would have been concerned only with Michael, with helping him and calming him, with what was, in fact, looking after him. She thought now, looking out of the porthole, how often Michael had seemed to her nothing less than a little boy.

There were moments when she felt tenderly maternal towards him, immeasurably wiser than he, a woman who must protect him from the world and from the vulnerability of his own character.

Yet she had felt the strength of Michael's arms round her, his mouth on hers.

She remembered the violence of his kisses after her wedding, and quite suddenly she yearned to see him again, to know what he was doing, to listen to the sound of his voice even if it was raised in anger.

It was then she heard someone coming towards the cabin. There was no time for her to return to the armchair which she had occupied when the steward had come in. Besides, for the moment she felt incapable of moving.

She thought she heard more than one pair of footsteps, and it flashed through her brain that it was perhaps the members of the crew coming to capture her, to imprison her as they must have already imprisoned Charles.

Then with a sense of utter relief she saw that it was Charles himself and that he was smiling. Without hesitating she ran across the room towards him.

"What has happened? Tell me!"

She put both her hands against his chest and felt his right arm go round her. He must have seen by her upturned, strained face that she had almost reached breaking point.

"It is all right, my darling," he said. "I only came back for a moment to tell you not to worry. We shall be rescued."

"But how? How? The ship has not altered course."

"I know," he said.

It was then she saw that he was not as immaculate as

187

when he had left her. His hair was untidy, one of the gilt buttons had been torn from his blazer and there was a great rent in the cloth where it had been.

"What has happened?" she repeated.

He glanced down at his blazer.

"I had a bit of a tussle with the wireless operator," he answered. "I did not want to disturb anyone by firing at him, but I had to knock him out. Unfortunately he was quite a hefty chap and knew how to use his fists. I shall have a sore jaw for weeks."

He put one hand up to his chin as he spoke, but his smile was very re-assuring.

"What have you done with him?" Toria asked.

"I have gagged him and locked him up in a cupboard in the wireless room," Charles said. "I must go back there in a moment in case he comes round and starts making a noise. I don't want more trouble on the yacht than is necessary."

"But aren't you going to make the Captain take us back to Monte Carlo?" Toria asked.

She did not move out of Charles' encircling arm.

It was somehow infinitely comforting to be close to him, to feel the strength of his chest beneath her breast.

"I did not feel capable of tackling the entire crew single-handed, so I sent for someone to help me."

"Who?" Toria asked.

"What could be better help than the British Navy?" Charles asked, "a portion of them at any rate."

"But where are they?" Toria questioned quickly. "Oh, Charles, do explain what you mean."

"I must not tease you, darling," he said. "You have been through too much already. All I want you to do now is to sit here quietly and to keep anyone who comes in from trying to awake that swine."

He indicated Billy with a gesture of his hand.

"In about twenty minutes' time, perhaps sooner, a Cruiser will come up alongside us and instruct the Captain to heave-to. After that all our troubles will be at an end!"

"You are quite sure they will not miss us?" Toria asked.

"Quite sure," Charles answered re-assuringly. "I am quite a capable navigator. I have told them exactly where we are."

"You are certain there won't be any mistake?" Toria asked.

She spoke insistently, but at the same time she felt curiously near to tears. Charles' arm tightened about her.

"You have got to be brave for just a little while longer," he said. "I must go back to the wireless room, but I will be back here before anyone comes along asking awkward questions, so try not to be afraid."

"You are sure you are all right now?" Toria asked.

"Quite sure, thanks to you."

Charles spoke very quietly; then he led Toria to a chair and made her sit down.

"I must go back," he said.

She felt herself incapable of speech. She could only stare dumbly at him while the tears gathered in her eyes; but he knew without any words that she would not fail him, that she was agreeing to whatever he suggested.

He smiled at her and then reached for the remains of his whisky and soda. He drank it off, then turned towards the door.

"Twenty minutes," he said quietly and was gone.

As soon as he was out of sight Toria reproached herself for her lack of control.

The battle was not yet over, but already she was collapsing. She was ashamed of herself, yet she knew that it was Charles' reassurance that they were to be rescued which had unnerved her.

She remembered her sense of horror when she had gone down to her cabin during the afternoon. She had thought then, though she hardly dared to formulate the idea even to herself, that it was hopeless to imagine they might be saved.

It had seemed almost a million to one against their escaping from the trap into which Billy had lured them.

"I am grateful," Toria thought; "Dear God, I am grateful."

She twisted her fingers together; then because it was impossible for her to sit still, she rose and went to the window.

It was possible to see out not only on both sides of the ship but also directly ahead. Toria's eyes scanned the horizon. There was not even a fishing-smack in sight.

She turned her head this way and that; she felt as if her eyes were strained with the effort of looking, looking and seeing nothing but blue sea, blue sky and gleaming waves golden with sunshine.

At last, when she felt despairingly that Charles was wrong and that no one was coming to rescue them, she saw the long grey silhouette of a Cruiser. Her heart leapt as it had never leapt before.

They were safe! They were going to live! The terrible dark cloud which had been ready to descend and crush the very existence out of them was gone.

She had never known until this moment how much she prized life. It was wonderful, glorious, miraculous just to know that one could go on living.

It was easy to talk as if dying was not important; but when the moment came, one knew that life was infinitely precious, a gift one forgot to value until it might be taken away from one.

Toria thought that never again would she forget to be grateful just for the fact of being alive.

It was better to be unhappy and miserable than not to live at all. She thought, as she stood there, that people who said they wished they were dead were committing the worst crime of all, the sin which Christ had described as being one against the Holy Ghost.

The great ship came nearer and nearer. The sun glinted on her, making her appear as if she were clothed in burnished silver, a St. George in shining armour come to rescue the traditional maiden from the Dragon.

Involuntarily Toria glanced down at Billy. She wondered what he would think when he awoke and found that he had been defeated by a girl.

She thought that it was perhaps the first time in his life that he had ever under-rated his opponent. He had been watching Charles and he had thought her too insignificant to be considered.

He had never for one instant been suspicious of her.

"Thank you, God, thank you, thank you," Toria found herself whispering the words over and over again.

There was a light flashing from the mast of the ship and she guessed that they were sending a message and she wondered if Charles was able to cope with it.

He would take it down, she thought, and find someone to carry it to the Captain.

Perhaps, if the messenger was the steward, he would not think it peculiar for one of Billy's guests to have taken the place of the ordinary wireless operator. The ship must have carried many strange passengers.

The Cruiser was signalling again and now at last Toria heard a bell ring and rhythm of the engines alter.

They were slowing down. Yes, at last they were slowing down.

It was then she felt the tension too much for her. She could not watch any more. She was shaking all over, her hands trembling as her fingers clenched and re-clenched themselves together, and her eyes were blinded with tears.

They were safe!

Someone was shouting instructions. The door of the cabin was burst open. A man dressed in a Mate's uniform came into the room. He glanced round quickly, then removed his cap at the sight of Toria.

He saw that Billy was lying on the sofa and went quickly towards him. Toria stepped forward.

"Mr. Grantly is asleep. You must not wake him."

"But the Captain wishes to speak to him," the Mate said with a pronounced foreign accent.

His face, Toria thought, was surly and disagreeable.

"He gave instructions that he was not to be disturbed under any circumstances," Toria said firmly. "He is very tired."

The man looked uneasy.

"The Captain wishes to speak with the master."

"You must tell the Captain that Mr. Grantly does not wish to be disturbed," Toria said.

The man looked down at Billy, put out his hands as if to touch his shoulder, then changed his mind and went from the room. He had reached the doorway when he came to face with Charles.

"Is anything the matter?" Charles asked.

"The Captain wishes to speak with the master," the man said, "and he is asleep."

"Tell the Captain that your master was insistent he was not to be woken up," Charles said, and he stepped on one side as he spoke.

The Mate hurried through the doorway and they heard his feet running along the deck.

"They are here," Charles said quietly.

The engines grew slower and slower and finally stopped altogether.

"The Cruiser is putting down a boat," Charles went on, walking towards the port-hole.

It was then that Toria said weakly:

"Charles, I think I am going to faint."

"Nonsense," Charles replied almost sharply.

He walked across to the bar and poured out a small glass of brandy.

"Drink this," he commanded, "and your nose wants powdering."

Toria said afterwards that it was being told that she looked plain which pulled her together far quicker than the brandy.

She finished the small glass, however, that Charles had given her and took her vanity case from her pocket.

She was smiling a few minutes later when a young Naval Commander came aboard and greeted Charles as an old friend.

"What the deuce are you up to now, old boy?" he asked, as Charles grasped his hand.

"You won't believe me," Charles said, "but all the same it is a good story."

He related what had happened to them in a very few words and the Naval Commander who rejoiced in the nickname of "Bingo" whistled softly.

"If I didn't know you, Charles, I should think you were writing for *Boy's Own* and this was instalment number twenty-two. It's as good as the hereoine being tied down on the railway line with an express thundering over her."

"I feel as if that is exactly what has happened to me," Toria said, and felt somehow comforted by the admiration in Bingo's eyes as he replied:

"I bet you do. Well, it's all over now."

Charles called a steward and sent him downstairs to re-pack their luggage.

"What do I do about that?" the Naval Commander asked, indicating Billy with a scornful finger.

"Leave him here," Charles answered.

Toria gave a little cry of horror.

"Leave him here?" she exclaimed. "But aren't you going to put him in prison or something?"

"If he is abducted off his own yacht by a British Cruiser on the High Seas, we shall have international questions of every sort. Can't you see the Foreign Secretaries enjoying themselves? No, leave him alone. I'll make it jolly difficult for him to re-appear in any of the free countries after this; but if we lay hands upon him, we touch dynamite."

"You're right," Bingo said. "What do we tell the Captain?"

"Tell him to continue his journey," Charles said. "He will find it difficult enough to waken his master and if his destination is where I think it is, the hospitals are putrid."

"Well, if that is all," Bingo said, "we'd better take you aboard."

It seemed to Toria a tame ending that they should climb from the yacht into the small launch, watched by the dark, unsmiling faces of Billy's crew.

"I thought at least someone would be made to walk the plank," she said wistfully as they drew away from *The Enigma* and set off towards the big grey Cruiser.

"Billy will do that when his chiefs get hold of him," Charles said. "They are not very tolerant of failures."

"You don't think that they will send him back to try again?" Toria asked, and then suddenly with a little spasm of fear she slipped her hand into Charles'. "They won't try to get you after this?"

"Not more than they have tried already," Charles said grimly. "But don't worry. When you get to know me better, you will realise I'm like a cat. I've got nine lives."

Toria made a little sound that was curiously like a sob.

"You must have used up at least eight of them already."

"That gives me another to go," Charles answered, "and I shall land on my feet somehow. I'm only sorry that you were mixed up in this. It was beastly for you."

He squeezed her fingers suddenly very hard.

"But I am damned proud of you all the same," he said.

Toria felt a sudden glow go through her.

"Thank goodness I had those sleeping tablets with me," she said. "It is a mercy I was so nervous and over-tired before our wedding. I generally sleep eight hours without the slightest difficulty."

"It is just one of those things that were meant," Charles said quietly.

"Do you really think that?" Toria asked. "It is just what I have been thinking myself. Everything seemed to have been planned."

"Even to your marrying me," Charles replied.

Then as Toria's eyes widened in surprise, he added: "Here we are," and took his hand from hers.

It was not easy for Toria to climb up the swaying rope ladder on to the deck of the Cruiser; but from the moment she set foot on board, the Navy's kindness and hospitality made her feel that she had come home.

She and Charles had to tell their story not once but a dozen times before the ship dropped them at Monte Carlo.

It was very late before they got back and as the little launch carried them from the open sea into the calm security of the harbour, Toria felt that with its lights shining Monte Carlo was the most beautiful place she had ever seen in the whole of her life.

It seemed a very long time since they had come aboard Billy's yacht at twelve o'clock that morning.

So much had happened. She had run through so many emotions that it seemed almost impossible that she could be the same person who had driven down to the quay, determined to have her own way and go on the cruise with Billy, however reluctant Charles might be.

They managed to get a taxi to carry them back to the Hotel de Paris.

As they drove up the hill, Toria, thankful that Charles could not see her face in the darkness, said:

"I am sorry, Charles. It was all my fault. I realise that."

She was glad he did not pretend to misunderstand her.

"You could not be expected to know what might happen," he answered, "but I mistrusted Grantly from the moment I saw him; and vaguely at the back of my mind I thought I had heard some rather unpleasant things about him. Yet I was not sure what they were. If I had had any sense I would have put a call through to London this morning and found out about him, but it is easy to be wise after the event."

"All the same I am sorry," Toria said. "I thought, when you left me alone with him, what a fool I had been."

"You need not blame yourself too much," Charles said. "All's well that ends well."

"If it is ended," Toria added. "Charles, I want to go home. I can't bear to stay here after this."

"We shall be quite all right."

"I could not be sure of it, I could not be sure of anything. Please, Charles, please let us go home."

"Of course, if you want it."

"I do!"

"Then we will go back tomorrow."

"Thank you."

Toria's voice was shaky and when they reached the Hotel de Paris she went quickly in through the swing doors while Charles paid the taxi. When he reached the hall, she had gone upstairs in the lift.

Their rooms were just as they left them. The flowers

which Charles had ordered scented the air. There was a sense of security in the shuttered windows and drawn curtains. But Toria knew she was still afraid.

It was there, lurking within her like some evil snake, and she knew she would never be free of it until she had reached home and was once again amongst the things which were familiar.

She felt, too, an almost overwhelming sense of fatigue. It was too much trouble to unpack her suitcase and she dragged out her dressing-gown and slippers.

When Charles came upstairs and called to her from the sitting-room, she was already undressed and brushing her hair at the dressing-table.

"I am here," she called, and he came to the door of her bedroom.

"Going to bed?" he asked.

"I am exhausted," Toria answered.

She went on brushing her hair, but she could see Charles in the mirror of the dressing-table.

She saw him look at her, his eyes resting on her shining hair and upraised arm; then with what appeared to her to be a little sigh he turned away.

"Call me if you are frightened, but I promise you there is no need for it."

"Good night, Charles."

She felt there was much more she wanted to say, much more that should be said between them, and yet she was too afraid to know what it was, too utterly fatigued to want anything save the feeling of a mattress beneath her and a pillow under her head.

She thought as she got into bed that she would be too afraid to sleep; but she remembered nothing from the moment she lay down until she opened her eyes to find the sun streaming through the slats in the shutters and the clock by her bed told her it was nearly half past ten.

She knew that the night's sleep had been dreamless; and she felt alert and sensible and no longer so terribly afraid.

All the same, she remembered Charles' promise that they should go home today. She could not bear to stay here, she thought. She wanted to be amongst the people she could really trust.

She thought of the twins, of Lettice, and of her father; and then last, because in reality he was so insistently in her mind, she allowed herself to think of Michael.

She rang for her breakfast and it was while she was sitting up eating it that she heard Charles moving about in the sitting-room. She called to him and he came to the door.

He was dressed and carrying a newspaper in his hand.

"Had a good night?" he asked.

"Perfect," Toria replied.

"I have been doing a bit of telephoning," Charles said. "I have arranged for an aeroplane to be at Nice at three o'clock. That will give us time to have a good luncheon and motor over afterwards. Will that suit you?"

"Thank you. I want to go home more than I've ever wanted anything in the whole world. You don't mind, do you?"

"Not particularly," Charles answered, "so long as you don't find the duties of taking up housekeeping too exhausting."

Toria raised her eyebrows.

"Housekeeping?" she queried. "Aren't we going home?"

"Home to England," Charles replied, "and to our new house. You remember I told you about it."

Toria felt her spirits sink.

"Yes . . . of course . . . our new house," she repeated rather stupidly. "I suppose . . . I didn't think it was ready for us yet."

"Fortunately it is finished," Charles answered triumphantly, "and I feel sure you will be pleased with it. It belonged to a friend of mine, Ronnie Wrotham, who designed it for himself. Personally I think it is an ideal house if one has to live in London, but I mustn't force my ideas on you. I'll wait and see what you think after we get there. I telephoned this morning and told the servants to expect us tonight. I even ordered dinner. I am really very domesticated."

He was smiling and Toria forced her lips to smile in response. It was somehow impossible for her to tell Charles that the only thing she wanted was to go back to the Castle.

She could not put into words her yearning for the twins and for her father. She could not explain that what had happened yesterday had made her shrink almost with horror from the idea of continuing to remain married to Charles.

It was not him, she thought. It was something else, something she could not explain. It was as if everything had grown too big, too overpowering and frightening for her.

She felt lost, a child who wanted to run to her mother's knee, a baby who wanted only security and comfort, nothing more difficult or hard to understand.

When she had asked to go home, she had meant to the only home she had ever known, the place which held everyone she loved—the dear, shabby, familiar Castle.

But she was Charles' wife and of course she saw that she was being utterly unreasonable in expecting anything but that he should take her to their new house.

She felt an unreasonable, overpowering hatred of it. It would be new and bright and clean, and she wanted something old and dirty and beloved.

She would hate it; yes, she would hate it, she thought; and yet all the time her lips went on smiling and she forced herself to say:

"Don't tell me any more about it. Let us wait until we get there."

"Very well, we will do that," Charles agreed, and she was not certain if he were disappointed or pleased.

Toria drank her coffee and put down her cup.

"I will get up," she said, "and we will go out and enjoy the sunshine. We have come a long way for it and we might as well have our money's worth before we leave."

"That is a good idea," Charles said. "Don't be long. I

will wait for you downstairs in the hall. There are one or two more things I have got to do."

"All right," Toria said. "I will be as quick as I can. Will you tell the valet to pack for you?"

"Yes," Charles replied.

"I will see about my luggage," Toria said.

She thought, as she spoke, that she sounded like a good wife, and was thankful that he could not know the tumult within her, the hatred and the resentment which she knew was wrong, but which she could not prevent herself from feeling.

When she was alone, Toria shut her eyes and wondered what was wrong with her.

Yesterday she felt herself almost torn in pieces because Charles might be killed. Today she almost hated him because he was alive.

She heard the door of the sitting-room close. Charles was gone.

Then instead of getting up she reached out her hand and picked up the telephone. She gave a number and was told there would be a delay of twenty minutes. She replaced the receiver with a feeling almost of guilt.

"Why shouldn't I tell them I am coming home?" she asked herself aloud and knew that she could in reality possess her soul in patience for the news of the twins.

It was Michael of whom she wanted news.

She got up and had her bath, then began to dress feverishly. She knew there was no need for so much hurry, no need to expend her energy, yet she knew she must do it.

She somehow felt it essential to put behind her not only the terrible events of yesterday, but also everything that had occurred between herself and Charles since they had left Lynbrooke with the old boots and the "Just Married" placard flapping behind them on the car.

At last the telephone rang, startling Toria even while she was expecting it.

She ran across the room and picked up the receiver. The French operator told her that her call to England was just coming through.

There was a long delay punctuated by cracklings, and

199

then at last, when she had almost begun to despair, she was told she was through.

"Hullo."

"Who do you want?"

The words were almost snarled into the receiver.

"Michael, oh Michael! It's Toria."

"Toria!"

"Yes, I had to ring up. What are you doing? What has happened?"

"Where are you speaking from? Monte Carlo?"

"Yes, we are coming home today. Things have happened, I can't explain now, but we can't stay any longer."

"Where are you coming to? Here?"

"No, London."

There was a sudden silence.

"Michael, Michael, are you there? What are you doing?"

"I am talking to you."

"Oh, Michael, don't be maddening."

Toria's voice was half laughing, half tearful.

"I must know what you have been doing since you won all that money."

"I'm feeling very rich, Toria."

"Is that a nice feeling?"

"Wonderful, of course."

"Are you at home? You are staying there?"

"If I wasn't at home, I shouldn't be speaking to you."

"Yes, I know. I am being terribly stupid, but I was afraid you might have gone away again."

"Back to the docks! Not likely!"

There was a sudden crackling on the line.

"Michael, we shall be back in London by six o'clock. We are going to our new house in Chesterfield Hill. Will you ring me up or shall I ring you?"

"What for?"

"Because I want to talk to you."

"There is nothing particular to say."

"But there is, Michael. I must talk to you. Promise you will telephone me. You will find the number in the telephone book under Wrotham. It's a queer name so there won't be many of them. Please ring me."

"I will have to think about it."

"Oh Michael!"

It was almost a cry of despair, but Michael seemed not to heed it.

"Good-bye, Toria. I hope you have a good journey back."

"But, Michael, listen to me. . . ."

He had gone. Toria knew it even while she kept on calling his name until the operator told her in French that the line had been cleared.

She put the receiver back in its place. It had been a hopeless, unsatisfactory conversation, and yet she had spoken to Michael, she had heard his voice, but it had not meant what she thought it would.

He had been difficult, in one of his moods, and she had been too far away to cope with it.

Why, she wondered, did he always leave her with that unsatisfactory, empty feeling?

It was almost as if he had submerged her, sapping her vitality until, when he was finished, she was nothing but a husk. She turned with a hopeless little gesture towards the window.

She did not understand Michael, nor herself, nor Charles for that matter. In fact it seemed to her that she misunderstood everything and everybody. She had done so many stupid things, made so many mistakes, and telephoning Michael was another of them.

She had upset both him and herself unnecessarily. It would have done just as well if she had telephoned Michael when she arrived in London; but because she was stupid, she had to go blundering on, even while she knew that the fact that she was telephoning from Monte Carlo, an expensive and unnecessary gesture, would be enough in itself to infuriate Michael.

He would not have altered because he had a little money of his own. He loathed what he called the ostentation of the rich.

Toria knew it was really a kind of resentment on his part, because he was unable to do the things which the rich could do. But now, she told herself, everything was altered.

Michael was rich. He could telephone Monte Carlo, New York or Hong Kong for that matter if he wanted to. He could buy her the things which he had always loathed other men for giving her.

She remembered how he had snatched a big spray of orchids from her shoulder and stamped on it. She could see his face now as he said:

"You look like a tart!"

He had turned and walked away slamming the doors behind him. She had not known then that he loved her.

She had only thought it was one of his strange peculiarities that he disliked her receiving presents from other men, just as he practically insulted every man with whom she became friendly.

And yet there was the other side of Michael.

She remembered the lilies-of-the-valley she found on her breakfast tray on St. Valentine's Day, the 14th February. He had gone to Covent Garden at five o'clock in the morning especially to buy them for her.

It was only a tiny bunch, for Michael never had more than a shilling or two in his pocket.

She had almost cried because she had been so touched that he had thought of it and had taken so much trouble because she had said a week or two earlier that the one thing she looked forward to in the spring was seeing the lilies-of-the-valley.

She remembered Michael carrying Brandy home once when he had hurt his feet in a trap in the woods. They had been out shooting with her father.

It was Michael who had reached the whimpering dog first and had released him. He picked Brandy up in his arms and carried him back to the house.

There he had bathed the wound with disinfectant and bound it up, talking all the time to the dog as gently and as tenderly as any woman could have done.

That was the Michael she loved, Toria thought, the Michael who could understand the suffering of a dog and alleviate it; the Michael who brought her lilies-of-the-valley because she liked them.

The thought of Michael suffering, being unhappy, being hurt and resentful she minded more than anything else. When he was happy, the whole world seemed enchanted; and yet how seldom lately had he been that.

It almost seemed as if his bitterness had accumulated, growing worse and worse as the days went by, until finally it had ended in the climax of her promising to marry Charles.

She had thought at the time that it was the right thing to do; yet now she knew it had been wrong and she had hurt both Michael and Charles and had done no good to anybody, especially not to herself.

She was ready. She must go downstairs to her husband who was waiting for her. She rang the bell for the chamber-maid, asked her to pack, and then, taking up her bag and gloves, she went towards the door.

She passed through the sitting-room, looked at the big bowls of carnations and thought that they would go on blooming long after she and Charles had left for England. They had been a symbol of Charles' kindness, a token of his thoughtfulness, yet somehow they remained only an expression of failure.

They should have glamourised and made lovely the beginning of their married life together, their honeymoon on which they should have got to know each other.

But the flowers had failed, even as she and Charles had failed to reach a proper understanding.

They were married, yet not married.

Husband and wife by law, two separate individual people by choice.

Her honeymoon had begun and ended; the flowers bloomed on; ahead of them lay England, a strange house and a new home . . . and Michael?

Yes Michael, waiting for her return.

10

The house was lovely! Toria had expected many things but not that she would be captivated immediately on entering the bright green front door.

The whole place was exactly like a doll's house. To begin with it was built on two floors. There was no basement and the dining-room opened on to a small paved garden which was bright with yellow and pink polyanthus.

The rooms were low and the windows large, and the drawing-room, with pale green walls and bright flame-coloured chintz, was the gayest room Toria had ever seen, while her bedroom was so exquisite that she found herself gasping and unable to express what she felt even to Charles.

The pale blue walls with coral silk hangings and a corolla of gilt angels were a perfect setting for her pale gold hair and pink and white beauty.

Charles did not tell her that he had furnished this room entirely for her and yet she knew it, and without wasting time on obvious questions she asked:

"But how did you get it done in time?"

"That is a secret," he replied, "but I assure you that I worked very hard."

"I am sure of it," Toria said.

"The decorations were half finished when I first met you," Charles explained. "I bought it as I told you from Ronnie Wrotham who had built it for himself and then had to go abroad at a moment's notice. As a matter of fact he is one of our newly-appointed Ambassadors. I went to dinner with him the night after he had news of his appointment and he told me that he loved this house so much that he could not bear to think of just anyone taking it over from him.

" 'Why don't you buy it, Charles? You will be getting married yourself one day,' he said.

"I laughed at the time, but to please him and because I was heartily sick of the flat I had occupied since the war, I bought it from him. Then I met you. It almost seemed like fate."

Toria laughed.

"It was either intelligent anticipation," she said, "or else, having bought your house, you felt you must acquire a wife to look after it."

She wondered then why she had made up her mind that she would hate Charles' house, why she had imagined it would never mean home to her.

She knew, as she sat in the small panelled dining-room that evening and moved when dinner was over into the charm of the green drawing-room, that it was her ideal house.

Charles' mother, she learned, had provided him with most of the furniture. They were all period pieces, valuable but chosen not for their worth but because they were lovely in themselves.

The care that had been expended on them by generation after generation gave them the look of old and familiar friends. The sofa and chairs were modern and Charles told her that he had insisted on choosing them himself; the covers were feminine but their breadth and comfort were essentially masculine.

Before she went up to her bedroom that night, Toria knew that she could not steel herself against the enchantment of her new home. She loved it.

Whatever she felt about Charles, she knew that she could have no feelings other than affection towards the home he had provided for her.

She undressed slowly.

She knew that she was happier that night than she had been since her wedding day, and yet, as usual, Michael had contrived to spoil the evening for her. He had never telephoned.

She had waited and waited until at last she could bear it no longer and when the big grandfather clock in the hall struck ten she said:

"I would like to telephone home to see how everybody is. Do you mind?"

"No, of course not," Charles replied. "I will get the number for you."

He crossed to the knee-hole writing desk set in an alcove by the window and dialled the number. Toria found herself watching him as he did so.

His expression was serious and yet she fancied that tonight he was not unhappy. For the first time since she had married him she wondered just how much she had managed to hurt him when he learned that she was in love with Michael.

He had said so little, so very little, and yet in that one moment when she had seen his face unguarded she had known he was in agony.

But that had been for just a fleeting second and since then he had never seemed to be off his guard.

He had kissed her on the yacht when he left her alone in the cabin with the unconscious Billy; but it was hard now for her to recall just how much that kiss had meant to him or to herself.

They had both been too overwrought, too intent on what was happening to be really aware of each other.

Yet now, as Charles stood with the receiver to his ear, she wondered if she was being unnecessarily cruel to him.

Had he dreamt of bringing her here as his bride, of their being man and wife together in the real sense of the word? Had his dreams like hers seemed a part of life itself so that in refuting the mental image one suffered physical bereavement?

If that was so, then this unnatural friendliness which went no deeper than a conventional civility must be almost unbearable.

Yet she could not think of Charles being so emotionally vulnerable.

It was Michael who was tormented, Michael who suffered a thousand deaths every day of his life. Charles was calm—"calm, cool and collected", as the saying went.

Uncomfortably Toria asked herself, was she not assuming that, because he had a rigid self-control, his feelings were not so deep or so easily hurt? She had an impulse to put out her hands towards him and say:

"Come and sit down on the sofa, Charles, and let us talk about ourselves."

But somehow it was impossible for her to voice the words, to be spontaneous and natural with this stranger whom she had married and to whom so far she had given nothing, not even frankness and honesty.

She had a momentary picture of herself and was ashamed.

"Charles," she said impetuously.

Then the words died on her lips, for Charles spoke into the telephone.

"No answer?" he queried. "Ask the supervisor to ring the number again." He looked towards Toria. "They say there is no answer."

"There must be," Toria said urgently.

She was no longer thinking of Charles. She was thinking of Michael, whom she had asked to ring her and who, it seemed to her now, was deliberately avoiding the telephone. She got to her feet and walked over to the writing desk.

"Let me hold on," she suggested.

Charles gave her the receiver. She took it from him and waited impatiently, drumming her fingers on the polished top of the desk. After a long time the operator spoke.

"I am sorry," he said. "I have had the number specially rung, but there is no reply. We can keep the call in hand if you like."

"Yes, please do that," Toria said.

She put the receiver down slowly. It usually happened that nobody heard the telephone when it rang at the Castle, but she knew that her peace of mind was ruined unless tonight of all nights she could get a reply.

"I am afraid there is nothing we can do about it," Charles said quietly.

She hated him because she felt he sensed her anxiety to speak to Michael.

"That is obvious," she replied rather aggressively.

207

They sat in silence for a few minutes and then Toria got to her feet.

"I think I will go to bed; I always feel tired after having been in an aeroplane. I suppose the telephone can be switched through to my bedroom."

"Yes, of course," Charles replied. "I hope you sleep well."

Toria sensed the disappointment he was experiencing even though his voice revealed nothing. For a moment she hesitated.

She wanted to say something nice, something gracious, she wanted to tell Charles that she could not help being upset about Michael. That was the way he always affected her.

She wanted to make him understand, but somehow she could not find the words.

"Good night, Charles," she said at length.

He opened the door for her. She passed through it and went up the stairs. She heard the door close behind her and for a moment she almost went back to tell Charles she was sorry.

She had a feeling that he might be able to help her, and then she almost laughed at herself.

Help her with what? To forget Michael, to stop her loving him? How could any man do that, least of all Charles to whom she was married?

She went up to her bedroom and shut the door. Michael had ruined the evening. She lay awake for a long time; in fact she heard a distant clock strike two in the morning before finally she fell asleep.

She was awakened by the shrill buzzing of the telephone bell. Sleepily she wondered for a moment where she was, then sat up in bed, realised it was morning and reached for the receiver.

"Hullo!"

It was a man's voice who answered her, but it was not Michael. To her astonishment it was her father.

"Is that you, Toria?"

"Daddy! What a surprise! I never expected you to telephone me."

"Michael told me you were coming back last night. I

want to see you, Toria. Will you be at home during the morning?"

"Yes, of course! Are you coming up to London?"

"Haven't I just said so?" Lord Lynbrooke asked.

"Yes, of course! How are the family? The twins and Lettice?"

"Tell you all about them when I see you," Lord Lynbrooke said. "Good-bye."

He put down the receiver with a sharp click and Toria had to laugh. She knew how much her father loathed using the telephone.

He treated it as an enemy, something that had to be fought and battled with until finally it was subdued. He always shouted into the instrument and the simplest and safest method when speaking to him was to hold the receiver at least two or three feet away from one's ear, otherwise one was likely to be prematurely deaf for some hours.

"I wonder what Daddy wants to see me about," Toria questioned to herself.

She wondered if it could be about Michael. She somehow thought it was unlikely.

"Perhaps he wants to talk about the twins," she suggested aloud to a fat and ancient looking cupid on the corolla.

She then wondered why, if that was the reason, Lord Lynbrooke should take it into his head to come to London. He would be far more likely to command her to come to the Castle.

She looked at the clock by the bed.

It was not yet eight o'clock, but she knew that her father would have been up since seven taking Brandy and Soda for a walk across the Park, looking into the stables to see if Daisy was all right, and watching the clock until Mrs. Fergusson should produce breakfast for him at eight.

He was always hungry in the morning and insisted on a big bowl of porridge to start the meal.

This he ate standing up, not because he was Scottish by birth, but because, when he was a small boy, he had frequently stayed with his godfather in Perthshire and

209

been told then that it was the only possible way for a decent man to enjoy his oatmeal.

Thinking of her father now, Toria found herself smiling. He had such an unusual character in that he never cared in the slightest what other people thought or said about him.

He did what he wished to do. If people did not like it, they could do the other thing. She had never met anyone in the whole of her life so impervious to world opinion.

It was so like her father not to ask why Charles and she had returned so soon from their honeymoon. He seldom if ever intruded into other people's business and did not like people to intrude into his.

If his family wished to walk about on their heads, wearing bathing suits in mid-December, he would accept their antics gravely, neither condemning nor condoning them.

Toria was almost asleep again by the time the maid came to call her at half past eight.

Her mind had wandered back into the past; and as she thought of the Castle and of her family, her imagination became almost part of a dream, so that she was with them again, running once more across the unkempt gardens, tumbling in the hay and forgetting everything except the happiness of being young and with the people she loved.

The curtains were drawn and a pale golden sun, very unlike the brilliance she had known at Monte Carlo, came shining through her windows.

Her breakfast tray was set down beside her bed and a dressing jacket of pale blue velvet trimmed with marabout was held out for her to wear.

She had finished her breakfast and was thinking she ought to get up when she heard a knock on the door and heard Charles' voice:

"May I come in, Toria?"

"Of course!"

He walked into the room and stood for a moment looking at her. She had no idea how lovely she looked, her head bright against the coral hangings of her bed, the blue of her dressing jacket accentuating the white magnolia beauty of her skin.

"I came to tell you," Charles said after a moment, "that I am going down to the Ministry to tell them about Billy Grantly."

"But of course," Toria answered. "There is all that to be dealt with. Do you think they can do anything to him?"

"Not openly," Charles replied. "So don't expect headlines in the newspapers; but I think we can make life very uncomfortable for Mr. Grantly; in fact I hardly think he will be seen again for some years at any rate."

Toria gave a little shudder.

"I hate even to think about him," she said. "Charles, did you think this morning that we might not be here but somewhere very different?"

"Forget it," Charles replied briefly. "It is a mistake to remember the unpleasant things in life."

"I know," Toria agreed, "but some times things cannot be forgotten very easily."

"Yes, I know," Charles said.

To Toria's surprise he crossed the room and sat down on the edge of her bed, then he put out his hand and laid it over hers.

"Listen, Toria," he said. "What has happened to us might happen only once in a million years. You have got to believe me when I tell you that it will never occur again. I don't want you to go about in the future anticipating trouble, being afraid that danger lurks round every corner. If you do that, you will be a nervous wreck and you will also be a very unhappy person. Think of the whole thing as an accident which is finished and done with."

"I will try," Toria said, "but I don't think I am a very brave person by nature."

"I think you are," Charles said quietly. "I have not thanked you yet, have I, for saving both our lives?"

His voice was low and tense. Toria suddenly felt embarrassed.

"Don't be silly, Charles. You can't thank somebody for a thing like that."

"I suppose not," Charles said, "one can only love them for being rather wonderful!"

He looked directly into Toria's eyes as he spoke. She felt the colour rise in her cheeks.

She felt there was nothing to say, and then in a sudden unexpected shyness she tried to take her hand away from his, but Charles held on to it.

"Have I never told you how lovely you are?" he asked.

"No, I don't think you have."

Toria tried to speak lightly, but somehow her voice against her will became low and serious. With a tremendous effort she tried to speak mockingly.

"Really, Charles!" she exclaimed. "Isn't it a little early in the morning to be making love to me?"

She knew even as she spoke the words that she had broken the spell between them, a spell that had for the moment held her despite her effort to escape from it.

"I don't agree," Charles said. "It is never too early to tell the truth. And you are looking very beautiful, Toria."

He turned her hand over in his as he spoke and pressed his lips on the palm; then he rose to his feet.

"I shan't be long," he said. "If you want to go to the Castle, we can motor down after luncheon."

Toria heard the door of the room shut behind him and he was gone before she was able to tell him that her father was coming to London. Indeed she had no time to do anything but strive to collect her thoughts and her feelings.

She could still feel Charles' lips on her open palm, she could still feel the blood warm in her cheeks. He had made her blush, yet at the same time she had felt embarrassed and a little afraid of him.

"I'm being ridiculous," she thought to herself, "and as coy as any débutante of seventeen with her first dance partner."

This was a Charles she did not know, someone unexpected, someone very different from the man she thought she had married. She found her thoughts dwelling on him continually.

Was this part of the friendship he had offered her, was this his plan of getting to know each other?

"It is a ridiculous situation!" Toria suddenly said out loud.

The maid, who was bringing her a dress from her wardrobe, looked surprised.

"Did you speak, m'lady?" she asked.

"I am sorry, Jean. I was talking to myself," Toria smiled.

She put on one of her new dresses and went downstairs to wait for her father. She had not long to wait. Lord Lynbrooke arrived almost on the stroke of eleven o'clock.

He was wearing the suit in which he invariably went to Church on Sundays and a moth-eaten old bowler hat which he kept for the few auspicious occasions when he visited London. He came slowly into the drawing-room and looked around him.

"Rather cramped," he said, his pale blue eyes taking in the antique furniture and the valuable pictures on the walls.

Toria laughed.

"It is a big room for London, Daddy. You must not compare London houses with the Castle."

"Never did care for them myself," Lord Lynbrooke said. "Always feel like a rabbit in a hutch. But if you like it, that is all that matters. Happy?"

"Yes, of course," Toria said, knowing that it would perturb him if she said anything different. "Will you have a glass of port, Daddy, or a sherry?"

"Sherry, please," Lord Lynbrooke replied. "The port nowadays isn't what it was when I was young."

Toria had heard this remark far too often for it to require any comment.

She poured her father a glass of sherry and set it on the table beside his chair with a plate of dry biscuits. Lord Lynbrooke took a sip of the sherry.

"Not bad," he said appreciatively. "I am surprised Charles knows about wines. Most young men nowadays only care for these poisonous concoctions called cocktails. Never could stand them myself. I remember when. . . ."

"Tell me why you have come to see me today," Toria interrupted.

She knew how easily her father got side-tracked into one of his interminable stories. To her astonishment Lord Lynbrooke looked uncomfortable.

"Yes, of course," he said. "I came up early especially to see you. I have something to tell you."

"What is it?" Toria asked.

"Fact is," Lord Lynbrooke said, then paused for a moment, and after a minute's silence the words came almost burbling from his mouth: "I have decided to get married."

"Get married?"

Toria's astonishment was so complete as to be almost ridiculous. She gaped at her father for a moment and then remembered to shut her mouth.

"But Daddy, to whom?"

"To Mrs. Hagar-Bassett," the Earl replied. "Now, wait a minute," he added quickly, as Toria appeared about to speak. "I want to explain this carefully to you. That is why I came to see you. I know this will be a surprise to you and to the rest of the family. I don't want you to think that I have gone into this matter hastily and without due consideration. I realise, of course, that Mrs. Hagar-Bassett is not exactly . . . well, how shall we put it? . . . not of the same family standing as my own, but I decided to ask her to honour me by becoming my wife and she has accepted."

"Daddy, do you really think you will be happy?" Toria asked. "I mean, is she nice, is she kind? Is she the sort of person who will look after you?"

The Earl tugged at his moustache.

"I have known Mrs. Hagar-Bassett for many years," he said. "I shall not, Toria, be marrying a stranger. We understand each other and I think we shall be as happy as it is reasonable to expect anyone to be in these difficult times."

Toria moved a little restlessly.

"But, Daddy," she said, "I can't quite understand. Why do you want to get married?"

The answer came unhesitatingly.

"Lonely, you know. No one to talk to at the Castle."

"But, Daddy, there has been all of us. We have talked to you."

"Yes," the Earl replied, "but you have never listened."

He spoke quite simply and without rancour, but Toria felt a pang of pity which she had never known before.

Of course he must have been lonely, and yet they had never realised it. They never listened to any of his stories.

She had said that they talked to him, but it was not really true; and if he joined in the conversation, they were almost impatient at the interruption.

He had been lonely, very lonely after their mother died. At first there were only children to talk to, and later Michael whom he had never liked and with whom he had little in common.

Was it surprising that he wished for a friend of his own and, having found her, was prepared to go one step further than the afternoon visits which must have grown irksome to both of them?

Impulsively Toria crossed to her father's side and sitting on the arm of the chair, she put her arms round his shoulders.

"If you are going to be happy, Daddy, that is all that matters. We will all try to like Mrs. Hagar-Bassett for your sake."

"A very pleasant woman," the Earl said; "what is more, an excellent cook."

"Daddy!" Toria exclaimed through both tears and laughter. "I never thought you cared for food."

"I like good food," the Earl replied. "It is one of the few passions left to anyone of my age. Never could stomach the rubbish Mrs. Fergusson served up, but I have had to make the best of it. Now she will be able to keep the house clean, which is about the only thing she is good for."

"Then Mrs. Hagar-Bassett will do the cooking?" Toria said in a bewildered way.

"Of course, of course!" the Earl said. "I tell you she is a very good cook. Prides herself on being able to turn out French dishes as well as any Chef. She does not want to set herself up in your mother's place, so you need not be afraid of that. That is what she asked me to tell you when I said I was coming to see you. She is not going to assert herself in any way; but she is going to make me comfortable and happy and clean the Castle up a bit. Heaven knows it needs it."

Toria sighed.

"What it wants is some money spent on it. We all know that."

"Well, Mrs. Hagar-Bassett is prepared to do that," the Earl said.

"But has she got any money?" Toria exclaimed in amazement, remembering the horrible little suburban house in which Mrs. Hagar-Bassett lived, with its laurel bushes and "in and out" drive.

"As a matter of fact she has quite a fortune. As I told you, she does not care for social life or ostentation of any sort. She has always lived very quietly, saving her money since her husband died and allowing the dividends to accumulate. So now she is very comfortably off."

"Daddy, this is too wonderful!" Toria exclaimed. "As long as you are quite, quite certain that you will be happy in changing your way of life after all these years."

"I have been thinking about it for a long time," the Earl said, "and I am not doing anything impulsively."

"And when are you to be married?" Toria enquired.

"Today," the Earl answered.

Toria gave a little cry.

"Today? But Daddy, how? I mean. . . ."

"I have got to be at Caxton Hall by twelve o'clock," the Earl said, pulling an old-fashioned gold repeater from his waistcoat pocket. "But I have time for another glass of sherry if you will give me one. Tell Charles his taste in sherry is surprisingly good."

"I can't get over it," Toria said, fetching the decanter almost mechanically from the table. "You are to be married today. And this is the first any of us have known about it. Have you told the twins?"

"I have not. Thought you might do that for me. Guessed you would be going home either today or to-morrow."

"But you? Where are you going?"

"Staying in London tonight," the Earl said. "Mrs. Hagar-Bassett thought it was more decent if we went on a short honeymoon to give the family time to get used to the idea. Not that either of us care for travelling, but she has a friend who keeps a small hotel on the South Coast. We are going there for a week and then will return to the Castle."

Toria stared at her father. Somehow she could not imagine him in a small hotel on the South Coast. What would he do with himself?

She was about to say so, but checked the words as they rose to her lips. It was not for her to interfere. He had made his decision and the only thing she could do was to wish him well and hope that he and his bride would be happy.

Somehow she could not think of Mrs. Hagar-Bassett as the Countess of Lynbrooke. They had referred to her for so long as Mrs. Hagar-Bassett and it seemed impossible for her to have a Christian name or any other identity save as the widow of the late Mr. Hagar-Bassett.

The Earl finished his sherry and got to his feet.

"Well, I will be moving along," he said. "May take me some time to get a bus. You don't know what is the right number by any chance?"

"A bus," Toria exclaimed. "But, Daddy, surely you can afford a taxi on your wedding day?"

The Earl looked astonished.

"A taxi!" he exclaimed. "I came up from Lynbrooke by bus and tube in the usual way, and I shall take a bus to Caxton Hall. I see no reason for unnecessary extravagance just because one is going to get married."

"No, of course not," Toria said meekly. "But Mrs. Hagar-Bassett—surely she is not travelling by bus?"

"Matter of fact she is not," the Earl replied, "for she stayed last night with her sister in London, and the sister is not only sending her to the Registry office in her car but lending it to us with the chauffeur for the next week. I hear there are some rather decent drives round the place we are going to, and Mrs. Hagar-Bassett is very keen on antique shops. Might find a few things which are wanted at the Castle."

Toria felt there was nothing she could say. She had expressed her astonishment so often and now to find Mrs. Hagar-Bassett had a rich sister who had a car was only one more surprise on top of the many.

As for her father poking about in antique shops, she could only imagine that he must be very much in love indeed, for ever since she could remember it had been very difficult to get him to go into a shop of any kind.

"I had better be on my way," the Earl said.

Toria walked with him to the door. As he picked up his old bowler hat, she put her arms round his neck.

"I do wish you every happiness, Daddy dear," she said. "If I have not said all the nice things I ought to have said to you, it is simply because I have been so surprised by your news."

"You are a good girl," Lord Lynbrooke said, patting her on the shoulder. "Don't make any mistake about Charles. Right man for you."

His last sentence surprised Toria almost more than anything else. As she stood in the doorway and watched her father walk down the street, she wondered exactly what he had meant by his last sentence.

How much had he guessed of the situation that lay between her and Michael? Somehow she had never expected him to realise anything about herself or her feelings. He had always seemed so aloof, just a figurehead in the family.

Now she wondered if in fact they had not under-estimated him and he saw a great deal more than they realised.

It was only as he walked away that she became aware

218

that she had never mentioned Michael's name since her father arrived nor talked about what was to happen in the future. It had all been too astonishing.

Hearing of the announcement that her father was to marry Mrs. Hagar-Bassett had been enough to put everything else out of her mind. It was difficult to recall even what she looked like.

Toria could remember her hat at the wedding and the frivolous gaiety of the tulle bow round her neck. She must have known then that she was going to marry again.

No wonder she had insisted on coming to the Castle that day, no wonder she had wanted to be present.

Toria stifled a desire to laugh at the whole thing. It was funny.

She wondered how she was going to break the news to the twins. She must try not to make it difficult for Mrs. Hagar-Bassett when she returned to the Castle as their step-mother.

Would they resent her, Toria wondered, or would they continue to laugh at her? The latter might be the more difficult situation.

At last the Earl reached the end of the street. Toria realised why he looked strangely pathetic. It was because he was walking along without the spaniels at his heels.

It was seldom one saw him unaccompanied by Brandy and Soda. Going into the house and shutting the door behind her, Toria walked from the hall into the drawing-room.

She thought, as she had thought a dozen times already, how lovely the room was. There were big vases of flowers set on a table behind the sofa and another on one by the window—spring flowers, daffodils golden as the sunshine, tulips crimson and purple, their leaves the vivid green of early March.

"I ought to be so happy," Toria told herself. "I have everything, yet I want more."

Even as the thoughts came to her mind, her heart ached for Michael, to know what he was doing, to understand, as she had understood for so many years, what he was feeling and thinking.

It seemed to her suddenly as if he was very near her, as if he stood by her side. Then as she heard the front door bell peal as if it were pulled by an impetuous hand, she knew instinctively that he was outside.

She did not wait for the servant to come from the pantry in answer to his summons. She ran across the hall and flung open the front door.

She knew he would be there, knew he would be standing hatless and without an overcoat, his hands thrust into the pockets of his old blue suit which was badly in need of brushing and pressing.

They stood staring at each other, and then, as Michael made a movement to enter the house, Toria exclaimed.

"Why didn't you telephone me? I waited and waited."

"What was the point?"

Michael seemed to push his way into the hall. Toria shut the door behind him; then he walked forward into the drawing-room.

"So this is the love nest," he sneered, looking round the room, seeming to dwarf it by his very height.

"It is lovely, isn't it?" Toria said, ignoring his tone. "Sit down, Michael, or do you want a drink?"

"Uncle Arthur has been here, hasn't he?" Michael asked.

"Yes, he has just left," Toria replied. "Did he tell you why he was coming?"

"No, he is not in the habit of confiding in me, as you well know," Michael replied. "I thought perhaps he had come to see you about me. I won't have him interfering and I hope you will tell him so."

"As a matter of fact he never mentioned you," Toria said. "He had other and far more important things to talk about."

For a moment Michael looked relieved, then he scowled.

"I might have saved myself a journey then," he said. "That is all I came to see you about."

220

Toria smiled.

"If you are trying to hurt me by saying that, you don't succeed. You wanted to see me, and I wanted to see you—terribly."

Michael's eyes rested on her then, but they did not soften.

"Apparently the honeymoon was a failure," he said. "Was it my fault?"

"That is rather a difficult question to answer," Toria said. "If you mean have you managed to upset my marriage, the answer is yes. You certainly did your best to do so, appearing at the wedding in the way you did and frightening me into making a fool of myself. But if you think that is the reason why we have returned home so quickly you are mistaken."

"So your marriage is upset? Well, what are you going to do about it?"

Toria made a little gesture with her hands.

"What can I do?" she asked. "I have married Charles. It is unfortunate that he found out that I loved you, but he has. What is done cannot be undone. What do you expect me to do, Michael?"

"I don't expect anything."

Michael got to his feet and walked across the room to stare at the flowers on the table by the window as if he had never seen flowers before. He was unhappy and miserable.

Toria could tell by the slouch of his shoulders, by the expression in his eyes, which always appeared resentful when he was most miserable.

She walked across to him and put her hand on his arm.

"Don't be unhappy, Michael," she whispered.

He turned then and stared down at her. She was startled by the pain she saw on his face.

"What the devil can we do about it?" he said in a low voice. "I love you, Toria. I can't live without you. I know that now. What can we do about it?"

She felt as if he was forcing her to give him an answer and almost instinctively she backed away from him.

"There is nothing we can do, nothing."

"Why not? You are mine, you have always belonged to me."

"That is not true," Toria replied. "You know it is not true. You are just making things worse, torturing us both by imagining things which were never there."

"And what if I am?" Michael asked. "If one has got to live in hell, it might as well be really hellish."

He turned and walked across the room away from her.

"I have been offered several jobs," he said, "since I won this money. It is extraordinary what an interest people take in you if you are rich enough to pick and choose what you will do."

"What sort of jobs?" Toria asked.

"One is with a Charter Service in South Africa," Michael replied. "That is the one Uncle Arthur wishes me to take. He has been nagging at me every day. He would seize at any opportunity of getting me out of the way. He never has liked me."

Toria did not bother to contradict this. She felt that her father's desire to be rid of Michael was not entirely unreasonable.

"What are the other jobs?" she asked.

"Oh, most of them are extremely uninteresting," Michael said. "Some of them depend, of course, on how much I will put into the firm, but others want to take me on probation without a contract."

"What do you want to do?" Toria asked, and even as she asked the question she felt it was a mistake.

"To be with you," Michael said roughly. "You know that."

He strode across to her and stood looking down at her. His hands were deep in his pockets and he did not attempt to touch her, but she felt as if he reached out his arms and put them round her.

"I suppose I am not really rich enough," he said. "I cannot compete with the unimpeachable Charles, the generous purveyor of all good things to all good people. I am only a ne'er-do-well, and what money I have is only a flash in the pan. Easy come, easy go! I know all the answers."

"Don't, Michael, don't," Toria begged.

She knew that tone only too well. He used it as a lash to whip himself.

"Well, what is the solution?" he asked. "Go to South Africa and get out of everyone's way? Stay here and make everyone as damned miserable as I am myself?"

"But, Michael, must you be miserable?" Toria asked. "You can be happy now. You have got money—enough money, to last you for a very long time. You can pick and choose what you want to do. You can find something to interest you."

"What very helpful suggestions!" Michael mocked.

Suddenly he put out his hand and put it under Toria's chin. He lifted her face to his and stood looking down into her eyes.

"So lovely," he said quietly. "Why couldn't you have waited for me?"

There was something in his tone which brought the tears to her eyes.

"That is not fair, Michael," she said. "You know it is not."

He released her chin and then very, very slowly, almost as if he were reluctant to do so, he put his arms round her.

"I can't go on without you, Toria," he said. "I can't."

The tears were blinding her. She hid her face against his shoulder. He did not kiss her. They just stood there wrapped, it seemed to Toria, in an unhappiness which united them far more completely than any kiss could have done.

How long they stood, silent and miserable, she had no idea. She was conscious only of Michael, a Michael who was unhappy, a Michael who needed her and whom she yearned to help.

It was the sound of a door opening which brought to Toria the realisation of where she was and what she was doing.

She raised her head from Michael's shoulder and

even as she did so he turned, his arm still about her.

Charles stood in the doorway.

There was something in the expression on his face which made Toria give a little cry of horror.

11

For a moment everyone stood very still.

Toria felt as if she was seeing a photograph in which, arrested in action, they faced each other as dramatically as in any incident in a film.

Then Charles spoke.

"Get out of my house," he said.

His eyes, steely grey, met Michael's, dark and lurid, and for a moment the tension between the two men was so dynamic that Toria instinctively put up her hands to her face as if she were already watching an act of violence.

She felt Michael move his arms away from her; then thrusting his hands into his pockets in a characteristic gesture, he walked a few steps across the room towards Charles.

There was something arrogant in his walk, something aggressive too in the way he moved close to Charles and stood staring at him.

"I am going," he said at last, and his voice was cool and defiant. "You think you have won, don't you? You think you have got everything; but Toria is mine. She has always been mine, and you won't be able to forget that easily."

Toria wanted to cry out, to deny what he had just said, but the words would not come to her lips.

Instead she could only stand as if paralysed, knowing that Michael was deliberately taunting Charles, showing himself at his worst, speaking in his most unpleasant manner.

"You heard what I said," Charles repeated. "Get out of here."

His tone had the calm, yet vibrant note of a man used to command, but Michael paid no heed.

Like a small boy who wishes to tease an animal he continued to speak in that mocking, sneering tone which invariably made his opponent, whoever he might be, lose his temper.

"Money can buy many things in life! You have found that, of course, but one thing it cannot buy, and that is Toria's heart. She gave that to me a long time ago. She is mine! Do not forget that when she is your wife. She is really mine!"

Strangely enough Charles did not lose his temper. Instead he said seriously and calmly:

"I think Toria at the moment belongs to no one. She has it in her power to give herself to whom she pleases, and when she pleases. You and I would do well to remember that, Gale."

It was perhaps his calm, unhurried voice which angered Michael more than anything else.

He drew his hand from his pocket and Toria saw with a feeling of horror that his fist was clenched.

She knew then that he was going to strike Charles, and swiftly with a quickness that almost preceded thought she flung herself across the room and clung with both hands to Michael's arms.

"No, Michael," she said. "No!"

Then, as he tried to shake her off, she added:

"Go! Please go!"

He looked down at her and she knew that the moment for violence was over. Michael was suddenly a little boy who was afraid that his threats and boastings might be challenged.

His eyes met Toria's and she knew there was an appeal in them.

But she could say nothing to comfort or support him, and after a moment with an almost pathetic effort to recapture his lost dignity Michael said:

"I will go because you ask me."

Without looking again at Charles he strode from the room.

They heard the front door slam behind him.

Toria felt relief sweep over her and realised that she was trembling. She was alone with Charles and suddenly she felt afraid of this calm, self-composed man whom she had married.

If he had said more, if he had hit Michael, she felt it would have been easier to understand than this rigid self-control.

She felt herself unable to look at him, and in a voice so low that she could hardly hear it herself she whispered:

"I am sorry, Charles."

He did not reply, and nervousness galvanised her into speech. Still without looking at him she went on:

"You must try to understand. Michael is desperately unhappy. He has always had me to turn to; I have always been there, and he cannot get used to the idea that I am married to someone else. If only he could get a job he would be different, I am sure of it. He has had so much to put up with in life. It has given him a feeling of frustration and bitterness."

She paused for lack of breath. Charles did not answer her. Instead he walked towards the window and stood there with his back to the room and looked out on to the street.

There was something uncompromising in the breadth of his shoulders and in his unbroken silence so that after a moment Toria went on:

"Please, Charles, do not be angry. You must not take anything Michael says too seriously. When he is upset, he very often loses all self-control."

There was another pause before Charles spoke.

"Are you telling me that what he said was not true?" he asked. "You are not in love with him?"

Toria clasped her hands together.

"I don't know, Charles. I honestly don't know. I have loved Michael always, but I never thought loving him meant anything more than the love of a brother and sister until . . . until just a few weeks ago. I don't know what I do feel. I only want to help Michael. It is agony to see him suffering so deeply."

"I see!"

It seemed to Toria that Charles sighed, but she was not sure. He turned from the window and came towards her.

"I came back to tell you," he said in a different tone, "that unfortunately I have to go down to the Air Ministry again this afternoon. They want a rather fuller report on what happened to us on the yacht. I thought perhaps you would like to go home. I have ordered the car for you at two o'clock."

Toria felt as if she had suddenly been let out of prison. Charles was going to say no more then about what had occurred this morning.

He was setting her free, releasing her from the embarrassment and discomfort which had seemed to hold her with a grip-like intensity from the moment he had come into the room and found her in Michael's arms.

It was with an air of relief and yet strangely enough with a feeling of emptiness and dissatisfaction that she forced herself to say:

"Thank you, I would like to go home. Will you come down yourself after you have finished at the Air Ministry?"

"I think not," Charles replied. "I shall expect you back in time for dinner."

"Very well," Toria replied.

She looked at her wrist watch.

"Luncheon will be ready in a moment. I had better go upstairs and tidy myself."

She almost ran from the room. When she reached her dressing-table and looked in the mirror, she exclaimed with horror at her appearance. Her cheeks were tear-stained, there were dark lines under her eyes.

She powdered her face and rearranged her hair, then went slowly downstairs again.

What had occurred between Michael and Charles had left her feeling curiously depleted.

She was beginning to feel that it was too much for her to cope with—all these emotions which seemed to revolve round her, forcing her to feel things that she had no wish to feel, compelling her into situations from which naturally she shrank in horror.

How difficult life was, she thought. She had no desire to hurt anyone, to make anyone unhappy, yet she was forced into doing that very thing both to Michael and Charles.

Michael was utterly miserable. She could not pretend even to herself that she was being anything but cruel to Charles.

He loved her, for he had told her so; and even if his love was not such an overwhelming and soul-destroying emotion as that which tortured Michael, the knowledge that she, Toria, was in love with someone else could not do anything but make him feel abjectly unhappy.

It was in very low spirits that Toria journeyed to the Castle.

Then as the car turned in at the Lodge gates, she felt a sudden warmth invade her at the thought of being home again. The bumpiness of the drive was cosily familiar and when she saw the ugly, dilapidated house she felt the tears start in her eyes.

She was home, home where she belonged, home with her own people.

It was impossible to be miserable from the moment she stepped out at the front door.

There was the usual pandemonium which invariably greeted one of the family when they returned home. She had telephoned to say that she was coming, and the twins and the spaniels were waiting for her on the doorstep.

It was difficult to know who made the most noise. There were shouts and cries and questions that no one could hear or attempt to answer, all mixed up with the yelps and barks that rose to a deafening crescendo as Brandy and Soda flung themselves on Toria, pawing at her in excitement and then rushed barking ferociously round and round the hall table.

"Why are you back so soon?"

"What has happened?"

"Do tell us everything!"

"Oh, Toria, it is wonderful to see you!"

The twins did not give her a chance to reply.

She could only hug them, feeling their cheeks warm

beneath her lips, knowing she had been hungry for the clinging affection of their arms round her neck.

At length they moved into the sitting-room.

The windows were open on to the garden, the sun was pouring in on the faded, threadbare rugs.

It was all very untidy, and it even seemed more threadbare and shabbier than Toria had remembered it, but it was home.

"Oh, darlings, tell me everything that has happened since I went away," she began; but the twins expostulated vigorously:

"Of course not! We want to hear about you. Why are you back so soon? Didn't you like Monte Carlo?"

She had agreed with Charles that the least said about their adventure the better, and so now she must lie to them, wishing at the same time that she could tell them the truth.

"Charles had to get back to the Air Ministry," she said.

"How mean of them interfering with your honeymoon," Xandra exclaimed. "What is your new house like? We are longing to see it."

"You must come up tomorrow," Toria said, feeling that this was on safer ground.

There were cries of delight, and when she had answered two or three dozen questions about the house, she at length remembered to ask:

"Where is Lettice?"

"She has gone over to see Susan Butler. She had left before your telephone message came. She will be as sick as mud to have missed you."

"Won't she be back for tea?" Toria asked.

"She might be, but I don't expect so," Xandra answered. "Lettice has become as thick as thieves with Susan Butler. They sit and talk about men for hours and hours. It is terribly dull and Susan cries because Michael does not love her. She is awfully sloppy but Lettice likes her. She has forbidden us to call her 'Phone and Photo' any more."

"Perhaps that is a good thing," Toria said. "It was rather unkind."

"She does not know what we call her, so I don't see that it matters," Xandra said. "She is a boring girl anyway. We are very glad Michael did not marry her."

"Is Michael here?" Toria made herself ask.

Olga shook her head.

"He went off to London early this morning. He is terribly disagreeable these days. We think he must be missing you. He does not even seem interested in the money he won. When we ask him what he is going to do with it, he says, 'Chuck it down the drain'."

"We are all missing you," Xandra said impulsively. "I wish you hadn't got married, Toria."

Toria refrained with some difficulty from saying that she wished so too.

It was difficult for her to believe that she could ever fill her life again as she had when she had lived at home —with her job, the twins, Michael and all the intimacies of a family life.

Suddenly she remembered that she had the news of her father's marriage to break to the twins.

So much had happened since her father had come to see her that morning that she had almost forgotten what a shock the announcement of his intending marriage had been to her.

Now she recalled it and hated the task he had set her of telling the children. But it had got to be done and it was no use shirking it.

Toria sat down in the window seat and drew Xandra and Olga down beside her.

"Listen, Twins," she said. "I have got some news for you about Daddy."

She saw the twins give a quick glance at each other, and went on:

"He has asked me to tell you something because he was rather shy of telling you himself."

"Bet you we can guess what it is!" Xandra said.

"I am sure you can't," Toria replied.

"We can, can't we, Olga?" Xandra said. "He is going to be married."

"How did you know?" Toria asked in astonishment.

"We heard him telephoning the Registrar one morn-

230

ing," Xandra said. "He was making enquiries about getting married, and Olga said: 'I am sure he is going to marry Mrs. Hagar-Bassett.' I said he couldn't be, but when she came to the wedding we were both certain of it, weren't we, Olga?"

Olga nodded agreement.

"We did not say anything about it to you or anyone else, because Olga said it would be wrong, because we had overheard Daddy talking and that was eavesdropping. So we have kept what we knew a secret. That was right, wasn't it?"

"Quite right," Toria said, and then suddenly she began to laugh. "You really are incorrigible, you know. One can't keep anything from you. I thought you would both be horrified. I was stunned when Daddy told me."

"We have thought about it very seriously," Xandra replied. "We don't mind, do we, Olga?"

"We did a little at first, but then we sort of understood it from Daddy's point of view. It is awfully dull for him here and he does like talking to Mrs. Hagar-Bassett."

"How do you know that?" Toria asked.

"He always looks so interested when he comes away from her," Xandra said. "You know, smiling and rather smug, with a sort of shining look like he has after dinner when some of his friends have been here and they have sat talking over the port. He never looks like that when he is with us."

Toria clasped the twins to her suddenly. How wise they were, she thought, and how much more they saw than anybody imagined!

Even as she thought this she realised that the twins should go to school. It was not good for them being here, watching grown-ups, being perceptive beyond their years, being perhaps too intuitive and sensitive.

They should not be worrying about grown-ups but be romping with children of their own age, playing hockey and tennis, and deciding who was going to beat whom in Form.

Yes, it was time they went to school. Charles was

right. But she did not say any of this aloud, instead she remarked:

"We must all try and be nice to Mrs. Hagar-Bassett. It will be hard at first to settle down with a family like ours."

Charles must find it difficult, too, she thought suddenly, and decided that if Charles with his wisdom, his common-sense and generosity found it difficult, what could one expect from a complete outsider, someone who had never lived their type of life, and knew nothing about it?

"I think, when we know Mrs. Hagar-Bassett better, we will like her," Olga said unexpectedly.

"Why do you say that?" Toria asked.

"We took a good look at her at the Wedding," Olga replied. "After all, Xandra and I thought that she might be our step-mother, so it seemed a good opportunity to get to know her, and when you and Charles had gone away, we went up and talked to her."

"What did you say?" Toria asked curiously.

"We started off by asking if she liked Brandy and Soda," Xandra explained, "and she said she did. We thought she must be nice if she liked animals. Then she started to talk to us. She was quite decent and ordinary, and did not speak peculiarly because we were children. You know that type of voice.

"She said how much she had wanted to see the Castle, how lovely you were. She was quite humble about it all and spoke of Daddy almost in an awed way as if she thought he was wonderful."

"Her eyes smiled when her lips did," Olga added quickly, "and though she was anxious to be nice to us, she didn't say anything that made one squirm. Not like Susan Butler's father who makes us feel as if we were sugar cakes and he might be going to eat us."

Toria laughed.

"I know exactly what you mean. People used to talk to me like that. I am not certain that some of them don't now."

"It is because we are pretty and the daughters of an
232

Earl," Xandra said in an unselfconscious manner, "but it makes me feel sick."

"Mrs. Hagar-Bassett said something else just when she was leaving," Olga remarked. "We had walked to the front door with her and she stooped down to pat Brandy. As she did so she said,

" 'There's a nice lot of you, isn't there? One wants a lot of people in a home, otherwise when one person goes away it makes such a terrible gap'."

"We knew exactly what she meant," Xandra said, "because supposing there had only been two of us and one had got married, it would have been awful for the one left behind. We hated you going away, Toria; but at least Olga and I had each other."

Toria got to her feet feeling that the twins had explained Mrs. Hagar-Bassett to her far more skillfully than she could ever have explained her to them.

In fact, the last remnants of the slight resentment she had felt at her father's marriage had gone.

A woman about the house might make all the difference, she thought, especially one who was prepared to see to the food, to mother the twins and be fond of the dogs.

And yet it was impossible not to feel that in some ways she herself was being ousted from a place she had held for so long. As the eldest she had tried to mother the family.

She had done her best, but she had not always been successful, in fact now she felt she had been a complete failure.

Her father had been lonely and unsatisfied, Michael was unhappy, the twins had grown too old for their years, and the house itself had not been well run.

With the indifference of youth towards food she had been quite content to leave the cooking to Mrs. Fergusson's incapable hands.

She had not realised that her father found it irksome, if not intolerable, to be served day after day with badly minced Shepherd's Pie or indifferently cooked fish.

She had not thought that he might have had preferences for other things than Tapioca pudding and fruit that was always stewed without sufficient sugar.

"I have been most inefficient," Toria thought, looking at a torn pelmet over one window and a curtain with a frayed hem hanging from another.

There were so many things she might have done which had been left either to Mrs. Fergusson or just ignored.

There is nothing more severe and unmerciful than youth's criticism of itself. Toria regarded with a merciless eye the past years when she had been at home and she felt guilty.

She would not listen to her own excuses of extreme youth or the desire to enjoy herself or of a happy-go-lucky nature which just did not notice when things were wrong.

She condemned herself utterly with a sudden return of the misery which had been hers earlier in the day. If she had been so inefficient at home, she would obviously be just as inefficient as a wife to Charles.

It was not even in her power to make Michael happy.

Then she knew that in whatever else she had failed she at least had the love and affection of her younger sisters. It was only too obvious in the way they looked at her, in their little hands clutching hers, in the manner Olga with a sudden sigh of satisfaction laid her head against her shoulder.

"It is lovely to have you back, Toria," Olga said softly.

"You look awfully pretty too," Xandra exclaimed, not to be outdone. "Are you happy, Toria, really and truly happy with Charles?"

Toria wanted to lie, to say the easiest thing which came into her head, but somehow she could not.

"I don't know," she answered at length. "It is rather difficult being married at first to someone you do not know very well."

"I wouldn't mind being married to Charles," Xandra said. "He is a nice homely sort of person. You feel warm and comfortable with him. You know he would never leave you out in the cold."

"I suppose that is true," Toria answered a little doubtfully.

She was thinking of Charles' face when he came into the drawing-room and saw her in Michael's arms. What was he thinking now? Was he angry with her?

Ever since she had been a child she had hated that anyone should be cross with her, that she should feel out of tune with those around her. As sensitive as the twins in their own way, a harsh word or an unkind criticism could always reduce her to pulp.

Now she knew that the misery which had encompassed her on her way down to the Castle was due to the fact that she believed Charles to be angry with her.

The dogs got up suddenly from the hearth-rug and ran towards the door barking savagely.

"Who is it?" Toria asked.

"Michael, I expect," Xandra replied. "They usually make that noise at him; I cannot think why. You would think they would know what he sounds like by now."

The dogs had disappeared through the sitting-room door which was half ajar. They heard the barks in the hall change to whines as if they were greeting an acquaintance.

Toria did not move from the window seat but the twins got to their feet as if they knew the moment of intimacy with their elder sister was at an end.

"Michael," Xandra called, "Toria is in here!"

He had been crossing the hall to go to his workshop, Toria decided, for she heard his footsteps stop and march briskly towards the sitting-room. He came through the doorway and stood looking at her.

"You didn't tell me you were coming here," he said accusingly.

"I did not know myself at the time," Toria replied. "Charles did not tell me he had ordered the car to bring me here until after you had gone."

"Have you seen each other already today?" Xandra enquired.

"Yes, I went to Toria's house," Michael said. "It is built of gold and upholstered in diamonds. Frightfully opulent and over-luxurious."

235

"Nonsense," Toria said sharply. "That is not true! It is a dear little house and very unpretentious."

"Just like its owner, of course," Michael remarked unpleasantly.

"Michael, don't be horrid," Toria pleaded.

He grinned unexpectedly.

"I am not feeling horrid, I am feeling excited. Shall I tell you why?"

"Yes, of course."

"I have had the offer of a job that will really interest me."

"A job!" Xandra exclaimed. "What sort of one, Michael?"

Michael looked at the three pairs of blue eyes staring up expectantly; then he stood with his back to the fire, his hands as usual in his pockets. Toria thought that he was preening himself a little and she felt her spirits rise.

If Michael had found a job which he really liked, everything might be all right.

"You have told me so often," Michael began, "that I ought to be on the films that I have begun to believe you. When I got a letter from a Film Company after my photograph had appeared in the paper as winning the football pool, I made an appointment to go and see them.

"They took some tests of me and while I was at the Studio I started talking to a chap who designed the sets. I made one or two suggestions as to how certain technical difficulties could be overcome. He was impressed and asked me to get out some sketches.

"I sent them to him yesterday, and to my surprise I got a telephone call first thing this morning asking me to call. I went there after I left you, Toria. I saw one of their executives from Hollywood. It is an American Film Company, by the way, working over here. To cut a long story short they have asked me to go out to Hollywood and work for them for a year.

"They are delighted with my suggestions, they like the sketches I have done, and they want more, many more of them. I am to specialise in mechanical inven-

236

tions; in short I have at last been offered a job which is just up my street."

Michael finished on a note of triumph. Toria jumped to her feet.

"Oh, Michael, how wonderful! It is the most marvelous thing I have ever heard."

"I have always believed that there must be an outlet for my ideas somewhere," Michael went on, "and now I have found it."

"Oh, but Michael, we would much rather you were on the films," Xandra exclaimed. "Now we shan't be able to go and see you act."

"Can you see me acting, if it comes to that?" Michael asked. "I should hate it, and I would be damned sorry for the leading lady if she had to put up with me scowling at her when they wanted me to smile. I never have been able to do what I am told."

"That is true enough," Toria said. "You would hate to be a film actor, Michael; but this sounds really interesting."

"They want me to make models too," Michael went on. "I shall like that, but it is the mechanical side which interests me the most. This fellow I saw today knew what he was talking about. He is the boss of the department and he told me I should have a free hand and pretty well as much money as I wanted. That's the stuff, no cheese-paring because they can't afford a dozen tintacks."

"Oh, Michael, it sounds wonderful," Toria exclaimed. "I am so excited."

"I want to show you some sketches I have done," Michael smiled. "Come along to the workshop."

He led the way, then stopped at the door.

"Not you, Twins," he said. "I will show them to you another time."

"But, Michael, that isn't fair," Xandra cried, "and Toria is not here for long."

"I can stay until nearly dinner time," Toria answered. "Get your coats and go up to the summerhouse. I will join you there as soon as Michael has finished with me."

"All right," the twins agreed, "but don't be long."

The summer-house was a place they had made their own. It was in reality an old and tumble-down tennis pavilion, but it was the twins' special and private den and no one could enter but by special invitation. On the door was a huge notice reading "PRIVATE—KEEP OUT—THAT MEANS YOU!"

Toria was well aware that Michael's suggestion about showing her his sketches was only an excuse to get her alone. In fact, no sooner had they reached the big, untidy workroom than he closed the door behind them and said:

"I want to talk to you, Toria."

"I guessed that," Toria replied. "All the same, I would like to see the sketches."

"They are not here," Michael answered. "I have left them at the Studio."

"I am so very glad about this job," Toria said. "You wanted to get away from here, and there's another reason why it is a good thing; Daddy was married at twelve o'clock this morning."

"Uncle Arthur! Good God! Whatever for?"

"He has married Mrs. Hagar-Bassett," Toria replied, "and actually we are all rather pleased about it."

"Pleased about it!" Michael exclaimed. "Then you must be off your head. Why, it . . . it is ridiculous at your father's age."

"He is not as old as all that," Toria expostulated. "And he has been very lonely for a long time."

"What has he got to be lonely about?" Michael enquired.

"Don't be horrid, Michael," Toria said. "The twins have been very understanding about it, and you are not to be beastly to Mrs. Hagar-Bassett when she comes here. She will be quite shy and frightened enough without your making it any more difficult for her than it need be."

Michael shrugged his shoulders.

"I can't stop your father making a fool of himself," he said, "but if you want to know the truth, I think it is

238

all rather disgusting—a man of his age marrying a common little woman like that."

"Michael, Michael, how little you see beyond the length of your own nose," Toria exclaimed. "You talk an awful lot about your own suffering, but you don't imagine that anyone else is ever unhappy or lonely or in the need of companionship."

"Most people can look after themselves," Michael said contemptuously. "I haven't got time for them and heaven knows they have not got time for me. But if Uncle Arthur likes to make a fool of himself, I can't stop him and I certainly shan't worry my head about it. I want to talk about you and me."

"Must we?" Toria asked a little wistfully. "Does talking make things any better, Michael? Now that you are going away, let us try and forget everything except the happy times we spent together as children. I shall be here, you will be in Hollywood, so don't let us tear ourselves into bits any more. I don't think I can bear it."

"I shall be in Hollywood," Michael said, "but you will be with me."

Toria looked up sharply.

"What do you mean?"

"Exactly what I have said," Michael replied. "You are coming with me, Toria. I am not leaving you behind."

"But, Michael, that is impossible!"

"Oh, no, it isn't. You married this man Drayton for one reason and for one reason only, because you thought it would help me. Well, it didn't. You were damned silly to imagine for one moment that it would.

"I ought to have stopped you, but I felt that, if you wanted to be such a fool, you might as well bear the consequences of your own folly. I did not know then that if you did go away from me, I wouldn't be able to bear it. But I had nothing to offer you, nothing save failure and incompetence.

"Now everything is different. I have got a large sum of money in the Bank, I have got a job which is going to bring me in thousands of dollars. You are mine, Toria, as I told that pompous husband of yours this morning.

You have always been mine! You are coming to Hollywood with me."

"But, Michael, how can I?" Toria asked. "I am married! I am Charles' wife."

"Are you?" Michael asked. "Are you really?"

Toria's eyes dropped before his and she didn't answer.

"I thought not!"

His tone was elated.

"I was sure of it when I saw you this morning. You are just as you were—mine, and now you will never belong to anyone else."

"But, Michael, I can't run away. Charles has been kind to me. He has never done anything wrong. He married me because he loved me. The only person who has behaved badly has been me in accepting him when I knew I loved you."

"Do you think you can make things better by staying with a man you don't love? My dear Toria, you will only make things worse. Come away with me, cut yourself free from your old mistakes. We will start a new life in America and we will be happy together, terribly happy. You know that."

"I wonder," Toria said quietly.

"You wonder what?" Michael asked frowning.

"If we would really be happy together," Toria answered. "You have not always been happy with me in the past, Michael. You have been moody, disagreeable and miserable, and I have not been able to prevent it."

"That is because I had no money," he replied. "It was impossible for me to be happy when I was depending on your father for every single penny I had in my pocket and for every bite of food I put into my mouth. I wanted to be independent, I wanted a life of my own, but I still wanted you."

Toria put her hands to her eyes.

"Wait, Michael, I have got to think what you are saying. I have got to think it out for—both of us. You say you wanted me, but did you really want me enough? Was it not just the fact that you could not have me that made you so bitter? I did not make you want to work for me, to strive at something you did not like so that we could be married and be together."

She felt Michael draw her fingers down from her eyes.

"What are you talking about?" he asked. "Are you trying to suggest that I don't love you? If you are, you are talking nonsense and you know it. I love you more than I have ever loved anyone else in the whole world. I love you and I intend to have you. You will come with me to Hollywood."

"I can't, Michael, I can't," Toria cried. "It would be wrong."

She broke away from him as she spoke, and moved across the room to the big chair she had occupied so often in the past. Hardly knowing what she did, she sat down.

"It would be wrong," she repeated.

Without looking at Michael she knew that he was drawing near to her. Suddenly he was down on his knees beside her, his arms were round her shoulders and his cheek was against hers.

"You have to come away with me," he whispered urgently. "I can't go on without you any longer. You have got to look after me, to love me and to make me all the things you want me to be. This is our one big chance, the only one I have ever had. You can't fail me now, Toria."

"But what can I do?" Toria asked. "I can't leave Charles; I can't just walk out on him. It would be cruel after all the publicity, after all the excitement over our wedding."

"Is that all you are thinking about?" Michael asked. "The publicity in the newspapers . . . 'England's war hero and the lovely daughter of an Earl'. I thought your feelings were stronger and finer than that claptrap."

"They are! They are!" Toria cried. "But you can understand what would be said if I ran away within a week of being married. If the newspapers got hold of it, it would be terrible and might damage Charles' career."

"Damn Charles and damn his career! What about

241

me? I can't go without you, Toria, and what is more I won't go unless you come with me."

"Don't say that, please don't say that, Michael," Toria begged. "You have got to go. As you say yourself, this is your opportunity. It can't depend on me; you mustn't make it."

"But it does," Michael insisted. "If you don't come with me, then I won't go. I will stay here and make life hell for Mrs. Hagar-Bassett."

His lips twisted in the ghost of a smile, but there was somehow a ring of truth in his voice which made Toria realise that he was not speaking jokingly.

"This is not fair, Michael," she said accusingly.

"What does it matter if it is fair or not?" Michael asked. "Toria, I have always loved you. You have never failed me yet; you can't fail me now. If you come with me to Hollywood, I shall be a success, I shall be rich, I feel it in my bones. This is something I can do and do well. I shall make a name for myself, but only if you are there with me. Charles will divorce you and we can be married within a few months. You have got to come, Toria, you have got to."

"It is crazy, insane," Toria exclaimed, trying to push Michael away from her; but he refused to move.

"Then it is a glorious, wonderful insanity. I love you, Toria. I love you so much."

His arms tightened round her, and now she could feel his mouth seeking hers.

"No, Michael, no," she pleaded. "Don't kiss me. We have got to think."

"I will do the thinking for both of us," he replied, and she was unable to answer him for his mouth was pressed against hers.

For a moment she was unable to free herself, feeling his possessiveness bruise her lips, while it sapped her mind, and then with a tremendous effort she wrenched her mouth from his.

"No, Michael, no," she stammered.

"I love you, Toria," he murmured in her ear, "and you love me."

"Yes, I love you, Michael," Toria answered a little

brokenly, "but not enough to do the cruel and beastly thing of ruining someone else's life."

Michael laughed.

"Do you really believe that?" he asked. "Charles will recover, even if he loves you as much as you think he does. If you ask me, I don't think he understands love, not as you and I know it. He is too complacent, too pleased with himself. It is not a fire within him as it is with us."

Michael's arms tightened round her again as he spoke.

"Don't kiss me again, Michael," Toria begged. "I must think, I must try. . . ."

She was unable to say more. Once again Michael's lips were on hers, demanding, compelling, possessing her it seemed almost completely, so that there was nothing she could do but surrender herself to him.

She felt as if she were sinking, drowning in deep waters from which it was impossible to rescue herself. She was sinking lower, the water was closing over her head.

She could feel the pressure of Michael's hands, she knew his heart was beating violently against her breasts.

She wanted to cry out, to stop herself from becoming utterly subservient to him, yet she was powerless to do anything but drown in this love, to slip into an unconsciousness from which she felt wildly there would be no return.

And then, just when she was certain that there was nothing she could do, that every coherent thought was passing from her, there came a shrill call through the window.

"Toria! Toria! Do come on! We are waiting for you!"

It was Xandra who shouted, and her voice brought Toria back from the depths. She moved in Michael's arms and he relinquished her lips.

It took her a moment or two to get enough breath to answer Xandra. Again the call came, more shrill this time:

"Toria, are you there? Do hurry!"

"I am coming, Xandra. I am coming now."

Toria thought her voice sounded strange, but apparently Xandra was satisfied.

"Come on then."

Toria looked into Michael's eyes.

"Let me go," she said.

Very slowly he took his arms from around her.

"For the moment," he replied, "but only for the moment. We leave in three days' time."

Toria's eyes widened.

"Are you going as soon as that?"

"If you come with me," he answered. "The contract is not yet signed. I can always tear it up."

He rose to his feet as he spoke and putting out his hand, drew Toria to hers, then he looked down at her. Her fair hair hardly reached to his shoulder.

"So little, yet so important," he teased, a sudden tenderness in his voice which was far more effectively compelling than when he tried to bully her.

"I can't do it, Michael, I can't," Toria whispered.

"You will come," he said confidently. "You can't spoil my life, you can't make me refuse the only decent chance I have ever had."

"You must go without me."

"I have told you that I won't. It is all settled. Don't struggle any more. You are mine and I won't give you up to anyone."

Toria made a sudden helpless gesture with her hands.

"I have said no, Michael, and it is no use going on talking about it. I can't come with you; you know I can't."

"Very well then, that settles it."

Michael drew a long foolscap envelope from the inside pocket of his coat. He held it between his hands and Toria gave a sudden cry.

"Michael, what are you going to do?"

"Tear up the contract."

"No, no, you mustn't, you mustn't."

She put both her hands on his, but his muscles were taut.

"Will you come with me?"

"Yes . . . no . . . I don't know. Oh, Michael, why must you behave like this?"

"Because I love you. That is obvious, isn't it? Well which is it to be?"

He bent the envelope slightly and began to tear the outer edge.

"You have got to accept this job," Toria cried. "You have got to go."

"Will you come with me?"

She shut her eyes for a moment. She felt as if the blood were draining away from her head and her heart.

"I suppose so," she said at last in a very small voice.

Michael put the envelope back into his pocket.

"I thought you would," he said.

He put out his arms towards her, but Toria turned away from him. She was crying as she left the room to run through the hall into the garden in search of the twins.

12

It seemed to Toria that the next two days had an unreal nightmare quality in which she moved as if groping in a fog with blinded eyes, unable to do anything but go on, even though she had no idea where she was going.

She felt as if there was nothing she could do, no one to whom she could turn for help, no escape from a dilemma which was so intense and so acutely personal that she could not think coherently or do anything but suffer because of it.

Where Charles was concerned, she felt an undisputable guilt; and because of it and also because she was afraid to relax for one moment from the part she must play in front of him, she made it impossible for them to be alone together even for a few minutes.

Frantically she telephoned her friends, filling the house with them, and making sure that, when finally the front door closed behind the last guest, there was no possibility that Charles would have even a few minutes' intimate conversation with her.

"I'm dead tired," she would say, as her friends rose to say good-night. "You won't think me rude if I slip off to bed? Charles will see you out."

Frantically she would rush to her bedroom and undressing with almost breakneck speed, would have the light out before Charles came upstairs.

She heard him hover outside her room for a moment and then walk slowly away.

It was not difficult to avoid Charles, who was apparently particularly tactful for some reason of his own, and took up his work again at the Air Ministry as if they had never intended to go honeymooning.

He left for the office at half past nine and returned at six.

Once Toria thought he was about to say something when he came to her bedroom after breakfast to say good-bye, and with a feeling that was almost frantic she reached for the little bell which lay beside her bed and pressed it.

It was only a minute before her maid appeared and the knock on the door checked the words which seemed about to come from Charles' lips.

"I must be off," he said hastily. "Have we got anyone dining tonight?"

"Yes, four," Toria replied, reeling off a list of names, "and I have asked two or three people in for drinks at six o'clock. Everyone is so anxious to see the house."

"Yes, of course," Charles said a little vaguely.

He went from the room, while Jean hovered in the doorway, waiting to hear why Toria had summoned her so imperiously.

The Twins came up the day after Toria had been to the Castle; they had luncheon in the house and were thrilled with everything they saw. They also brought a message from Michael.

"He wants you to telephone him," Xandra said, "at half past four. Don't forget. He made us promise to tell you to ring him."

When half past four came, Toria made an excuse to

slip out of the house and go to the telephone box up the road.

There was no reason why she could not have telephoned to Michael from her own bedroom. They would not have been overheard; but she had a sudden reluctance to speak to Michael from Charles' house.

It took her some time to get through, but at last the Operator told her to press Button A and she heard his voice.

"Is that you, Toria?"

"Yes, Michael, what do you want?"

"I want to tell you that everything is arranged. Our aeroplane leaves on Wednesday morning. We have got to be aboard by seven o'clock."

Toria said nothing and after a moment Michael said: "Are you there?"

"Yes, of course," Toria replied. "I was thinking."

"About what?"

"How I can get to the aerodrome."

She felt suddenly limp and helpless.

"It is quite easy," Michael said impatiently. "You will have to order a car. You may not be able to pick up a taxi so early. You had better leave at six o'clock before anyone is up."

"Yes, of course."

It was almost as if she could not take in what he was saying.

"I must say you don't sound very cheerful about it."

"I am not particularly," Toria replied.

"Oh, don't fuss about that idiotic husband of yours," Michael snapped. "He will be all right. Better leave a note for him telling him to divorce you as soon as possible, and then we can be married out there. I must say the more I hear about the job, the more it appeals to me. It is going to be extremely interesting, there is no doubt about that. We shall have a lot of fun, Toria, as well."

"Michael, listen, won't you go without me?" Toria pleaded. "You won't want me when you get into a new place with new people. You will be all right then. Leave

247

me behind. It is going to make everything in such a mess our going off together."

"You have got to come." Michael's voice was angry now. "I have told you that I won't go without you. If you fail me, Toria, you will ruin my life. That is what you will do, ruin it for ever."

"All right!"

Toria's acceptance was dull and hardly above a whisper.

"Don't be afraid of that pompous airman you have married," Michael went on. "We are going to have a wonderful time together, you can be sure of that. Now just arrange everything and I will be waiting for you at the aerodrome at half past six. Don't bring a tremendous amount of luggage. It is so expensive. You can have your other things sent on by sea."

"All right," Toria said again, and the conversation ended.

She thought as she walked back to the house that it was so typical of Michael to leave her to make all the arrangements. It would have been nice if he could have picked her up.

She dreaded leaving the house alone and having that lonely drive to the aerodrome.

She felt that she was running away not only from Charles, but from everything that was right and conventional.

"I don't think I was cut out to be an adulteress," Toria thought to herself with a little wry twist of her lips as she went into the house.

She had left the twins in the dining-room, eating a large tea of iced cakes and chocolate biscuits; but now as she opened the door she realised that they were not alone. Charles was with them.

She felt her heart give a sudden jump as if she had been caught out in doing something wrong; then she realised that he could not have known where she was, as he would have approached the house from a different direction.

He rose gravely to his feet and smiled at her.

"I got away early today," he said. "I remembered

that you had said the twins were coming to tea, and I wanted to see my new sisters-in-law."

"Is that what we are?" Xandra exclaimed. "I had not thought of it. Doesn't it sound grand?"

"It is nice having a brother-in-law," Olga said.

Toria slipped into her place and picked up the silver teapot to pour herself out some tea. Charles sat down again and began to chatter with the twins.

He had a way of being easy and completely at home with children, Toria thought. He was not unnaturally jovial or irritatingly facetious. He was just simple and unaffected and it was obvious that Xandra and Olga were completely at their ease with him.

In fact they were so absorbed in Charles that Toria felt a pang of jealousy. This was her family and for the moment Charles seemed more at home with them than she did herself.

She knew it was her guilty conscience that was making her feel as if she were an outsider, and combined with that was the recollection that she was cutting herself off from this kind of life.

It was not that she would not be able to see the twins or be with them when she was married to Michael; it was just that she knew instinctively that, once Michael was established in Hollywood, he would not want to come home again.

Since the war he had not been happy in England. He had not settled down. He had been nothing but frustrated and disagreeable. If this job really suited him, he would be a voluntary exile, and Toria's whole instinct cried out at the thought.

She loved England. She was, though she did not often announce it to herself in such a manner, intensely patriotic. The place where she was born, the people to whom she belonged, meant a great deal to her.

She had never been to Hollywood, but her mental picture of it was of a place bright with sunshine and far too full of glamourous and exotic people.

She knew that, once Michael was really interested in a thing, his energy was almost dynamic. He never seemed to get tired.

When he was working on something that interested him, the whole of his concentration would be pinpointed on some particular object to the exclusion of everything else. At times like that he would be indefatigable.

At the thought of it Toria suddenly felt very tired herself. She foresaw, as Michael refused to see, many difficulties ahead of them. It was not going to be easy to explain her own and Michael's position with each other.

Even if she was unknown in America, she at least had a title and that would make her interesting to a certain number of people.

There would be searching questions, there would be moments of intense embarrassment. There would be times when she would hate Michael because he had destroyed so much and given her so little in return.

She tried to tell herself that love counted for more than anything; and yet, as she balanced Michael's love against losing the twins, the Castle, her friends and all that was dear and familiar to her, she felt as if by going away with Michael she was losing everything and gaining nothing.

It was wrong to feel like that, Toria told herself not once but a thousand times. She would lie awake at night trying to recapture the moments of happiness that she had felt with him.

She would try to tell herself how vitally important it was that Michael should have his chance and that she ought to be proud to give it to him. But somehow the only thing of which she was really acutely conscious was a heaviness within her.

It seemed to grow hour by hour, this heavy lump between her breasts, until it was almost like acute indigestion and she could not escape from it.

"Michael must have his chance," she said not once, but a thousand times to herself until the words became meaningless, almost like a slogan in a foreign language which was quite unintelligible.

Michael must have his chance; but if he did not?

She thought of his unhappiness, of his sullen, difficult moods when he was disappointed in anything; his frustration would make it more difficult than anything else could ever be.

She knew that she could not face the future if Michael were to tear up his contract with Hollywood because of her. There was nothing she could do but go with him.

As she tossed restlessly on her bed, she would wonder sometimes if it would not be better to die and let the world go on without her. It is always so easy to make a tremendous decision; but it is the little things which follow it which are far more nerve-racking, far more upsetting.

Having said that she would go with Michael, Toria had to scheme how it could be done. It was easy to order a car to come for her just before six, but it was a little difficult to explain why it should wait at the corner of Hill Street rather than drive up to the front door.

"There is somebody ill in the house," Toria said at last. "I do not want them to be awakened."

The man who took the order said he understood, but she felt suddenly ashamed that she must lie even to the manager of a garage.

That having been done, she had somehow to get hold of her suitcase and pack it. Jean had arranged all her clothes carefully into the fitted wardrobe, which were so contrived that they formed part of the panels of the room and were quite indiscernible when closed.

When everything was unpacked, Jean had taken Toria's suitcases away to the box-room, where they were piled neatly until they were wanted again.

Toria wondered for a long time how she could get hold of a suitcase as well as her dressing case, which she had discovered was kept in a cupboard on the top floor for extra safety.

She knew, if she suggested packing anything, Jean would offer to do it for her, and it would be difficult to explain why she should want to pack her own things.

It was also too dangerous to tell Jean that she was going away in case one of the other servants repeated it inadvertently to Charles.

There was another problem, too, which every woman

251

knows is the most difficult of all. What clothes should she take?

The March winds were very cold and there was still frost in the morning. People were still walking about wrapped in fur coats and wearing felt hats.

Toria had an idea, although she was not certain, that it was hot in Hollywood. Would she want cotton dresses, straw hats and sandals? What sort of things did people wear every day? Smart London clothes or casual country ones?

She felt there must be many women amongst her acquaintances who could answer these questions, but she was afraid to ring them up.

Not only was there the chance that they would ask her if she was going out there, but she also knew only too well how later her words and actions would be criticised.

"My dear, she actually rang up to ask what she would wear, and never breathed a word that she was actually running away."

She could hear their voices saying it, their heads nodding together as they sat over a women's luncheon at Claridges' or met in some comfortable little cocktail club where gossip filled the air like cigarette smoke.

Another difficulty was how to waken herself at the right time. If she were to leave the house at six, it meant that she would have to get up about five.

She had no alarm clock. She was sleeping so badly that she felt it was more than likely she would lie awake all night; yet often after hours of wakefulness it was easy to doze off about dawn.

She could not contemplate what would happen if Michael refused to go without her and found that she was late owing to having overslept.

Round and round her mind went, like a bird in a cage, trying to find a solution to not one problem but half a dozen.

There was her father. Should she write to him and tell him what she had done?

He would be upset, she was sure of that, not only because she was doing something which would react unfavourably on the family, but also because she knew in her heart of hearts that he had never liked Michael from the first moment he had come to the Castle—a dark, sullen, unaccountable schoolboy.

Michael had always been truculent, resentful of what he called taking charity, and though they imagined that the Earl saw very little of what went on in his household, he was not so blind that he could remain unaware that Michael was a continual problem. Someone who disturbed the atmosphere and who seldom appeared grateful for anything that was done for him, however kindly it was meant.

There was someone else whom Toria would have hated to hurt, and that was Charles' mother.

Mrs. Drayton had been kind to her from the moment they first met, and Toria had loved her when, after Charles had introduced them, she said:

"I know you will make Charles happy. You are so lovely, and lovely things were put into the world to make us all happy."

Mrs. Drayton adored her only son, Toria knew that and was well aware what pain it would give her to learn that Charles had been deserted, that his wife not only had run away from him, but had contrived to make him look a fool as it had happened so soon after a big and much-publicised wedding.

But at least Charles would have a mother to comfort him. Toria thought a little wistfully of the close bond which lay between mother and son.

She could still remember very vividly the sweetness of her own mother, and often it seemed to her that everything had gone wrong since Lady Lynbrooke died.

The twins could hardly remember her, but Toria yearned for her with an intensity which was at times frightening.

Every year as she grew older she realised how much she had missed in losing her mother, but she knew that in remembering her she was luckier than the twins and therefore must be the more responsible towards them.

Yet she had failed them!

She had failed to be a mother to her sisters, a companion to her father, a housekeeper for their home.

And now she was to fail yet another person—her husband. She wondered, if her mother had been alive, whether she would have wanted her to marry Charles.

Her mother would have known that she was not in love with him and she would undoubtedly have tried to guide her to be sensible.

She would have asked them to wait, to get to know each other better, to be quite sure they were suited before they became husband and wife.

There was another question, too, which Toria dreaded asking herself. Would her mother have approved of Michael?

Michael was her first cousin. Her mother, she knew, like most mothers would not approve of first cousins marrying each other.

She wondered if the old wives' tale that first cousins might produce idiot children was true or merely one of those traditional superstitions which are handed down from generation to generation.

Then as Toria tried to laugh at the idea as being obsolete and out of date, she shuddered.

She wanted children, she wanted babies of her own, but the idea that they might be born idiots through her fault was terrifying.

"I am sure it is not true," Toria cried aloud in the darkness.

But the doubt remained, like a speck of poison at the back of her mind.

Gradually the hours and the days passed, seeming to drag and linger as if she travelled endlessly down a dark corridor.

When Toria went up to bed on Tuesday night she knew it was the last time that she would sleep in the little house Charles had chosen for her.

She heard the voices of their guests outside her window.

"It has been such fun," someone exclaimed. "Goodnight, Charles. You and Toria must come and dine with us next week."

There was a slam of a car door, the sound of the engine starting up and then they were gone.

They had gone! Soon Charles would be coming upstairs.

Quickly Toria began to undress and then frantically she felt that she would not be in time. But she could not talk to Charles tonight, she simply could not. She rushed across the room and turned out the light, although she was not yet in her nightgown.

Then she hesitated and locked the door.

There was something final about the action.

It was as if she deliberately and for the last time refused Charles. She heard the click of the key in the lock and then flung herself face downwards on her bed.

"Why should I mind?" she asked herself. "I am not Charles' wife. I have never really belonged to him. It is Michael I love."

And yet she knew, even while she spoke in defiance of her better self, that she was straining her ears for the sound of Charles' footsteps coming upstairs.

First he would turn out the lights, close the windows, make sure that he had remembered to bolt the front door and put on the chain. Now he was coming.

She could hear his footsteps, slow and resonant. He had reached the landing and turned down the little passage which led to her room. She heard him hesitate outside the door.

She knew he was listening, hoping against hope perhaps that she would call him; and then slowly he turned away.

She felt as clearly as if she could see him that his shoulders had sagged, his eyes had become very tired, and that there was something almost pathetic in the expression on his face.

He was going to his own room. She heard the door close.

This was the end of her marriage, a marriage which had lasted for a very short while despite the good wishes of so many and such a variety of people.

She lay for a long time on the bed; then at length she roused herself, switched on the bedside light and finished undressing. She was shivering and her teeth chattered a little.

A pale blue chiffon nightgown trimmed with écru lace was little protection against the cold. She took her dressing-gown of sapphire velvet from the chair and wrapped it round herself.

Then she sat down at the dressing-table and began to brush her hair.

She thought of the twins' golden heads and wondered who would remind them to brush their hair.

It was the one thing she had fussed them about, feeling a personal satisfaction in seeing the burnished shine on the short waves which framed their little faces. Olga was invariably conscientious about brushing, but Xandra often forgot.

"I ought not to have got married at all. I ought to have stayed at home and looked after my sisters," Toria said aloud.

It was no use relying on anyone else, she thought.

She had imagined that Lettice would take her place, but it had been very obvious to her since she returned from her honeymoon that Lettice had no idea of taking on responsibilities which were not hers by right of birth.

Toria had learned that she spent most of her time at the Butlers' and was even at this moment staying with Susan in London.

There was no reason why Lettice should not enjoy their company. They were rich and could afford to entertain and go to theatres and do all the things which she most enjoyed; but somehow Toria felt that by being away so much she deliberately neglected the twins.

It was unreasonable, yet she resented Lettice's indifference.

Suddenly she remembered that Charles had promised to take the twins to see "The Crazy Gang" next week.

They had wanted to go for such a long time but had had neither the opportunity nor the money. Charles had told them that they could come to London and stay at the little house and that he would get seats for the first evening performance.

Toria, watching their faces alive with excitement and

gratitude, had forgotten for a moment that she would not be there. Now she remembered! Would Charles still take them?

Even as she asked the question she knew the answer. Charles would not break his promise.

He had a great sense of integrity. However upset or even affronted he might feel, he would never punish the twins for what was not their fault.

No, Charles would never break a promise.

Her thoughts shied away from the idea that she herself was breaking one far more solemn, far more sacred. It was almost as if she heard someone beside her say:

"Marriage is a sacrament, not to be entered into lightly."

She remembered the last time she had a feeling that someone was with her. She recalled almost too vividly that moment in the cabin on the yacht when she had known that her Mother was beside her.

"I am imagining things," Toria cried in sudden terror.

She jumped to her feet, she ran into the bathroom, switching on all the lights.

There was nothing she could do about it now but set forth on the course into which fate and Michael had persuaded her. It was too late to retract, too late to go back.

She had got to go forward, however wrong, however despicable it might seem to leave Charles, to leave England.

She washed her face in cold water and then taking a book from the table she got into bed and sat upright to read it. She had decided that the only way to be quite certain she would not be late for Michael was to stay awake all night.

She had tried to think of some excuse for borrowing Jean's alarm clock, but had been unable to make the request.

Anyway, there would be little time for sleep. It was already after twelve o'clock, and as soon as Charles was asleep she must go downstairs and bring up a suitcase.

She must also creep up to the top floor and fetch down her dressing-case.

She started a story called "My Heart's Desire"; but after she had turned over several pages, she realised that her brain had not taken in one word of the sentences which her eyes had followed. She lay back against the pillows. Was Michael her heart's desire?

She supposed he was, but somehow the expression did not fit him. What indeed did she know of her heart? It had brought her so far nothing but trouble, nothing but worry.

Perhaps it was not her heart which was to blame but her face? If she had been born plain, no one would have wanted her.

There would not have been this tearing sense of unhappiness. Michael would have gone happily to Hollywood alone and Charles would still have been living with his mother in contented bachelorhood.

Is beauty a blessing or a curse? Toria asked herself. And she smiled at the question. It was almost like the title of a newspaper article.

"My Heart's Desire!" She repeated the words to herself, trying to think what her ideal man had been before she became involved in this tangle of Michael's love for her and hers for him.

She remembered telling him that she would not marry Lord Pennington because she was not in love with him. How, then, at that moment had she thought of love? She could not remember.

There was some vague, shadowy man who had always lurked at the back of her mind as a kind of Prince Charming who would come along one day and sweep her off her feet, but she had never been able to put a face to him. She had only known that he was handsome, strong and brave.

What idiots girls were, Toria thought bitterly. They expected so much and never asked why an Adonis or a Sir Galahad should be expected to fall in love with them.

"Oh, Michael, Michael!"

The words seemed to be forced from her lips. She had got to save him, she had got to look after him. But he was not the hero of her childish dreams, he was just a man tortured and unhappy who could not live without her.

She lay thinking of Michael and Charles and the way she was entwined into both their lives and her eyes were wet.

It was almost with a sense of shock that she realised it was two o'clock. Now was the time to go downstairs.

She got out of bed, put on her dressing-gown and slipped her feet into the satin mules which matched it; but having put them on, she realised that they would make too much noise. The heels would tap behind her as she went downstairs.

There was nothing for it but for her to go barefooted. It would be quieter that way.

She went to her bedroom door and tried to open it. She had forgotten that she had locked the door.

As she turned the key, it seemed to her that the lock slipped back into place with an almost sinister quietness.

She opened the door and looked out.

Everything was very still. She moved silently along the carpet and down the twisting oak stairs.

The chill cold of the linoleum which was laid along the passage to the box-room was very unpleasant to her bare feet; but she found the suitcase she wanted, and making as little noise as possible, she crept back again upstairs.

The case was clumsy and awkward to carry even when empty and she wondered how she could manage to get it downstairs again when it was full. But it was no use wondering.

The die was cast! She must, whatever happened, get from the house without arousing Charles.

She felt she could not bear a wordy argument at the last moment, when she would have to tell him what she was about to do, knowing that he would never understand just why and how she was compelled to obey Michael's commands.

She got the suitcase safely into her bedroom and went upstairs for her dressing-case.

The cupboard where it was kept was next to the

maid's room, but Jean and the cook were strong country girls and Toria felt quite rightly that they would sleep soundly and not be easily disturbed.

It only took her a few seconds to open the door, take out the dressing-case and creep back to her room.

Inside it she stood breathless, her heart beating quickly.

She had done it.

The first difficulties were over, and now she must pack. She had tried again and again to come to a decision as to what she was to take with her, but now it seemed completely unimportant and she piled in the dresses which came first to hand.

The pale mauve wool dress which she had worn in Monte Carlo, the blue frock she had gone away in after her wedding, a dress of brown crêpe which she had been told was just right for cocktail parties, and a simple dinner gown.

The suitcase was full, but not too full. She hesitated whether to add an elaborate evening dress, one of the lovely filmy tulle creations which had been fashioned by one of the greatest Court dressmakers in the country.

She even took it off its hanger, then she put it back again with a decisive gesture.

She was going to Hollywood surreptitiously, a woman running away from her husband and her family. Even if she were asked to parties, she ought not to go to them.

She was someone who was behaving badly—a woman living in sin.

Toria stopped suddenly and put both hands to her throat. She had not thought of it like that before. She, Toria Gale, would be living in sin.

She remembered saying that sin was so untidy, now her life would be untidy, and because of what she had done other lives like Charles' would be in a similar state. She hated the thought of it, she felt ashamed and humiliated.

She could almost see the glances of curiosity and disdain which would be cast at her. She could hear voices whispering, people repeating who she was and what she had done.

"I can't do it, I can't."

She said the words aloud; but even as she said them she glanced at the clock.

Time was passing. The night was creeping on and Michael would be waiting for her.

She had got to be unselfish, she had got to think of someone else beside herself. What did it matter if she suffered, as long as Michael was happy, as long as he got what he wanted?

The hands of the clock crept slowly onwards. She began to dress, choosing a plain travelling dress and a small, rather severe hat which had never been particularly becoming.

Then she looked at her mink coat hanging in the wardrobe. It had been Charles' present to her.

It was the only really warm coat she possessed, and yet she knew she could not take it with her.

It would be wrong, almost indecent, to run away with Michael in the expensive present which Charles had given her for her wedding.

Instead she took a short tweed coat from the wardrobe and put it on. It did not match or tone with either her dress or hat, but somehow she did not care.

She was filled with an overwhelming desire to be off, to be free of the house once and for all. She felt as if it was holding out its hands to her, clutching at her and begging her not to go.

She was afraid of the silence, of a voice that seemed to be speaking to her out of the shadows of the room, of the presence which still seemed to be hovering near her.

She must get away. She would wait at the corner of the street for the car. She shut her suitcase and took a last look round the room.

She had only stayed in it for such a few days, yet already it seemed imprinted with her personality.

The clothes-cover of pale blue satin trimmed with lace which lay over the chair, the photographs of the twins in a blue frame which stood on the dressing-table, a bunch of primroses from the Castle by the bedside were all part of herself, part of the past which she must leave behind her when she set out into an unknown future.

She picked up the photograph and slipped it into her handbag. She already had another photograph of the twins in her suitcase, but somehow she could not bear to leave this one behind.

The frame was rather old and battered now, but it had been with her everywhere since it was taken five years ago. The twins were younger then, plump and rather fat. They stared out of the photograph with a solemnity which was very different from their usual sunny smiles.

It was no use thinking of the twins now, Toria thought suddenly, she had got to leave them behind.

Tomorrow they would learn what she had done. She shrank from the thought and started to collect all her belongings; a suitcase in one hand, the dressing-case, bag and gloves in the other. She turned out the lights by the bed.

When she opened the door she saw that dawn had broken.

There was a pale light coming through the skylight above the landing. She crept to the top of the stairs. It was not easy to tip-toe down them, carrying the big suitcase; but somehow she managed it.

She put her case in the hall and went into the sitting-room. It smelt a little airless. The windows were closed and she resisted an impulse to open one. Instead she went straight to the desk and sat down to write a note to Charles. She picked up a pen.

Somehow she could not begin. She stared at the writing-pad and it seemed to stare back at her. The thick white paper embossed with the name of the house was almost fascinating.

It was as if it had an identity of its own, as if it seemed to be telling her of all that she was leaving behind.

This was to have been her home, this was where she would have lived and been happy, had children and made it a place of joy and happiness for her sisters.

Toria looked away from the writing-pad. She wondered why everything was trying to make things more difficult for her.

It was hard enough to go, hard enough to remember that it was Michael she must think about, not herself, without it seeming that everything was enchanted and had a voice of its own.

Suddenly she began to write. It was only a few lines, but that was enough.

"Charles,
I am going to Hollywood with Michael. He needs me, and he won't go without me. Forgive me if you can. I am ashamed and miserable at what I have done to you and to your life.

Toria."

Without reading what she had written Toria folded the sheet in two and slipped it into an envelope. She wrote "Charles" on it and propped it up against the inkpot so that it could not fail to be seen by anyone coming into the room.

Now she was ready to go. As she rose from the desk, the telephone shrilled. For a moment Toria held her breath. She could not answer it; she must not.

And then just as swiftly she reached out and took the receiver off.

The bell would waken someone—perhaps Charles. If he should hear it, he would come downstairs to answer it and that must be avoided at all costs.

"Hullo!"

She spoke into the receiver.

"Toria, is that you?"

It was Xandra, her voice high and agitated.

"Xandra, what is the matter? Why are you ringing me at this hour?" Toria asked.

"Oh, Toria, do come at once. Something awful has happened! It is Olga! I think she is dead."

"What do you mean?"

Toria could hardly say the words.

"It's the balcony. She has fallen off it. It broke."

"Why was she on it? Explain, Xandra, quickly!"

"Brandy and Soda got shut out. No one remembered when we went to bed that they had gone for a walk and they must have come back a little while ago and started whining. Olga heard them and got out of bed to see what was the matter. I heard her, Toria. I woke just as she was walking across the room. I asked her what was the matter and she said something about the dogs. Then she went on to the balcony. I heard her say something and then . . . then she screamed. There was an awful crash . . . and oh. Toria . . . I ran to look and. . . ."

Xandra's voice broke.

"Try and tell me the rest," Toria said quietly.

"I could see her . . . below the window, lying on the ground . . . the stones from the balcony . . . all round her. I . . . I rushed downstairs. She did not speak . . . or move and I screamed for Mrs. Fergusson. . . . Old Fergie carried her upstairs and . . . and they told me to telephone . . . you."

"But, Xandra, you must get a Doctor at once."

"I tried, I tried first," Xandra answered. "Mrs. Fergusson said, 'Get the Doctor and then your sister'. But he's out. . . . He has gone to a baby case and . . . and they don't know when . . . he will be back."

Toria drew a deep breath.

"Now listen, Xandra, listen carefully," she said. "That was Dr. Gray you rang, wasn't it? Well, ring Dr. Jackson, you remember he is the young man. You will find his telephone number in the book. Get on to him. He will come if you explain there has been an accident. I am coming down to you now at once. I shan't be long, darling, but ring Dr. Jackson immediately. Do you understand?"

"Yes, Toria, I will do . . . what you say. But hurry . . . please, please hurry, I am so . . . frightened."

Toria heard the click as Xandra put down the receiver. Without remembering her suitcase in the hall she ran from the house.

She rushed up the street to the corner. With a relief which almost made her cry she saw there was a small car drawn up at the side of the kerb.

At the sight of her the driver got from the front seat and opened the door at the back. She stumbled into it.

"Drive as quickly as you can," she stammered.

"Yes, Madam, to the aerodrome, I believe."

"No, no, to Lynbrooke Castle."

She told him the way, sitting forward on the edge of her seat. It seemed to her as if the changing down of the gear, the slowing down at the corners was an agony that was almost unbearable.

She kept seeing that broken balcony and Olga falling from it. It had been unsafe for years.

They had spoken of mending it so often, but nothing had come of it, and in the usually inefficient manner of everything at Lynbrooke Castle it had remained as it was, only deteriorating a little more every winter.

There ought never to have been a balcony outside that particular window. It was one of the hideous discrepancies added by their grandfather in his desire for elaborate ornamentation.

The twins both knew it was dangerous; the window-cleaner on his periodical visits invariably pointed out that "that there balcony be unsafe and some'at ought to be done about it."

Something would be done now, Toria thought, when it was too late.

It seemed to her as if the car was crawling along.

"Can't you go faster?" she asked.

"We are going over seventy, Madam," the chauffeur replied.

"Go faster still, please. There has been an accident," Toria commanded. "I must get there quickly."

Yes, there had been an accident! How could she bear it? An accident to Olga!

13

As the car drew up at the front door of the Castle, Toria sprang out, thrust a pound note into the driver's hand and ran up the wide, shallow steps to the front door.

Xandra had obviously been waiting in the hall and as Toria appeared she ran forward and flung her arms round her sister's neck.

"Oh, Toria, Toria . . . thank goodness you have come! I have been so . . . frightened. I am sure that Olga . . . is dead. She is so white . . . and she does not speak. I tried . . . and tried . . . to waken her, but she does not . . . answer."

Xandra's little body was racked with sobs and her words were almost incoherent.

"Hush, darling, do not upset yourself so terribly," Toria soothed her. "Is the Doctor here?"

She had not seen a car as she drove up to the front door, but that was not surprising.

Nobody local used the bumpy, pot-holed front drive, but everyone came to the Castle by the tradesman's entrance instead, a longer, but smoother roadway which led through what had once been the Home Farm.

"Yes, he is here," Xandra answered through her sobs, "but he . . . turned me out."

"We will go up and see what he says," Toria said.

With her arms round Xandra, who was completely blinded by her tears, she led the way to the staircase.

"If Olga dies, what shall I do?" Xandra asked, stopping suddenly and clinging to Toria with both hands. "I shall only be half me, shan't I?"

Toria understood. The twins had always spoken as if they were one person rather than two. For a moment she hardly knew what to answer.

Like Xandra, she felt that the future would be intol-

266

erable without Olga. Then she said firmly and reassuringly:

"I am sure Olga is not going to die. We have got to be brave. It won't help her or anybody else if we panic."

Her words seemed to pull Xandra together for she loosened her almost convulsive grip and walked upstairs beside Toria in silence.

"You are frozen with cold," Toria said.

While Xandra's face was pale from agitation, she was also shivering from waiting in the unheated hall, wearing nothing but her night-gown under a flannel dressing-gown threadbare with age and long outgrown.

"You must go and put on something warm," she added; but Xandra shook her head.

"I must know about Olga first," she answered. "Ask the Doctor to tell us what is wrong—please, Toria."

They had reached Olga's room, but before Toria could open the door Doctor Jackson came out.

He was a young man who had recently come to the neighbourhood, but he had had the experience of working in the Glasgow slums and during the war had been a Surgeon in the Royal Navy. Toria had not actually met him, but she had heard of him from many people who spoke highly of his ability.

She liked him at first sight. He had a lined, intelligent face, tired grey eyes and thin, scrupulously clean surgeon's hands which seemed somehow to proclaim efficiency and reassurance even in the way he shook hands.

His eyes lightened at the sight of Toria.

"I am glad you are here, Lady Victoria," he said. "I was wondering how I could get hold of someone in authority."

Toria felt for a moment as if she must choke. Did this mean the worst, she wondered; and then something in Dr. Jackson's face told her it was not as bad as might be feared.

"How is my sister?" she stammered.

"She has broken her collar bone," Dr. Jackson replied, "and I think a rib or two. At the moment she is suffering from concussion and I don't want to move her more than is absolutely necessary. What is imperative is

267

that I should get her to the hospital immediately so that she can be x-rayed for any injuries which I cannot diagnose."

Toria drew a deep breath, but before she could speak Xandra gave a little cry.

"Then she is not dead! Olga is not dead!" she cried.

Dr. Jackson put a hand on the child's shoulder.

"Your sister is very much alive," he said, "only we will have to take a great deal of care of her for some weeks at least."

Xandra put her hands over her face and began to cry. They were not the frantic tears she had cried on Toria's arrival, but quiet, almost soothing tears of relief.

Toria put her arms round her and held her close.

"They are twins," she said to Dr. Jackson over her little sister's head as if in explanation.

"Yes, I know," he answered; "and now may I use the telephone? I will get an ambulance to come here right away."

"You will find the telephone in the hall," Toria replied. "May I go in to Olga?"

"Yes, of course," he said. "You will find her unconscious, but your housekeeper is with her just in case she moves before I return."

"Can I come too?" Xandra asked through her tears.

"Just for a minute," Toria said, "and then you must promise me to go and put on something warm."

They went into the room together. Olga's face was almost as pale as the pillow and her fair hair was tumbled about her forehead which was scratched and bleeding.

She looked so very small and pathetic, with only her face showing above the blankets and eiderdown which had been pulled on top of her, that Toria found it impossible to prevent the tears blinding her eyes and flowing down her cheeks.

Mrs. Fergusson rose from a chair beside the bed. She was wearing an old red flannel dressing-gown and her hair was in curlers. She had forgotten to put her teeth in and this gave her a curiously withered expression.

"It's thankful I am to see you, m'lady," she exclaimed. "The poor child! It's only by the mercy of God that she's not dead. Over and over again I've said to Fergusson that there balcony should be repaired."

Toria did not answer.

She could only stand looking down at her little sister, feeling there were so many things which ought to have been done and so many things which ought not to have been done.

The balcony should have been repaired, the twins should not have been left alone in the house with only old Fergie and his wife far away in the kitchen wing. If the dogs had not been forgotten and Olga had not heard them whining, all this would never have happened.

There were so many ifs, so many mistakes one way or another, yet no one was actually to blame for the whole thing. There was no reason why their father should not have gone away for a few days or Lettice should not be staying in London with some friends at the same time.

It was just an accumulation of trivial mistakes, but Olga was the sufferer.

Toria felt, as she stood there, that children were too precious a heritage to be treated lightly or forgotten even for a few minutes.

They should be remembered always, loved and cherished and protected; and she thought to herself that when she had children of her own, she would never take risks with them—never.

She could feel Xandra trembling against her and with an effort she forced herself to be practical.

"Would you be very kind and make us some hot tea?" she asked Mrs. Fergusson. "Xandra is cold, and I expect you could do with a cup yourself."

"That I could, m'lady," Mrs. Fergusson agreed; "and I'll have the kettle on in a jiffy."

She hurried away, obviously glad of an excuse to be doing something, and as she went down the passage, Toria could hear her shouting at old Fergie, who had obviously been waiting to know what the Doctor's verdict might be.

Going to the chest of drawers, Toria took out a jumper and cardigan and a warm tweed skirt which she gave to Xandra. The twins' underclothes were thrown untidily over an armchair.

"Go and put them on in my room," she commanded, and Xandra with a last look at Olga did as she was told.

Alone, Toria touched Olga's cheek very gently with her fingers.

The child felt horrifyingly cold and for a moment Toria wondered if she had died after all; but even as she sat there almost too frightened to ask the question even of herself, the door opened and the Doctor came in.

"The ambulance will be along in about five minutes," he said.

He bent over the bed, moving the blankets back from Olga's arms so that he could take her pulse.

"Your housekeeper brought me one hot bottle, but I would like at least another two."

"I will go and get them," Toria said, and added in a low voice: "She is all right, isn't she?"

Dr. Jackson nodded.

"It is not nearly as bad as it might have been," he said. "She fell into the flower bed, I gather, and the ground was soft from the recent rains. Fortunately the window is not so very high from the ground."

"She looks so terribly white," Toria muttered.

Dr. Jackson put Olga's hands back under the blanket.

"We shall know more when we have got her to hospital," he said quietly. "You'll go with her in the ambulance, won't you?"

"Yes, of course," Toria replied.

She went from the room and hurried along the passage to her own bedroom. Xandra was there, dressing. She was still crying and her face was dirty where she had rubbed the tears with her hands.

"What did the Doctor say?" she asked Toria as she came into the room. "I saw him come upstairs."

"The ambulance is coming for Olga in a few minutes," Toria replied, "but the Doctor wants more hot-water bottles. I think I have got one here in the chest-of-drawers."

"No, you haven't," Xandra answered. "Lettice borrowed that two nights ago. Her own burst in the bed

270

and she was awfully angry. Mrs. Fergusson said there wasn't another one in the house; then I remembered yours. I told her where it was and she took it."

"I suppose she has taken it to London with her," Toria said, knowing that there was no likelihood of Lettice having replaced anything she had once taken.

Lettice was an inveterate borrower and once anything was lent to her it became her own automatically.

"I expect so," Xandra replied.

"Are you quite sure there is not another one in the house?" Toria asked.

"Mrs. Fergusson might have one," Xandra suggested.

"So she might," Toria said and ran down the back stairs to the kitchen.

Mrs. Fergusson was standing at the stove. The kettle had just come to the boil and she was warming the pot before making the tea.

"A hot-water bottle, m'lady?" she replied to Toria's question. "Never had such a thing in my life. A hot brick was what my mother always used in bed; and when I first went into service, they used the old-fashioned warming pans. I never did care for such things myself, and I always says my old man is as good as a hot-water bottle any night."

"The Doctor wants one for Lady Olga," Toria said, "but we can't give him what we haven't got."

"No indeed, but there are plenty of blankets we can wrap round her ladyship. I filled the bottle she had with water that was just off the boil."

"I am afraid we can do no more," Toria said a little helplessly. "Shall I take up the tea? I expect the Doctor would like a cup too."

"He'll like it well enough if he is anything like the other Doctors I've met."

Mrs. Fergusson put three cups down on a wooden tray, the brown kitchen teapot beside them, and fetched a small jug of milk from the larder.

None of the cups matched each other, and two of the saucers were badly cracked. Some milk had keen upset on the tray, leaving a white patch on the brown wood, while the teapot had a chip out of the spout.

"It is typical of what we always put up with," Toria thought, and felt ashamed as she entered Olga's room to find the Doctor sitting by the bedside, Xandra standing beside him.

She set the tray down on the table and poured them both out a cup of tea. She was just going to pour one for herself when she heard a car draw up outside.

It was the ambulance and the Doctor hurried downstairs, Xandra running after him.

It seemed to Toria only a second or two before the Doctor was back again, followed by the ambulance men.

They lifted Olga very carefully, wrapped her warmly in blankets and then carried her with professional smoothness down the stairs to the ambulance.

"Please, can I come with you? Please let me." Xandra begged.

Toria glanced over her head at the Doctor and almost imperceptibly he shook his head.

"No, I want you to wait here, darling," Toria said. "I will telephone you the moment we hear what is wrong with Olga, and I will be back just as soon as I can. Help Mrs. Fergusson to get things straight!"

Xandra did not plead any more; but there was a look in her eyes as they drove away which reminded Toria of the expression in Brandy and Soda's eyes when they were parted from the person they loved best in the world.

It was fortunately only a short way to the County Hospital. It was a low, well-built house set back from the road in its own garden and staffed by what appeared to Toria to be an extremely efficient collection of nurses.

Within a few seconds of their arrival Olga had been taken away upstairs and Toria found herself sitting in front of a warm fire in the Matron's sitting-room.

It was then, when she was alone, that she began to think of herself for the first time since she had left London. She was vaguely aware that her head was aching, and putting up her hand, she drew off her hat.

As she did so, she glanced at it and realised it was

one she had never liked. The memory of why she had chosen it came back to her.

For the first time since the telephone rang as she was leaving the house in Chesterfield Hill she remembered Michael. She had been going to America with him! He would have been waiting for her at the aerodrome!

She felt her heart give a frightened thump; then after a moment of startled surprise she felt the blood run in a crimson wave into her cheeks. She had forgotten Michael! How awful! How ghastly!

She had never given him a thought since Xandra's frightened voice had come over the telephone wire.

She had been thinking only of the twins, of Olga falling from the balcony. It seemed incredible, almost impossible, that even Olga's accident could have been so tremendous that it had put every thought out of her head.

Yet it was true. It was only now that she remembered where she had been going and that Michael would be waiting for her.

She looked at the clock over the mantelpiece. It was nearly eight o'clock.

Slowly she felt the blood recede from her cheeks. What would he think? What would he say? How could she possibly explain that she had not even remembered his very existence?

She knew now that she ought to have stopped at a telephone booth on the way down to the Castle. She should have telephoned him, told him what had happened; or if that had been impossible, she might have tried to get through to him after she had arrived home and realised that Olga was not dead, only injured.

And now—now it was too late! He would have cancelled his passage, and he would be coming in search of her.

Toria put her hands to her eyes, and in that second of tribulation she knew the truth. She did not love Michael, she did not want to go to America with him. She had never wanted to go.

She was sorry for him, desperately sorry, as she always had been. There was something about him which

273

tore at her heart, made her yearn over him as she yearned over Xandra and Olga, because they were helpless and childish.

Michael had never grown up. He, too, was a child, a child who had clung to her, who wanted her help and her protection. He had demanded her love and she believed she had given it to him; but in reality it had been nothing but pity.

She had never been in love with Michael; she had only loved him as one might love a difficult and yet at times adorable small boy.

And now what could she say to him? Toria felt suddenly helpless. It was all too big, too overwhelming for her. She felt that she could not cope with any of it.

Michael's life with its difficulties and dramas, Michael's temperament with his moods and sulks and moments of overwhelming intensity, Michael's demands upon her.

"You are mine, mine, mine!"

She could hear him saying it, and she suddenly shrank from its very implication. What was she to do? She asked herself the question, but could find no answer.

Above all, how was she to get hold of him so that she could explain what had happened? She sat there, feeling exhausted and very weak.

Then the door opened and Dr. Jackson came in. Toria started to her feet. Before he spoke one look at his face told her the news was good.

"What have you found?"

She heard herself ask the question, although she was not aware that she had meant to ask it.

"Very little," Dr. Jackson replied. "Your sister has been amazingly lucky. As I have told you already, she has a broken collar bone, and we find there are two ribs cracked on the left side. She has splintered three small bones in her wrist and she is very badly bruised, but otherwise there is nothing of any consequence."

"Thank God!"

Toria's voice was low and her exclamation was almost a prayer.

"I had not dared to hope that things could be as good as they are," Dr. Jackson said. "It is difficult to ascertain yet how badly she will suffer from shock, but she has already come round and I expect you would like to see her for a moment. After that she must sleep."

"Yes, of course I would like to see her," Toria said.

The morning sun from the casement window glinted on her hair. The Doctor looked at her appreciatively as he stood aside to let her pass.

Olga had been placed in a bedroom facing south. The windows on to a balcony were open and there was a sweet-faced sister with grey hair by the bedside when Toria came in.

"Do not talk to her unless she talks to you. I will leave you only for a minute or two," she said in a low voice.

Toria sat down beside the bed. Someone had washed the blood away from Olga's face and smoothed back her hair. She looked very small and neat, almost like a child out of a story book.

Toria felt her heart contract. She sat there for a few seconds, then Olga opened her eyes.

"Toria," she exclaimed in a husky whisper. "I felt you were here."

"You have had a nasty accident, darling," Toria said, bending over her, "but you are all right now."

"Yes, I know," Olga said. "They told me. My head aches rather, but I expect I fell on it."

"I am afraid you did," Toria answered, "but we will soon get you well again."

Olga closed her eyes for a moment as if she were very tired, then she opened them again.

"Toria, there is something I want to say," she whispered.

"What is it, darling?"

"Something I dreamt. I can't remember whether it was before I fell . . . or afterwards. There was a lot of darkness . . . but . . . I dreamt a strange dream about you."

"I shouldn't worry about it," Toria said soothingly. "Dreams are soon forgotten."

"This was a horrid . . . dream," Olga insisted. "I dreamt you . . . you were going away . . . from us. It was wrong . . . very wrong for you . . . to go, and I was pleading with you . . . begging you to stay, but . . . you would . . . go. Oh, Toria, I hated it."

Toria bent down until her face was very close to her little sister's.

"Listen, Olga, you are not to think of that dream any more. I am not going away, I am staying with you for always."

"Staying with us?" Olga repeated. "For always?"

"For always," Toria said firmly.

"And Charles too?" Olga asked, her voice very faint but happy.

Toria hesitated. Olga's eyes were closed and yet she felt the child was waiting for an answer.

"And Charles too," she repeated at last.

Olga was asleep; and then as she stood watching her, Toria was aware that the Sister had come silently into the room.

"You must leave her now," the Sister said. "Was she talking sensibly?"

"Yes, absolutely sensibly," Toria answered.

"She seemed rather distressed when she first regained consciousness. The Doctors thought she was delirious, but it struck me there was something on her mind."

"I think there was something on her mind," Toria replied softly, "but she won't worry about it any more."

She moved through the doorway into the passage and Sister followed her.

"I am glad about that," the latter said. "Visible ailments are always so much easier to cure than mental ones."

"And are often far less painful," Toria said.

The Sister nodded.

"Isn't it strange how often we forget that?"

She took Toria to the top of the stairs, then smiled and left her. It was only as Toria was walking down to the hall that she knew that she must telephone the aerodrome. She must find out about Michael, find out if by any chance he had left a message for her there.

She went back into Matron's room, but it was empty, and without waiting to enquire if she might do so Toria went towards the telephone on the writing desk.

The four London telephone books were by the bed on a small stool beside the desk. It took Toria only a few seconds to find the number of the aerodrome, and then she dialled for the operator.

She found she was trembling. It was absurd to be so frightened, and she tried to laugh at herself, but she felt suddenly as if her knees would no longer hold her.

She sat down in the chair and waited.

After what seemed to her a century of time she heard a voice and in a tone that she could hardly make audible, she asked:

"I wish to enquire about a traveller due to leave this morning on the seven o'clock aeroplane to New York."

"Hold on a moment, please," the operator said.

There were several clicks at the end of the line and then at length a courteous voice said:

"Can I do anything to help you?"

"I am ringing to enquire if Mr. Michael Gale travelled on the seven o'clock aeroplane to New York this morning," Toria said. "He and Lady Victoria Gale had booked their passages, but I think it is likely that they cancelled them at the last moment. I should like to make sure."

"Yes, of course; will you hold on, please?"

It seemed to Toria that she held on for a very long time. She was still trembling. She could feel her whole body shake and quiver, and then at last the voice said:

"Are you there?"

"Yes," Toria replied.

"I have made enquiries and Mr. Michael Gale left on the seven o'clock plane. Lady Victoria Gale's place, however, was not claimed and was taken by another passenger at the last moment. Is that all the information you require?"

Toria tried to speak, tried to answer, but the words simply would not come.

"Are you there? Is that all the information you require?"

277

The question was repeated rather sharply this time, and Toria at last was able to stammer.

"Thank you . . . thank you . . . that is all . . . I wanted to know."

She put down the receiver. Michael had gone!

For a moment she could not realise it, could not understand why she felt so different, and then she knew that she was no longer trembling.

The room seemed to be suddenly very sunny and she knew it was a relief—a glorious, wonderful relief flooding over her. She was free!

She could hardly breathe the words even to herself; then as they came to her mind, she repeated them again and yet again.

She was free! She was free, free of the cloud which had hung over her for the last few days, free of the chains which had bound her so that she was afraid to move, afraid even to acknowledge to herself that they were shackles. She was free!

She lay against the back of the chair, feeling a lightness in her mind which made her spirit soar like a bird into the open sky. She was free! She drew a deep breath —there was so much to be done.

First of all she must telephone Xandra, then she must go back to London.

She almost heard Olga's voice saying: "And Charles too?" She must go back. Toria knew in that second exactly what she must do.

She must go back to Charles, she must tell him it had all been a mistake. He would understand—she was sure he would understand. With a feeling of shame she remembered the letter she had left propped up on the writing desk.

Charles would have read it by now. He always rose early and when he went down to breakfast he would have seen the note waiting for him.

Toria put out her hand towards the telephone receiver, then hesitated. Her first impulse was to ring Charles, to tell him what had happened to Olga, to explain about Michael; then somehow it seemed impossible. How could she just ring up on the telephone?

No, she must go and explain everything to him in person. She must ask him to forgive her, try and make him understand what she felt about Michael and how at last she was free, free of the spell which he had cast over her.

But first Xandra! Never again she swore to herself would she neglect either of her little sisters. They would have Mrs. Hagar-Bassett to help look after them in the future. It would be at least something to have a woman in the place; but apart from that Toria swore to herself that they would always be her responsibility and one which she would never neglect.

She got through to the Castle and heard Xandra's quick, excited voice answer her.

"There is little more the matter with Olga than what Dr. Jackson found when he first examined her," Toria said. "She has gone to sleep now, but she spoke to me quite sensibly and did not seem to be in pain."

"I expect they have given her something to take it away," Xandra said practically.

"Yes, I expect so," Toria answered.

"And now are you coming back to me?" Xandra asked.

"Yes, I am coming right away," Toria replied.

"Oh, be quick, be very quick," Xandra pleaded. "I want you so."

Toria put down the receiver and turned to find that Doctor Jackson had come into the room while she was speaking.

"I think it would be wise if you kept your other sister as quiet as possible today," he suggested. "She has had a terrible shock, and shock is often just as bad as an injury. If you can get her to stay in bed, well and good. If not, keep her quiet. I should not leave her alone if you can help it."

"Very well," Toria said. "I have used Matron's telephone for two calls. I hope she won't mind."

"I am sure she won't," Dr. Jackson replied. "She hoped to see you, but she is in the Operating Theatre at the moment, so you will have to meet her next time you come."

"When do you think that ought to be?" Toria asked.

"May I telephone you this afternoon?" Dr. Jackson answered. "If the patient is restless and seems to want you, it might be a good idea for you to come out late this afternoon. If not, I think tomorrow morning would be better. The quieter she is kept today the better."

"Yes, of course," Toria said, "and thank you very much."

She held out her hand.

"I am so glad I was able to help," Dr. Jackson smiled. "I will get in touch with your own Doctor and explain to him what has happened."

"Yes, do," Toria agreed, "and I must speak to him too. Thank you very much once again."

She left the Hospital and walked down the street. There was a garage not far away where she knew she could hire a car to take her to the Castle.

She was back with Xandra within twenty minutes and when she had had a look at the child's face, she was glad it had not been longer.

There was no doubt about it, Xandra was suffering from shock, and after Toria had insisted on her eating some breakfast she took her upstairs and put her into bed.

"It is silly, but I can't stop crying," Xandra sobbed. "I can't think why, because I am not unhappy."

"I want you to try and go to sleep," Toria said, "and when you wake up, I will read to you. You will like that, won't you?"

"Just like when I was a little girl. Do you remember how Olga and I used to beg you to read to us, but sometimes you were too busy?"

"I will never be too busy again," Toria wanted to say, but she knew it would not be true.

They might not be so frequent in the future, but there would nevertheless be times when she would be too busy to do what the twins wanted. That was life!

There would always be things one could not do however much one tried.

She drew Xandra's blinds, tucked her in, and made her promise not to think about anything, but to try and go to sleep. It was when she went downstairs that she knew she had to go to London. She had got to see Charles.

Dr. Jackson might tell her not to leave Xandra alone, but there were other people who must not be left alone either. Charles could not be left in ignorance of what had happened, believing, as he must, that she had gone away with Michael and left him for ever.

Toria called Mrs. Fergusson.

"I must go to London," she said. "Will you promise me that you will look in on Xandra every ten minutes? If she wakes and wants me, tell her I will be back very soon. It won't take me more than forty minutes each way, and I won't stay a second longer than I have to, but I have simply got to go to London now."

"That's all right, m'lady," Mrs. Fergusson said. "If you ask me, that child is real worn out. She'll sleep, I'm certain sure of it. You hop off to London, m'lady, and be back as soon as you can. I'll keep my eye on everything while you're away."

"Thank you, Mrs. Fergusson."

Toria ran out of the house to the garage.

Her father's old Austin was housed there. It took her a little time to get it started because, as usual, the battery was run down and she had to fetch old Fergie from the house to swing the starting handle before the car could be galvanised into life.

Then at last she was off. She drove faster than she had ever attempted to do before, usually having far too much respect for the old Austin to dare to coax it over a comfortable thirty miles an hour, but today she was in a hurry.

Clanking along, puffing and blowing on the hills, they covered the miles far more rapidly than Toria had dared to hope for, and it was only half past twelve when she drew up outside the house in Chesterfield Hill.

She jumped out, opened the door with her latchkey and went in. She had expected Charles to be at home.

Somehow she could not imagine that, having received her note, he would go off to the Air Ministry as though nothing had happened. But his hat was not in the hall

Then suddenly she remembered that her suitcases had been left at the bottom of the stairs. She wondered what Charles had thought.

Had he imagined that at the last moment she had felt that she could not take anything she owned with her, feeling that they were part of the past?

Toria felt she could not attempt to unravel any more of the problems which confronted her.

It was Charles she wanted, Charles whom she must find. There was no one in the drawing-room, but on an impulse she ran upstairs to her own bedroom.

She opened the door and then stepped back in astonishment.

Someone was sitting in front of her dressing-table, trying on a hat, turning her face this way and that to get the different angles in the triple-sided mirror.

For a moment Toria did not speak; then the girl at the dressing-table turned round and saw her. It was Lettice.

"Toria!"

Her exclamation was one of sheer astonishment. Toria came further into the room.

"What on earth are you doing here, Lettice?" she asked.

Slowly Lettice got up from the dressing-table and took from her head the hat she had been trying on. Toria recognised it. It was one which had been in her trousseau, a model of black velvet trimmed with white feathers.

"I thought you had gone away," Lettice said. "Charles told me you had gone to America with Michael."

"Charles told you that?" Toria asked. "When?"

"I telephoned this morning," Lettice explained, "thinking I should speak to you, but Charles answered the telephone. He sounded rather strange at first, and then he told me what had happened.

" 'Come round here and have luncheon with me,' he said. He wanted to see me!"

Lettice said the last words almost defiantly. Toria

stared at her. Lettice was lying. Toria always knew when she was lying.

She put on a defiant air which was somehow not unlike Michael's. Charles had not asked her to luncheon, Toria thought suddenly; she had asked herself.

She felt suddenly angry and irritated. There was something about Lettice's attitude she did not like.

"So you are lunching with Charles," she said. "What time is he coming home?"

"Half past one," Lettice said.

Toria raised her eyebrows.

"You're early, aren't you?" she asked. "Is that why you are passing the time by trying on my clothes?"

Lettice flushed.

"I don't see why I shouldn't," she replied sullenly. "They were not going to be any use to you if you did not take them with you."

Toria said nothing. Lettice chucked the black and white hat down on the bed and turned towards her with an air which was peculiarly aggressive.

"Why have you come back?" she asked. "I thought you had gone for ever. Charles thought you had at any rate."

"Perhaps I changed my mind," Toria said; "and anyway, you don't seem very pleased to see me."

"Why should I be?" Lettice asked, and now her voice was shaking with some strange emotion.

"Why should I?" she repeated in a louder tone. "You've got Michael. Isn't he enough for you?"

"I don't know what you mean," Toria said in surprise.

"Yes, you do," Lettice retorted. "You have always had everything, everything. Michael always loved you better than he did me. You took him away from me. When we first came to the Castle we were very close friends, but after that I didn't matter any more. It was you who mattered most, you who were first, I was only his stupid little sister who could run away and play by herself.

"Oh yes, you took Michael, as you took everybody else. It was always Toria who was so beautiful, Toria

283

who was so charming, Toria whom people admired. I would have been a success if I hadn't been held up in comparison with you. And then Charles came. . . ."

Lettice paused for a moment. Toria stood staring at her unable to move. She was beginning to understand so many things.

"Yes, Charles came," Lettice repeated. "I liked him from that very first day he came to luncheon. No, like is not the right word. I loved him, I wanted him. He might have loved me, too, if you hadn't set your cap at him. You had to get him in the bag just as you had got all the other men, just as you had got Michael.

"You didn't really want him, but you took him just the same; and having got him, what do you do? You run away and leave him. You've gone off with Michael. Michael, who will make you as unhappy as you deserve, Michael who has never cared a damn in the whole of his life for anyone except himself. This is my opportunity, mine, and I won't have you coming back to spoil it."

Toria stared at the girl whom she had thought of as a sister and who had suddenly become an utter and complete stranger to her.

She felt nauseated. It was all so horrible. Lettice's contorted face, her spitting lips, her hands clenched together, her body shaking with the violence of her feelings.

Toria felt as if she had never seen the truth before of these two cousins who had come into her home and who had been treated as part of the family.

Now for the first time she realised that neither Michael nor Lettice had been anything but alien.

They had never been "us", never been a part of herself and the twins, but always strangers, outsiders, resenting kindness, suspicious of affection, distrusting everybody and everything.

She suddenly felt as if she could not bear to stay there any longer. She could not argue with Lettice, could not answer her, could not do anything to make the atmosphere any the less horrible.

Without a word she turned, went from the room and

downstairs. She crossed the hall, opened the front door and walked out into the sunshine.

The old car was standing outside. Automatically she got in to it. As she started the engine, she wondered where she should go. Xandra was waiting for her. Should she go back to the Castle?

Then she knew, knew with a certainty and a clarity that was indisputable that it was Charles she wanted.

Charles who would make everything all right. Charles with his quiet, calm wisdom, who could transform what appeared to be a nightmare of perplexity into sound, common, everyday sense.

Toria put her foot on the accelerator. She would go to the Air Ministry. Charles must have gone there despite everything that had happened.

Perhaps he had important commitments, a meeting which could not be postponed. Besides, by sitting at home and suffering what good could he do?

It was always difficult for him to come home to luncheon so that was why he had fixed to return today at half past one. At this moment he would still be in his office. She would find him there.

Toria drove down Clarges Street into Piccadilly. The traffic was bad and it took her a little time before she could turn off into St. James's Street.

The old car got very hot in traffic and the radiator was steaming as she turned into Birdcage Walk. All of a sudden as she hurried towards the Horse Guards Parade she saw Charles.

He was coming from St. James's Park, carrying his hat in his hand, his umbrella on one arm. She saw him and realised that he was about to cross the road, but for a moment she was unable to stop the car.

About a hundred yards further on she managed to pull into the kerb and jamming on the brakes she switched off the engine.

She jumped out. Charles had crossed the road and was walking away from her. He was going home, Toria thought, home to where Lettice would be waiting for him.

She knew then that never to Lettice or to anyone

would she relinquish Charles. He was hers, he loved her.

Strangely and unexpectedly she had come to love him too. It was not as she had expected love to be, a violent and tumultuous, overpowering emotion.

That had been Michael's type of love.

This was different. A feeling of utter reliance and contentment, a desire to lean on Charles, to know his strength, to be certain of his gentleness, his tenderness and his understanding. But it was love, and infinitely precious.

Toria could see Charles ahead of her, see his broad back, the proud carriage of his head.

Suddenly she loved him almost overwhelmingly. It was as if a flame rose within her, warm and brilliant. He was hers, and she would never, never give him up to anybody or for anything.

She started to run towards him.

"Charles!" she called. "Charles!"

But he did not hear her. She ran faster and only as he was turning into St. James's Street did she catch up with him.

"Charles," she panted, breathless from the speed of her hurrying. "Charles!"

He turned round to see who called his name, and she saw his face for a moment blank with astonishment, then lit with a joy and a happiness that was almost indescribable.

"Toria!" he ejaculated. "Toria, my darling, where have you come from?"

"I have . . . come back to . . . you," Toria gasped. "It was all a . . . mistake. Oh, Charles . . . Charles, don't ever . . . let me go . . . again."

Her hands were reaching out to him. Suddenly his arms were round her. People passing by stared at them curiously, but neither of them had any idea where they were or of anything save themselves.

They were a man and woman on the edge of the world and everything else was forgotten.

"Oh, Charles . . . I didn't know. . . . I didn't understand . . . until now that I . . . loved you," Toria whispered.

She thought she had never seen anything so wonderful as the expression on his face.

"My darling, my little love," he exclaimed. "And I thought I had lost you."

"Never . . . never." Toria answered. "I am yours . . . yours for ever . . . and ever. Do you . . understand?"

"Mine?" Charles repeated. "Mine! Oh, Toria, are you sure?"

"Quite . . . sure," Toria answered, and lifted her face to his, her lips parted.

are you missing out on some great Pyramid books?

You can have any title in print at Pyramid delivered right to your door! To receive your Pyramid Paperback Catalog, fill in the label below (use a ball point pen please) and mail to Pyramid . . .